maxim's promise

AN ARRANGED MARRIAGE BRATVA ROMANCE

THE COMMISSION NOVEL SERIES

HAVEN FOX

HAVEN FOX BOOKS

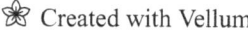

for all those looking for their potential companion for the zombie apocalypse — these things are important 🤍

and to the silent hero ... the em dash —

and to my husband, who makes it possible for me to write my novels

content warnings

Dear Reader,
This is a novel with dark themes. Meant for 18+

This book is not recommended for sensitive readers.
* Graphic violence and death (including torture)
* Physical assault (against the FMC, not by MMC)
* Gun violence
* Drinking
* Open-Door & descriptive spice
* Off-page description of past spousal violence & trafficking by father

None of the situations in this book are meant to be real or are condoned in real-life settings.

CHAPTER ONE

maxim

MAXIM - AGE 12

MY FATHER'S hand clamped down on the back of my neck, his grip relentless, his nails pressing into my skin so hard I knew they'd leave marks. With a growl, he shoved me forward, and I stumbled, but I didn't resist. I didn't have the size or strength to push back— not yet. But I held onto a tiny, powerful hope: one day, I would grow. One day, I'd be stronger than him, and when that day came, I'd make sure he never laid a hand on me again.

I would kill him. I swore it on all that was holy and everything unholy.

We stopped in front of a nondescript building with darkened windows in the roughest part of New York, a place where even the daylight didn't seem to reach. I was only twelve, but I knew places like this weren't suitable for children. Although those were details that my father didn't care about. Men like my father didn't bother hiding their business in a nice part of town. In fact, they preferred these shadowy corners.

The bouncer at the door nodded to my father, not even glancing at me. "Mr. Volkov," he acknowledged, stepping aside like I was invisible. I could try to resist, but it'd only make things worse.

"Over there." My father jerked his chin toward a corner booth, and I moved forward, knowing better than to drag my feet. The thumping bass of the music rattled the floor as a woman on stage slinked around a pole, her movements mechanical, her gaze vacant. She looked drugged, and I wouldn't be surprised if she were, but there wasn't anything I could do about it — yet. A few men sat around the room, glassy-eyed and looking like they'd been here for days. But in the back, at the booth where my father's gaze was locked, there were men of a different breed—calculating, cold-eyed, and each with a boy my age by his side.

One of them called out to my father with a drunken, cheerful voice, "Alexei! It's been a while!" He was already half-slouched over, his thick, meaty hand resting possessively on a boy beside him—a kid who grimaced at the touch.

My father narrowed his eyes at the boy and then addressed his friend. "Yianni, it's good to see you." He squinted, looking at the boy. "Is this your youngest?"

"This is Ilias." Yianni ruffled his son's hair, and Ilias jerked away, clearly disgusted.

My father gripped my shoulder, pressing hard enough on his latest belt marks to make me flinch. He pushed me forward, and I caught a quick, subtle glance from Ilias that said he knew exactly what I was feeling. "This is my oldest, Maxim."

I nodded politely, staying silent. I knew better than to speak up in front of these men. I'd learned that silence was survival, especially when my father was around. I scanned the booth, eyeing the other men and the kids they'd brought along, trying to figure out why I was there. He'd never brought me into something like this, and my mind raced with the worst possibilities. Was he trading me off? Using me as collateral? With my father, nothing was off the table.

The boys looked tense, with a quiet, uneasy energy between them. Except for one—an older kid with reddish-brown hair who stared defiantly at the stage, his jaw set, refusing to acknowledge the men's presence. I admired him for that; he was stronger than me in that way. I tried to mimic his look, setting my gaze on the stage, but I could still feel the sharp stares of the men at the table. It made me uncomfortable to look at the woman, so I finally had to look away.

After a few minutes of lewd comments and laughter, one man finally got to business. "Where's the lawyer?" he grumbled, irritated.

As if on cue, a thin man hurried over, out of breath. "Apologies, gentlemen," he wheezed, pulling out a stack of papers and a small, polished box. "Traffic was a nightmare."

No one laughed, but he seemed immune to their indifference, setting the papers on the table and flipping them open with a flourish. "Right, let's get started. These are the terms you discussed in the previous meeting. I outlined them for you."

He pushed a piece of paper toward the center, and each man took it in turn. My father scanned it, nodded in satisfaction, and said, "I'll sign first."

The lawyer opened the box, revealing an ink pad and a short protruding tack that looked very sharp. My father pressed his thumb to the tack without hesitation, wincing only slightly as a drop of blood formed. He smeared it onto the pad, then pressed his bloody thumbprint onto the paper beside his signature.

I blinked, surprised by the ritual, until the lawyer looked at me, his eyes cold and expectant. "Your turn, Maxim."

My father leaned over, his breath hot against my ear. "Remember Dimitri," he hissed in Russian. "You don't want anything to happen to him, do you?"

The weight of his words settled over me, and I knew exactly what he was doing. Dimitri was all I cared about, the only person who mattered. My father discovered years ago that my baby brother was my weak spot. I wouldn't be so foolish as to risk his safety. I skimmed the document, ignoring my father's glare, catching phrases like "alliance," "open lanes of trafficking," and "the Commission." This contract bound us—the Volkovs, O'Kellys, Santellis, and Anthakos'. A twisted pact that tied us all together through blood and, one day, through marriage.

Marriage. My stomach churned, but I shoved the thought aside. That was a problem for the future, something to worry about later. What did I care about marrying some dumb girl? I pressed my thumb down on the tack, harder than necessary, feeling the sting as my skin broke. With a grimace, I left my mark beside my father's, the blood seeping into the paper.

I wasn't so stupid or so young that I didn't understand what it meant to put my blood and my name onto a document. In the bratva, or any mafia, you were making a promise — a bond that couldn't be broken.

"Feck, he's a bloodthirsty one," commented a red-haired man across the table—Cormac O'Kelly, head of an Irish gang of some kind. He chuckled, nudging his surly-looking boy named Conall, who barely reacted. "Watch him, Conall," Cormac muttered, but Conall's gaze stayed fixed on his father, his expression defiant yet detached.

There was a brief commotion when the Italian boy, Angelo, refused to sign. His father snapped, grabbing him by the collar and delivering a harsh slap across his face. Angelo snarled, swearing in Italian but finally relenting, pressing his bleeding thumb to the paper with a sneer.

I admired his defiance, his resistance. But unlike him, I didn't have the luxury of rebellion. I had a baby brother to protect, and there was no room for bravado when Dimitri's life was on the line.

"Remember, gentlemen," the lawyer said as

he rolled the document up. "You'll be expected to provide a female from each of your families. This is a blood oath, and it cannot be broken. Copies will be mailed. The original will be held for safekeeping."

The joke was on them. I had no female siblings for my father to marry off.

The document was passed around, and the final thumbprints were made, sealing a bond thicker than ink. I leaned back, biting down on the nausea rising in my throat. Today, I'd bound myself to a future I didn't want. But for now, it was just another hill on the road, another step toward the mountain where my father's shadow loomed.

"My comrades. A toast," my father declared. "To the newly formed Commission."

One day, I would be ready, I promised myself. One day, I'd be strong enough.

And on that day, the blood I'd spill would be his.

CHAPTER TWO

maxim

PRESENT

"ANGELO, YOU DRIVE LIKE AN OLD LADY," I complained as Santelli seemed to slow even further and stopped at the yellow light. "It's yellow. That means go faster, you asshole."

"No, that means caution, you dick," he argued.

Santelli babied his 1968 Lamborghini Miura like it had just come off the showroom floor instead of it being old as fuck. It drove us crazy.

"It's a special car. I need to be careful with it."

I rolled my eyes. It was a nice car, but

Angelo was absolutely ridiculous about it. The day he got it, he sat next to it in a lawn chair and stared at it, making us listen while he told us all sorts of random car facts that we didn't give two fucks about. We weren't even allowed to drive it, and I'm surprised he let us ride in it.

"We're going to be late."

He sent me a slow look. "We're almost there, you impatient fuck. You're the one that insisted that I pick you up."

"I don't like to drive," I grumbled.

Angelo pulled his car into the familiar lot of the lounge where we'd all met what seemed to be a lifetime ago. It had become upscale partly because we'd burned the building down and started revitalizing the area and partly because we had our enforcers keeping crime down in the neighborhood.

As if he were reading my thoughts, Angelo said next to me, "That was a good night."

"Yeah, it was," I agreed. Even now, the memory was sweet. "The old place was an eyesore."

The four of us had snuck out, came to the old strip joint, and had a couple of beers. We'd been teenagers then, except for Ilias, the baby of our little squad. Dawn had been creeping over the horizon when we lit the match and set the whole thing on fire. We had sat on the curb for a few minutes until we heard sirens, watching the place burn. Then, we ran like the wind, cackling like mad hatters.

"You were slow even then," I added as we walked into the club.

What used to be dingy and tacky had become a classy gentleman's lounge with low lighting, wood floors, and scattered plush couches. The idea had started small at first to rebuild it into something we could use — a headquarters, and then it took on a life of its own. It had taken many years to come to fruition.

Today, we had our club, *Fortune*.

I couldn't claim too much credit in the venture. This was Angelo's baby. Well, money. I'd put my twenty-five percent in. That was the deal. The four of us agreed that we'd invest in rebuilding the club, but how we wanted — a place to hatch our plans and see our businesses grow. It would be a piece of our revenge. The four of us were all about revenge, but Angelo had the vision, so credit should go to him.

"Looks good."

"I know," he smirked, throwing an arm around my shoulder. "Come on, asshole, they're waiting for us."

I could just make out the two men waiting in the back corner. Conall and Ilias sat in the low light of the brass lamps in one of the private booths, their drinks already sweating on the table. They looked up as we approached, each of them giving a nod. Conall lifted his glass in a silent toast, his eyes sharp, as always, assessing. On the other hand, Ilias leaned back in his seat, arms spread out over the backrest, looking like he owned the place—to be fair, we all did.

"You two took your damn time," Conall said, raising an eyebrow. "Did Angelo drive like someone's granny again?"

"Only because Maxim's too much of a princess to drive himself," Angelo muttered, releasing me with a good-natured shove as we slid into the booth.

I grinned, lifting my own glass after a waiter appeared to set it down. "Someone has to balance out all the tough guys around here. Besides, I have a reputation to maintain," I joked.

Ilias laughed, his effortless demeanor never entirely masking the cunning lurking underneath. "Some things don't change. You still bitching about everything, Maxim?"

"Are you still pretending you're the responsible one?" I countered, grinning at him.

The easy banter between us slipped into silence as we settled into our seats, each of us falling into our thoughts. We rarely got together like this; responsibilities pulled us in different directions, and we now ran our own crews, organizations, or businesses. But when we met, there was a certain gravity to it, as if the four of us coming together signaled something important, something inevitable.

Conall leaned forward, his tone dropping. "How's the business on the West Coast?"

I took a sip, then set my glass down. "It's good. The restructuring is taking longer than I'd like, but it's working. Besides, it has been quiet, which helps. Boring, honestly."

"Quiet isn't always a good thing," Angelo pointed out, swirling his whiskey. "Sometimes it's the calm before the storm."

"Well, I'm more than ready if anything kicks up." I wasn't concerned about trouble. There were measures that I'd taken for my West Coast operations, and now that Dimitri had resurfaced, I felt more comfortable than ever with how things stood. "How's New York?"

Angelo shrugged. "Good. Lots of turf issues."

Ilias nodded in agreement. "My guys tell me there's talk that the Olivetos are trying to take over some of the Scarpato's turf."

Angelo's gaze narrowed. "Oh, are they?" He scoffed. "Are we intervening or letting them hash it out?"

There were essentially five prominent Italian families in New York, but Angelo had been itching to take over and consolidate. He'd love to expand the Santelli family's reach. Angelo's mafia family was small but ruthless and efficient. While others in the Italian sector were hapless and without direction, Angelo kept a tight ship, and his men were loyal. It helped that the Santelli mafia was directly allied with all members of the Commission. It made a lethal combo. Cross one of us, and you crossed us all.

I shrugged. "For now, let's see what happens. But if they step too far, we'll act. We have enough to deal with."

Conall raised his glass, nodding in approval. "That's why we're here, isn't it? To keep each other informed and prepared. Stronger together."

Angelo was the first to break the moment. "Well, enough with the serious shit. I didn't build this place to sit around brooding. Let's celebrate—*Fortune* is open, business is booming, and we're all under one roof for the first time in years."

Ilias's face lit up, his grin widening. "Now that's what I'm talking about. Let's live a little."

He signaled the bartender for another round, and soon enough, drinks were flowing, laughter echoing off the walls of our new club. We'd come a long way from the reckless teenagers who set fire to that crumbling dive.

I glanced around the table at the faces of these men who had been through it all with me —fights, bloodshed, betrayal, and laughter. In a world where trust was a rare and precious thing, we'd managed to build something out of the ruins.

As the drinks flowed, Conall leaned in, lowering his voice, and his tone slipped from celebratory to strategic. "Maxim, we've heard rumors about a bratva outfit in the city. Their leadership is weak—infighting and lost alliances. It could be… ripe for the taking. It'd be nice to have someone in our corner here." He wagged his eyebrows at me.

I raised an eyebrow, intrigued but cautious. "New York has been a no-man's-land for the Volkovs for years. They're barely hanging on, then?"

Ilias nodded, his expression serious. "Yeah. They're running on fumes. From what I've heard, they've lost the loyalty of their men. Lost the respect of their allies, which means every crew in that territory is looking for a way in. If you step in, you can consolidate what's left and bring order. With us in your corner, you could do it. Bring your men, and it'd be a slam dunk."

Angelo leaned back, swirling his whiskey, but his gaze sharpened. "But leaving the West Coast? That's no small thing, Maxim. You've spent years building up your presence there. You walk away, even briefly, and someone will start circling."

I nodded slowly, my thoughts weighing the possibility against the reality of what I'd be leaving behind. "I get it. But I've established my foothold out there. New York would double our leverage. It would give us a strategic advantage, not to mention the control over trade routes."

Conall smirked, but there was a hint of concern in his eyes. "The problem is, there's no guarantee. The bratva here might be weak, but there are still others lurking. Some of the other families... they'll want a piece of it, and if you show up on their doorstep, they'll push back hard. Are we ready?"

Ilias chimed in, a note of caution in his voice. "Plus, your absence on the West Coast could send the wrong message. You've got rivals there who'd love to chip away at your territory while you're distracted."

I ran a hand over my jaw, absorbing their words. They were right, and I knew it. My empire in California was stable, but only because I was there to enforce that stability. The East Coast could bring new power, but it could also bring new problems. The idea of being close to my friends again was enticing. When we were young, it was something we had promised.

"I don't plan on abandoning the West Coast," I said firmly. "If I go, it's for the long game. And I'd be smart about it—split my time, keep my men in line. Build a bridge between both."

Angelo gave a slow nod, his calculating gaze fixed on me. "You'd need someone you trust to handle things in California while you're gone. Someone who commands respect. You have anyone like that?"

For a moment, I paused, picturing the men loyal to me who could handle the pressure. "There are a few. I'll need to put them to the test, but it might be worth the risk if it means expanding the family's reach and solidifying control coast-to-coast."

Conall raised his glass, his smirk returning. "Then here's to risk—and to new territory. If anyone's crazy enough to pull it off, it's you, Maxim."

The others joined in, and I lifted my glass, feeling the thrill of the unknown mixed with the cold, calculating drive that had been guiding me for years.

Conall lowered his glass, his tone shifting from the thrill of expansion to something heavier, more serious. "There's something else we need to discuss, lads. That old arrangement our fathers put in place—the blood oath."

I felt the weight of his words settle over the table and glance at the others. Conall's face was set, Angelo frowned, and Ilias looked annoyed. We all knew what he was talking about: the pact that bound our families together when we were kids, signed in blood and sealed by each of our fathers. They promised each other that we, their sons, would marry into each other's families to keep our alliance secure and unbreakable.

Conall was the oldest of us, and he was the one that kept us on track. He wasn't wrong. It was past time that we thought about this. It was a topic we'd avoided for a long time, but we'd been racing along toward honoring that blood oath in all ways but one.

Angelo rolled his eyes, looking unimpressed. "So? Are you saying it's time we followed through on that mess? We're grown men now, Conall. I think we should be able to choose who we marry."

Conall raised an eyebrow, holding Angelo's gaze. "That oath was no small thing, brother. It's not just a promise—it's a blood bond. And in our world, blood oaths aren't taken lightly. Don't be thinking we can break it. We have our blood on that feckin' thing. If we're going to expand—if Maxim's going to expand to New York—it might be time to solidify that bond. And like it or not, the best way to do that is through family." Conall sighed. "I'm getting older, and I'll need an heir soon. Like it or not, that's just how our world works."

Angelo huffed, running a hand through his hair. "And what if we disagree? If any one of us refuses, what then? The other families come for us? We've ignored it this long. Why can't we just keep ignoring it?"

Conall's jaw tightened. "Criminal organizations have short memories for good deeds and long ones for broken promises. You know as well as I do, Angelo—nobody breaks a blood oath and walks away unscathed. Do you want to be the one to test that theory?"

Angelo leaned back, still skeptical. Ilias scoffed, his eyes narrowing. "We're talking about marriage here, not business. Why should we be forced into something because of a promise our fathers made? I was fucking ten when he made me put blood on that paper," Ilias said sulkily.

"Because it's not just a promise. It's our

legacy." I spoke up, meeting each of their eyes. "Our fathers may have built this alliance with their shitty trafficking, but we tore that to the ground. We swore to each other that we'd build something better — something true and honest. It's up to us to keep our word and our promises. We might not have signed willingly, but we promised. Our word is our bond. If it means marrying into each other's families, so be it. I'll go first."

They knew I was right, and I saw resignation on Angelo and Ilias' faces. I didn't mention that I had other motives. It had only been recently that I'd found my half-sister Galena — my father's little secret. This agreement with the others would provide for her. Right now, she was on the fringes of the underworld — a target. Marrying one of my friends would protect her. I had left her to her normal life, but it was only a matter of time before she was discovered.

There was a pause as the others considered my words. Conall nodded, the corner of his mouth lifting in approval, while Angelo sighed, looking as if he were facing a firing squad. Ilias ground his teeth but finally shrugged, muttering, "Fine. Whatever."

"Good. I'm glad you all agree." Conall reached into his jacket pocket and pulled out four scraps of paper. "If we're doing this, let's keep it simple. Draw randomly, and that's the family you're marrying into. No arguments, no deals. Fate decides."

He folded each piece and tossed them into a tumbler before clearing his throat.

"Let's draw," he said, shaking the tumbler.

I narrowed my eyes at him as I watched him look at the glass before gingerly picking one of the scraps out before he indicated that the rest of us should draw. One by one, we drew until each of us was left holding a slip of paper. I unfolded mine. The name inked in dark letters stared back at me: *O'Kelly*.

The others revealed their slips. Conall smirked when he saw his—*Santelli*. Angelo, looking slightly amused, had *Anthakos*. Ilias frowned at his paper, turning it over in his fingers as if he could change it by force of will: *Volkov*.

So it would be Ilias who would have Galena's safety in his hands. I could live with that. The room fell into silence as we absorbed what this meant. Conall broke it, raising his glass again. "Looks like the plan is in motion."

Angelo chuckled, though there was a hint of tension in it. "Well, here's to alliances and to these poor girls that are stuck with us."

We all laughed, but underneath was the understanding that things were set in motion

26

now. There was no backing out. The blood oath had spoken, binding us not just by loyalty but by marriage into something deeper, more permanent.

If it was what was needed to secure our empires, then so be it.

CHAPTER THREE

cora

I LOVED TWO THINGS: *photography and watching zombie flicks. Luckily, even though I'd been exiled to Dublin, I could still do both.*

I CROUCHED BEHIND A BIN, tucking myself out of sight. My fingers lightly grazed the crumbling brick wall as I adjusted my camera, searching for the perfect angle. The narrow alley around me hummed with tension, every noise sharper, every shadow longer. The unmistakable rawness of this part of Dublin kept pulling me back, day after day, like a place out of some hazy memory.

Blanchardstown had its own pulse, a heart-beat that thrummed beneath the grit and graffiti, the boarded-up shopfronts, and chipped paint. It was nothing like the manicured streets where my uncle lived, with their trimmed hedges and clean front lawns, the kind of neighborhood that felt like a lie. Here, everything was laid bare. Life was raw and exposed, painted in harsh strokes that the rain couldn't wash away. Something in that honesty, even in the danger, made me feel more myself.

Being behind a camera excited me. I loved capturing people's lives when they weren't looking.

Their secrets.

Their arguments.

Their passion.

A psychologist would probably have a field day with me — the voyeur. Sneaking around and living vicariously through other people.

I was good at it, though. The sneaking.

My brothers would have a fit if they knew this was my passion project. I was supposed to be safely hidden away in my uncle's nice suburban house. I'd been here in Dublin for over a decade now since my older brother Conall shipped me off. I'd gone to school, and now … well, now I was just looking for trouble. I wasn't sure where I belonged anymore.

I steadied my camera and focused on a group of kids at the corner, hands jammed into their pockets as they shared a cigarette. One of them glanced my way, but I ducked before they noticed, letting the wall shield me. I held my breath and waited, the thrill of capturing this city's edges making my pulse quicken. It was the feeling of being on the brink of something bigger than myself, something I wasn't sure I understood but couldn't stay away from.

Blanchardstown had a reputation, one my uncle warned me about whenever I left his house. "Don't be daft, Cora, it isn't safe for ye' out there," he muttered every time I stepped out, reminding me that I'd be safer staying away from neighborhoods like this. But safety felt like a cage. My life had been about running from things unseen, the stained legacy my father left, and the enemies my brothers said lurked everywhere. With its broken glass and weary eyes, Blanchardstown didn't pretend to be anything other than what it was. It was a place where people survived, where life pushed through even when the odds were against it. Where fist fights broke out, where men paid for a quick blow job in a back alley, where kids stole a wallet here or there. I took pictures of it all.

I shifted, tightening my grip on the camera, capturing the rawness in every shot. A stray dog sniffed around a pile of trash, scrappy and fearless like it knew how to survive no matter how hard things got. I snapped a picture of it as it moved, hoping to capture the stubborn resilience in its eyes.

A pair of men walked by, hunched over and talking in low voices, heads bent as if shielding secrets from the world around them. I raised my camera, snapping a quick photo before they vanished around the corner. Here, everyone had a story—dark, twisted, or desperate—and I wanted to capture it all, every fleeting moment. This part of Dublin might be rough around the edges, but it was real in a way I couldn't turn away from.

I leaned against the wall, letting the cold seep into my bones, and wondered if my brothers ever felt the pull of a place like this. I wondered if they'd understand why I'd rather be here, surrounded by Dublin's harshness, than tucked away in my uncle's suburban bubble where the most exciting thing that happened was Maude next door arguing with her husband, Fred. I did catch Fred alone one day while Maude was at the market, but it wasn't that exciting. He was putting on her underwear. I only took a picture of his fingers running over the polyester lace and the expression of longing on his face, but I deleted it. Seemed wrong.

My brother Conall thought he was doing me a favor, keeping me in Dublin. "You'll be better off with Uncle Tommy," he'd said. But I knew what he meant: I'd be better off far away from him, from the life he and my brothers had chosen. I'd be out of reach from the secrets and threats woven into our family history. I'd be out of the way. I wouldn't be a bother.

We used to live in a fancy house with our father in a ritzy neighborhood in New York, but one night, Conall had bundled me up in my coverlet, stuffed my doll in my arm, and walked me out of the house. He'd held my head to his chest and told me not to look, but I had peeked. There had been splashes of red everywhere. Even then, I'd known what they were.

From then on, we'd lived in a crappy walk-up in Jersey with my other brothers. I'd only been four, but I wasn't stupid. I knew we were all hiding. I just hadn't been sure from what.

Conall worked like a dog for years to support us. He was the oldest. At the time, my brother Brody was only six, and my brother Paddy was eight. It was years before Conall had any help to put food on the table. Still, I ached for my brothers, even if they were a pain in my ass.

I snapped a shot of two people arguing behind a bar, then a man shoving his finger hard into the other person's chest, his breath coming out in white puffs. I skipped a few blocks, humming to myself.

My camera's shutter clicked away, capturing lives that were simple every day. Ordinary. Sometimes, I imagined what it would have been like to be ordinary myself. Instead, I had brothers an ocean away doing Irish mob things, and they'd put me over here like I was an unwanted item. Conall said I'd be brought back when it was safe. I was guessing I would be brought back when it was "necessary."

I tried to imagine his face the last time we spoke, his steady gaze as he said goodbye, the weight in his eyes. If I was honest, I didn't know who he was anymore, not in this life he'd chosen. I knew he was out there, wading into things I'd rather forget and business I wasn't sure I wanted to be part of. For now, I was left here, stranded.

I lingered by the river, watching how the overcast sky made everything softer as if Dublin knew how to keep secrets. This was a stark difference from the sharp edges I remembered America having. Every sound there seemed to pierce the air as if the city demanded to be heard. Here, the noise was a hum, a heartbeat. I lifted my camera and took another gray, endless photo of the quiet water.

Conall had some faulty ideas about the state

of things in Dublin. He sent me to live with my mother's brother, our uncle Tommy, from the McElroy side of the family. Uncle Tommy was decent enough as long as he was sober, but he could be a mean drunk. I'd lived with him since I was twelve, attending school and keeping to myself. Conall visited every few years for a day or so to check that my grades were up to par, but I was twenty-four now and wondering what the rest of my life looked like.

Conall said the O'Kelly name and the grudges our father left behind still lingered in certain corners. He told me to be careful, but honestly, he didn't understand that there weren't any "corners" here where I would talk to people who cared, nobody I would whisper secrets to. When I came to Dublin at twelve, I knew nobody and had no friends. Twelve years later, I still knew nobody and had no friends. My uncle was protective and strict when it came to outsiders.

I had been too young to remember the things my dad had been involved in, but I knew that Conall killed our father. There were two theories. One was that it was to take over the businesses that our father had, and the other was that Conall killed him finally in retribution for our mother's death.

Either way, I was sure my father deserved it.

I headed home. Maybe I would put on *Zombieland*, order takeout, and edit my pictures from today. It sounded like the perfect evening.

Maybe I would consider getting a job or a boyfriend. I sighed.

Maybe not.

CHAPTER FOUR

maxim

I LEANED against the grimy leather booth in the back of the club, scanning the room. New York differed from San Diego, where everything had sharp edges and glitter, but it was still built on the same foundation—power, influence, and fear. The bratva here was just as the boys said — fractured, led by weak men with big mouths and little reach, ripe for the taking. That was why I was here, after all.

The thought of it excited me, and nothing had truly excited me in years.

Beside me, Lev leaned casually against the wall, arms crossed, his hawk-like gaze on the room. Lev had been my right hand since I was young. He glanced over, raising one eyebrow as a smile tugged at the corner of his mouth.

"So," Lev said, voice low, "you plan to sit here all night and brood, or are we going to make a move on this place? Get our blood pumping?"

I smirked. "Well, you know that this brooding look works, Lev. It gets people nervous. People make mistakes when they're nervous."

Lev rolled his eyes. "You know what else makes people nervous? A couple of Russians kicking in doors."

Lev wasn't much for standing still and doing nothing. He was ready for action and knocking some heads together. Things had been a little stale lately on the West Coast, and he hoped for blood and guts in this takeover.

"Patience, Lev. I need to get the lay of the land. Can't charge in like bulls," I teased.

Lev snorted. "Sure."

I glanced at the bar, tracking the men gathered there. A cluster of bratva lieutenants sat around the corner, oblivious to us for now, caught up in their petty conversations. The head of this fractured crew, Vladimir Slavsky, was set to arrive any minute, thinking we'd come here to discuss terms for a partnership. What a laugh. The fool didn't realize we were here to kick him to the curb.

If this were my territory, no way would I allow some mudaks like us into my joint without being challenged. They were fools. If Slavsky had any brains at all, he should have known what was about to happen. A Volkov at his gates? Fucker should have shot me on sight.

"Here he comes," Lev muttered, nodding toward the door.

I straightened, my eyes narrowing as Vladimir strode in, a thick coat draped over his shoulders and two guards flanking him. He scanned the room briefly, but I didn't miss how his eyes skimmed over us carelessly. Vladimir was too confident for a man with so little power and so little control over his men. I'd already bribed half of them, and the other half had already agreed to work with us.

"Maxim Volkov," Vladimir drawled as he approached. "I was surprised when I heard you wanted to meet."

I offered a thin smile. "I thought it was time we cleared the air."

His eyes flicked to Lev, dismissing him immediately, and my respect for him waned further. It was a mistake that was going to cost him.

Vladimir leaned against the table, trying to look casual. "Clearing the air… That's a polite way of saying you want in on my territory.

You're not the first man to try, Volkov. New York's different from your little operation out West in the sunshine and the beaches. We don't take kindly to outsiders."

"Outsiders?" I echoed, feigning surprise. "Last time I checked, the bratva doesn't recognize borders. And from what I hear, Slavsky, your bratva hasn't successfully held on to your territory."

Vladimir bristled, his hand twitching toward his belt before he stopped himself. Lev's eyes caught the movement, and he stepped closer on guard if Vladimir decided to pull his piece.

"Let's keep this civil," Vladimir sneered. "What do you want exactly? A piece of the action?"

My elbows rested on the table as I leaned forward. "Civil? By all means, let's keep it civil. Here's my offer—I take over your territory, and you get a choice. Walk away now, and I'll let you live. Stay… and I'll be less generous."

Vladimir made a short, harsh sound. "You think you can just waltz in here and take over? You can't be serious."

I tilted my head, giving him a cold, appraising look. "Yes."

Lev was already moving before Vladimir's hand finished reaching for his gun. In one swift motion, Lev twisted his wrist behind Vladimir's back, forcing him to his knees. The guards snapped into action, but I didn't give them a chance. I stood, throwing a punch into the jaw of the nearest man, then drove my knee into his stomach before pulling out my H&K and shooting him in the head when he tried to pull his piece. The guard crumpled, and Lev's knife found the throat of the second.

The room erupted into chaos. A few patrons tried to slip out the back, but most stayed glued to their seats, eyes wide with fear. No one dared to interfere or help.

"You're making a big mistake," Vladimir gasped, struggling in Lev's iron grip.

I crouched down beside him, my voice low and icy. "The only mistake here is yours, Vladimir. You let this territory slip through your fingers; now, it's mine. You were too weak to hold it."

Vladimir's face twisted with fury. "You won't get away with this. New York isn't like fucking Hollywood. You'll never have control here."

I sighed, glancing at Lev. "You hear that, Lev? He doesn't think we can take control."

Lev grinned, giving Vladimir's arm a painful twist. "Maybe we should show him otherwise?"

"Good idea," I agreed. I reached into my

pocket, pulling out a slip of paper. "This is a list of your allies. Those who aren't with me by midnight will be dealt with. One way or another, you're done here, Vladimir."

"You're insane," Vladimir spat. "They'll come for you."

I gave him a thin smile. "Let them try." I wasn't sure who Vladimir thought 'they' were, but his bratva here was a joke. He shouldn't have even been calling himself a pakhan. I would give his men a chance to prove they could be part of the Volkov Bratva, and then we'd weed out the disloyal ones.

With a nod, Lev hauled Vladimir to his feet and pushed him toward the exit. "Consider this your farewell tour, Vladimir. Get out of New York, and if I see you again, it'll be the last time you breathe fresh air."

I kept my promises. He could walk out a free man.

As Vladimir stumbled out, cursing, Lev straightened his jacket and shot me a satisfied look. "Not bad for a night's work."

I chuckled, finally pulling out my cigarette and lighting it. "Well, Lev, I think New York is starting to feel like home. Wish I could have killed that mudak, but I keep my word. Maybe he'll have an accident soon." I emphasized the last part, knowing that Lev would catch my drift.

"You got it, pakhan." Lev winked, telling me we were on the same wavelength. "It'd be most unfortunate, but the world is a dangerous place."

I recognized a few of the men we'd spoken to in Slavsky's ranks. They stood at attention.

"Pakhan," a man said, bowing his head. "Your orders?"

"Clean this shit up." I lit a cigarette as I indicated the bodies. "Lev will be in touch."

Around us, a few curious onlookers peered cautiously out of alleys, their faces lit with nervous energy as they realized this part of New York had a new owner. I took a long drag on my cigarette, ignoring the weight of their stares.

Lev's mouth quirked into a grin, his eyes glinting with satisfaction as we left the club. He scanned the empty street.

"What now?" he murmured, his eyes gleaming in anticipation.

I exhaled a slow ribbon of smoke into the chilly night air, feeling the rush of satisfaction. "Now, we send a message. Call the men. I want them to hit all of Vladimir's operations—ports, warehouses, and clubs. Silence any resistance before anyone has a chance to sound the alarm."

Lev nodded quickly, his bloodthirsty grin wide. "All at once?"

I flicked the cigarette to the gutter and ground it with my heel, a slow smile creeping over my face. "All at once. Vladimir's men swear loyalty or get out of our district. No exceptions. Any resistance at all — wipe it out."

Lev didn't hesitate, already barking orders on his phone in clipped Russian, his voice sharp and decisive. I watched him out of the corner of my eye, savoring the anticipation building in my chest. Taking the bratva here in New York wasn't just about Vladimir. It was time to show people what operating under the Volkov Bratva meant.

"Vlad's men are heading for the East River docks," Lev said, his phone pressed to his ear. "Kolya's crew will take Queens."

"Perfect." I nodded, watching the night absorb his words. "Ask Conall's men to support. Make sure there's no chatter. We don't want a word out until it's done."

Lev smirked. "Nothing like a clean slate."

The crisp air felt charged with purpose as we stepped out of the alley, our car just across the street. We were halfway there when Lev stopped short, his eyes narrowing at a figure lurking near the doorway. I knew him before I even saw his face.

Dante Caruso.

I took in his smirking expression, the easy stance. He was more of a snake than an enforcer, but that hadn't stopped the low-level asshole from sneaking around and causing problems. Even as a teenager, he was a thorn in our sides. He worked with the Olivetos if memory served and wouldn't work with Angelo if he were starving. I never had figured out why he hated us so much.

"Well, well," Dante drawled, his voice low and taunting. "So it's true."

I met his stare head-on, my voice sharp. "Caruso. You should know better than to slink around in shadows. I could have shot you. You know … by mistake. What a shame that would be." We both knew I didn't mean it.

He just laughed, shaking his head. "Not sneaking, Volkov. Just here to let you know you aren't welcome in this city. You should have stayed out West and away from here. Or died," he said maliciously.

I stepped toward him and said, "I couldn't care less what you think. I'm here to stay. You can tell that to the Olivetos."

Dante's face tightened, but he masked it quickly, his easy smirk snapping back into place. "Is that so? Plenty of people around here might take issue with a Volkov taking a seat at their table. You're all dirty scum. All the Volkovs are. Like your father."

The dig hit hard. I was nothing like my father. The man was a piece of shit.

I felt Lev tense beside me, his hand drifting subtly toward his side, but I raised a hand, keeping my gaze steady on Dante. If I couldn't handle Dante Caruso on my own, then I shouldn't be a pakhan. "New York's changing. I don't care who has an issue with me being at the table."

Dante's smirk faltered briefly before he laughed, low and quiet. "You're a stain. You and your pops did unspeakable things. You're no man. One day, I'll make sure that everyone knows it."

I said nothing, just kept my eyes trained on him as he shook his head and turned, fading into the night's shadows. When he was gone, I glanced at Lev; his eyes were slick with hate as he looked after Dante. Both Lev and I had our reasons for hating my father and the things he had done. To be blamed for the small parts that we had to play was unfounded and unkind. That asshole didn't know what he was talking about, but still, my gut twisted with the words that Dante had thrown into the universe.

Fucking Dante Caruso.

I was sure that other people thought I should have made a move sooner than I had.

Done more.

When I was twenty-one, I'd barely scraped together enough power and backing to keep myself and my brother alive. Youngest pakhan ever in the history of the bratva. If I had been alone, without Dimitri to worry about, maybe I could have found a way to end my father sooner.

Fuck Dante Caruso.

"He's a problem," Lev muttered, his tone dark.

"Yeah." I acknowledged before stepping toward the car. There wasn't much right now that we could do about Dante hating that we were back in New York. We had another focus right now. I'd worry about Dante later. It wasn't like I could take him out unless we wanted war with the Olivetos. "I want Vladimir's men to feel the shift by dawn," I said, pulling our focus back to the job at hand.

Lev's grin matched mine as he slipped behind the wheel. "They won't know what hit them."

The hours blurred together as we drove between districts, our men slipping into Vladimir's old haunts and bringing his empire under our control one step at a time. Each warehouse, dock, and club fell into place, the pieces clicking together like they were always meant to be mine. By the time we were done, the city was silent, the weight of our work hanging over New York like a new bloody dawn.

At sunrise, I stood in the courtyard of my new townhouse in Manhattan, the first light gleaming off skyscrapers in the distance. My phone buzzed, Lev's message glowing on the screen: *It's done. New York is ours.*

I pocketed my phone, a smile tugging at the corner of my mouth. New York might be a beast, but now? It was my beast. And this was only the beginning.

* * *

Me: done

Conall: elaborate, you tool, it's six in the morning

Me: took over Vlad's operation

Conall: good for you

Angelo: took you long enough

Me: it's only been a month 😕

Ilias: I'd have done it in a week

Conall: you want a cookie or something?

Me: yes

Ilias: 🍪

Me: I hate you all

CHAPTER FIVE

cora

THE LATE AFTERNOON light in Dublin was softer than I expected. It seemed to settle like a gentle haze over the brick buildings and narrow cobblestone streets. When I lifted my camera, I spotted one of my favorite kinds of prey—a pair of young lovers parked on a side street, wrapped up in themselves.

I was fascinated. Each desperate grab and clutch was another click until the clothes started coming off, and then I felt like a creep.

I probably was a creep anyway.

Photography was my solace, the one place I could escape all of this—my family, the mob, the weight of expectations I never asked for. I'd always been the quiet watcher with a lens to hide behind. My brother, Conall, said I could capture a ghost if I set my mind to it. I'm not sure that he was complimenting me.

I ducked into a quieter street, my boots echoing softly on the damp cobblestones. The shadows were longer here, stretched by the dimming light as the sun dipped behind the horizon. I raised my camera again, framing an abandoned storefront with graffiti scrawled across its glass. Through the lens, I saw layers: the bright, chipped colors, the empty alley, and the flicker of streetlights beginning to warm up for the night.

I adjusted the focus, moving slightly to get a better angle, and that was when I saw them.

Two men, just across the alley, their faces partially hidden in the shadows. One of them had his hand gripping the other's collar, and even from this distance, I could see the sheer force of his hold.

Click.

The second man, smaller and looking like he was on the wrong end of a miserable evening, sputtered and stumbled as he was pulled up against the wall.

Click.

They were too far for me to hear what was being said, but I could read the menace in the posture, the hard glint in the taller man's eyes, and see the knife as it was raised and lowered over and over.

Click.

Then, the blood on the cobblestones—too much blood. I knew what that meant.

Click.

My pulse quickened immediately, the gravity of what I'd done sinking in as I pulled the camera away from my face. The shutter's click felt too loud, an accidental flag waving in their direction. I turned, hoping they hadn't heard, but just as I did, I caught movement out of the corner of my eye.

The man's head jerked in my direction.

Run.

It was the only thought I managed before my legs responded, propelling me back toward the main street. My footsteps were quick and light, but I could feel him picking up behind me, the sharp sound of someone else's boots closing in. I clutched my camera to my chest, my breath coming in shallow, panicked bursts.

A glance over my shoulder confirmed my worst fear: the man had followed me, his face hard and eyes narrowed like a predator who'd caught the scent.

Dublin was a maze of alleys and side streets, and I slipped down the first turn I saw, hoping to lose him. My heart pounded as I ducked past an overturned trash can. My pulse roared in my ears. If I could make it to the next block, I could disappear into a crowd, blend in, and vanish.

Shit. I'd been stupid before, but this was really stupid.

I nearly tripped as I rounded a corner, the cobblestones uneven beneath my feet. My lungs burned, but I couldn't slow down. I knew how these things went; Conall made sure I understood from the time I was small. He'd been a thug even then. Stealing food and working in low-level gangs to put food on the table. Some people witnessed things and lived to tell the tale. And then, there were the others that didn't live at all.

If you could, you should run.

Another turn, another empty street. The sky was dimmer now, casting deep shadows that seemed to swallow everything whole. I couldn't hear him anymore, but I was not foolish enough to think I'd outrun him. I ducked into a recessed doorway, pressing my back against the cold, damp stone as I tried to catch my breath. My grip tightened on my camera, my only weapon, the evidence that could get me killed.

I waited, willing myself to stay still and blend with the shadows. But a flicker of movement near the end of the street made my stomach drop. He was there, his face half-lit by a weak streetlight, his eyes scanning the alley like a wolf sniffing out prey.

For a moment, I thought he'd missed me. That he'd keep walking, but then his gaze snapped to my hiding spot, his expression hardening. He'd found me.

My body reacted instinctually, pushing off the doorway and sprinting in the opposite direction. I could hear him behind me, closer this time, his footsteps pounding against the stones. The alley opened onto a broader street, busy enough that people glanced up at me with idle curiosity as I dashed past, but no one stopped me or intervened.

Up ahead, I saw the faint glow of neon and the hum of a pub alive with chatter. I veered toward it, slipped inside, and pressed myself against the wall by the door, heart racing. The noise, the warmth, the crowd—it was a sharp contrast to the cold terror that had been chasing me.

I scanned the room, looking for somewhere to hide and blend in. Just as I started to move, the door swung open, and he stepped inside, his gaze sweeping the room, searching.

For fuck sake. Why wouldn't he just give up? A back alley murder. Who cared? I wasn't going to the Guards or anything. I shouldn't have been taking pictures in the first place.

I held my breath, ducking my head and hoping he'd pass me by, but he was too close, and I could feel his eyes lingering, his footsteps slowing as he looked in my direction.

I pressed myself further against the wall, trying to disappear into the dimly lit corner. The pub's noise swelled around me—a shield of voices, laughter, and clinking glasses. He was scanning the room with the intensity of a predator. I saw his eyes flicking over each face, searching, calculating.

Desperation coursed through me. If he found me now, if he knew what I saw…

Stupid. Of course, he knew.

The man stepped further inside. His shoulders tensed, his sharp gaze narrowing as he caught sight of the camera strap slung across my shoulder. For a split second, our eyes met, and my stomach dropped. His expression shifted, a flicker of recognition like he'd caught me in the act. He knew.

I didn't wait. Before he could react, I pushed through the crowd, elbowing past people with mumbled apologies. I could hear him moving after me, the subtle disturbance he left in his wake as people looked back, confused by the tension simmering beneath his steady, deadly pace.

I spotted an exit door toward the back, marked for staff. It was a gamble, but I didn't have a choice. I burst through it, finding myself in a narrow, damp alley lit only by a flickering light above the door. The smell of stale beer and garbage filled the air, and I resisted the urge to gag, pulling my coat tighter as I raced down the alley.

There was a pounding in my ears, a drumbeat of adrenaline and fear. My shoes slapped against the wet pavement, and I fought to keep my balance as I navigated the slick cobblestones. Behind me, the door swung open, and I knew he was still relentlessly following me.

At the end of the alley, I spotted a wrought-iron gate. Without thinking, I leapt for it, hoisting myself over the bars, my fingers scraping against the cold metal as I pulled myself to the other side. I landed with a jolt, knees buckling slightly, but I forced myself upright, glancing back just in time to see him stop on the other side of the gate.

He stared at me, a flicker of irritation passing over his face as he realized the obstacle I'd put between us. The following look was even worse—a cold, calculated amusement. Like this wasn't over. Like he was just getting started.

I took a shaky step backward, unable to tear

my eyes from his. The message was clear. I wouldn't be able to outrun him forever.

I forced myself to turn, bolting down the narrow street. I didn't stop until I reached the open plaza, my lungs screaming, my heart slamming against my ribs. Only when I was among the scattered evening crowd did I let myself slow, blending in with the people milling around the square. I turned my head, peeking back the way I'd come.

He was nowhere in sight. I exhaled shakily, barely daring to believe I'd lost him.

I slipped into a café on the corner and sat by the window. I clutched my camera tightly, its familiar weight grounding me amid the fear still coursing through my veins. I turned it on with trembling fingers, scrolling through the photos, praying they were not blurred.

The shots were clear. Crisp. Damning.

I'd captured everything—the tension in the tall man's stance, his iron grip on the other man's collar, the cold fury in his eyes as he delivered what I now realized was a death blow. Holy shit. Murder.

The pictures were great, though I thought with satisfaction.

I bit my lip, struggling to piece together what I'd just witnessed. Whatever it was, it landed me in a shitstorm. I didn't think the man who chased me would stop until he found me. That was a problem. The last thing I needed was for some rando to chase me around Dublin.

The barista approached, startling me from my thoughts. I ordered a coffee, keeping my voice as steady as I could manage, and then took a shaky sip as I thought through my options.

I could delete the photos and erase everything, and I hope he didn't find me, but I didn't think that would do me any good. Conall always said information was power. The photos contained information and proof. If I had to, I could use them. Right?

A soft chime broke the café's quiet, and I looked up, my heart in my throat. A figure stood just outside the window, looking in.

It was him.

And he was watching me with that same cold gaze.

Weighing my options, I knew one thing with certainty. I didn't think that I had the tools to run from this guy if he was chasing me around Dublin. I was bored here anyway. Maybe it was time to go home. With shaking fingers, I sent my brother a text.

Me: I need to come home. Now. Urgent.

Conall: OK. I'll be there for you at midnight. Pin your location. I'm sending a car.

Dropping a pin as he instructed, I watched

the door until two competent men walked in thirty minutes later. I breathed a sigh of relief when one of them said, "O'Kelly sent us to escort you to the airport."

Nodding, I followed them, keeping one eye on the periphery of the building, but I didn't see any sign of the man. I still felt the tingle on the back of my neck. It wasn't until we were in the car and gone that I felt somewhat safer.

THE PLANE SHUDDERED with the force of the gangway touching the pavement, and I could already see Conall's broad shoulders in the doorway. Typical Conall, sharp, intense, always a little too much in everyone's face. He waved me over, and his impatience was as visible as the leather coat that stretched tight over his shoulders. I hadn't seen him in over three years, but he didn't look much different. Harder maybe.

There was a concern there, though. I'd never doubted that my brother loved me with every particle of his being.

"Thanks for coming, Conall." He wrapped me in a fierce hug, kissing the top of my head.

"What happened?" he said, voice low, as we

settled into the plush leather seats. The jet hummed to life as the pilot readied for takeoff back to New York.

I shrugged, trying to keep my face neutral. "Just… felt like it was time." I wondered if I'd been hasty when I asked him to come. Maybe it would have blown over if I had just gone back to Uncle Tommy's.

He didn't look convinced. His eyes narrowed as they studied me. "Don't be an eejit. You texted me that it was urgent. That was the word you used." He tilted his head, a smirk forming. "Cora, you've never been one to run unless you're being chased."

"I was bored."

He frowned. "I had them collect your things from Uncle Tommy's since you wouldn't go back."

"Thanks."

I busied myself looking out the window, watching Dublin shrink below us as we climbed into the clouds. I was not ready to tell him about what I saw in the alley or the strange man who had nearly caught me. I could feel Conall watching, waiting for more than I gave him, but it wasn't really important. Was it? That guy wouldn't be following me to New York.

"Are you being chased?" he pressed, and I

glanced at him, feigning innocence. His gaze searched my face. "Did something happen?"

I met his eyes, forcing a small smile. "Nothing happened that could follow me here."

He didn't look satisfied, but he dropped it. Instead, his expression softened a fraction, and he leaned back. "It was time for you to come home, anyway."

The way he said it, like a loaded gun just waiting to go off, sent a chill through me. "Why do you say that?"

He hesitated, just for a second, but it was enough to make me wary. "The family has been... adjusting. There's been a lot going on. We need everyone in place."

It was deliberately vague, and I felt a growing unease twisting inside me. Conall didn't leave things up to interpretation, not like this. If he was dancing around the truth, it meant there was something big he was trying to shield me from. Conall always had big plans — grand schemes. If I was being included, I didn't like the sound of that.

"Are we in trouble?" I asked quietly.

"No," he said, a little too quickly, forcing a reassuring smile. "But you're not going back to Dublin. It's time for you to be where you belong."

I didn't push further, but his words didn't bode well.

CHAPTER SIX

maxim

BEING the swanky fucker that Conall was, he bought an entire building in Vinegar Hill to house his operations. He was also extra paranoid, so I had to wade through bodyguards before I could get upstairs to his apartments to bang on the door.

The guard at the door perked up as he recognized me, smiling. If he were in my bratva, I'd kick his ass for smiling like that at people. "Good afternoon, Mr. Volkov. Glad to hear that you're going to be around permanently."

"Thank you, Owen," I nodded, giving the guard the answer he was looking for.

Permanently wasn't precisely the word for it. For the last six months, I'd traveled back and forth to San Diego to manage operations on both coasts. Then, there was the whole business with my cousins. Natasha had been attacked in Arizona, but by some stroke of luck, she had been on a video call with Conall, and he'd spotted someone in the courtyard with her. We got her help just in time.

Thankfully, things were finally stable there, but I'd been busy.

Enzo and Dimitri had a firm handle on the West Coast operations, so it would mean that I should be able to keep my visits to twice a year. It had been a rocky road to get things to that stage. Enzo had been loyal, and he deserved the promotion. I had hoped that Dimitri would have a more active interest, but he'd been adamant about remaining in Arizona, where his family and friends were. It pissed me off, but I understood. He'd agreed to step back into a role with the bratva — something he swore he'd never do, so I would take what I could get.

Vladimir had an unfortunate accident in Jersey — we were all terribly sorry, and so far, Caruso had sent two threats to the new townhome I'd bought.

"Your boss in?" I asked, indicating the door.

"He's expecting you."

I stood outside Conall's apartment, listening to the muffled sounds of life inside. I usually didn't make house calls, but Conall was adamant earlier. Ringing the bell, I waited for him to answer. Honestly, I didn't have time for this, but Conall was Conall. There was no way that I wouldn't have come.

When the door was pulled open, and it was not Conall's face, my brain couldn't compute. Instead, there was a curvy black-haired beauty standing there. She looked like she stepped out of a Disney adaptation of Snow White. Fuck, she was gorgeous. Her cheeks turned rosy as if she were imagining all the dirty things I was thinking while looking at that mouth of hers.

"Don't just open the feckin' door like that, Cora!" Conall stormed forward, and I tried to catch up as I stared from her to him. "You wait for Owen to say it's okay first, you spanner."

"Somebody knocked," she said like it was the logical thing to do. "Looks like a friend of yours," she added derisively. Something told me she didn't think much of Conall's occupation.

"Gah, I need to get you a keeper. Like yesterday."

Cora.

The sister.

My soon-to-be wife.

My cock twitched at the thought.

The last time I saw Cora, she was a tiny thing hiding behind her brother's leg at some godforsaken gathering. Conall had called her his "little shadow," which was fitting enough. She'd been all big green eyes and dark hair, watching everything as if she understood more than a six-year-old should. Conall had already assumed responsibility for his family, but I was still struggling under my father's control.

"Cora," I managed, and it came out rougher than I intended. As I took her in, I felt an unfamiliar jolt akin to surprise. She had grown up. That much was obvious—the kind of beauty that stopped a man in his tracks. Black hair fell down her back, and those eyes—emerald green and intense— searched me just as openly as I was her. She was dressed like an urchin in torn jeans and a t-shirt, but even that couldn't hide her lush, soft figure. Already, my mouth was watering. "Can I come in then? Or should I stay out here?"

"Let him in," Conall said, and Cora moved to the side, but her face gave nothing away, which was disconcerting. There was no recognition, no trace of the little girl she used to be. Her gaze was unflinching, guarded as though assessing a stranger. Although I'm not sure why I thought she would remember me.

For a second, I was unmoored. I hadn't expected her to look like this—hadn't expected her to look at me like this. Like I meant nothing to her. Sure, I'd thought about the moment I'd marry Conall's sister, but it was an abstract idea

—a name on a piece of paper, a duty to be fulfilled. A box to check. But now, staring at her, I felt that reality settling heavily onto my shoulders. She wasn't just a name or a promise. She was very real and very much a woman. Now that she was standing in front of me, reality smacked me in the chest, and it took my breath away.

I was starting to catch up and couldn't tell if I was scared shitless that Conall wanted me to honor the promise I had made to go first or if I was excited. Was Cora coming back planned when he brought it up? It wouldn't surprise me. Conall was a strategic thinker, and he could be a sneaky fucker.

"So," she said finally, breaking the silence that had stretched too long. Her tone was neutral, but there was a flicker of something behind her eyes. "Who are you?"

Clearing my throat, trying to find my usual charm, I smiled at her. "You were right. I am a friend of Conall's. I'm Maxim Volkov."

"Friend of Conall's. I'm Cora. The sister they've been hiding," she said the last a little bitterly, and I heard the hurt in it.

"Let's talk in my office, Maxim," Conall suggested. "That meeting I wanted."

"Sure." Tucking my hands into my slacks, I

gave Cora a nod. "Maybe we'll have a chance to get to know each other later."

"Maybe."

Oh, zayka. *Little rabbit*. I promised. I definitely would be getting to know her. Intimately.

Conall led us down a hallway lined with polished wood and tasteful art. He'd made sure that the crappy apartments he'd had to put his siblings in were in his past. We stepped into his office, which was more like a fortress than a workplace. It had a wall of screens, polished mahogany furniture, and floor-to-ceiling windows overlooking the river. The man knew how to make a statement.

The door clicked shut, and Conall gestured toward the leather chair opposite his desk. I took a seat, leaning back as he settled in. He had that look in his eye, something hard-edged that wasn't there when we were kids, and I knew it meant he had a plan—or a concern he wanted to address. I was pretty sure I knew what it was, but I waited.

"Thanks for meeting me here," Conall started, reaching for the crystal decanter on his desk. He poured two glasses of whiskey and handed me one. "How was San Diego?"

"Solid," I replied, taking a sip. The whiskey burned just right. "Enzo and Dimitri have the West Coast running smoothly, so I'll stay on this coast for a while. Natasha is good. That has all smoothed over. She and her man Pike are doing well now. Pretty sure Ronnie has settled too."

"Good." Conall nodded, but there was tension behind his gaze. He hadn't brought me here to discuss San Diego.

I gave him a look that said to get to the point, and he didn't miss it. He set his glass down, lacing his fingers together.

"About Cora," he said finally, his tone lowering. "She called me out of the blue. Wanted me to pick her up from Dublin—no explanations, nothing. Just told me to come, and…" He shook his head. "She's never asked that before. She has been happy there. Never complained. Much. Something spooked her."

I stayed quiet, watching him. I knew this was hard for Conall. He had always been protective of her, more so than I had imagined, but he had always been a closed book on the subject of his sister. He'd kept her away from our world, from everything. None of the O'Kellys ever talked about Cora once she left for Dublin, and I was too busy to bother asking. Yet here she was, back in a world that didn't forgive or forget.

"She's not a kid anymore," I said carefully. "She's old enough. If she wanted to come back, there's a reason for it."

What Conall said didn't sit right with me. If something scared her enough to call her brother, I wanted to know what happened to freak her out. "Did she have anyone in her life there?"

Conall's eyes flicked to the side. "I don't think so. Tommy made sure to keep her protected. I can't be sure," he admitted.

I wasn't so old-fashioned that I expected my wife to be a virgin, but I wasn't sure I could marry her if she were in love with someone else.

"She won't tell me why she messaged," Conall continued as if that was of no consequence. "And the way she looks at me... it's like she's watching every word, looking for something I haven't said."

I leaned forward, catching his gaze. "Is there something you haven't said?"

His silence was answer enough. He broke my gaze, then exhaled, the barest hint of vulnerability showing through the cracks. "It's time to move forward with our fathers' arrangement."

I was expecting it. The weight of his words settled over us, heavier than anything else in the room. We both knew it was coming. That old blood oath would tie us together in an unbreakable alliance, but knowing and acting on it were two different things.

"Was that why you brought her back?" I asked. "So we could... honor that agreement?"

He stared at his empty glass, expression hard. "She's here, and you're here. I would have brought her back eventually, but she called me. I think it's time." He looked back at me, all sharp edges and conviction. "We all have our territories to solidify. Marrying into each other's families only strengthens us. It's how our fathers built their crews and how we'll keep ours. The safety of our families should be considered. I know you'll take care of Cora."

I took a deep breath, absorbing the reality of it. In our business, wives lent us credibility, and we all knew it. It was an old-fashioned custom, but we worked with the systems that we had. I heard what Conall didn't say. The system was a way of protecting our sisters. Protecting our women. Cora was one of Conall's greatest treasures and greatest weaknesses. He was passing her on to me to protect. "I'll honor it," I said quietly. "I'll go first."

Conall's eyes met mine, satisfaction flickering there. He knew the weight of that promise, and so did I. "Good," he said. "Then it's settled, but Maxim."

I knew what he would say, and I squared my shoulders. "I'll treat her right, Conall. You have my word." His throat bobbed, and I saw him tapping the desk with the knife he kept on the blotter.

The conversation shifted to logistics, and we focused on territories and operations. I discussed my plans for the Bratva and how I'd handle the fractured groups that needed to be brought in line. Conall offered advice, and we mapped out a plan. If some of the other groups knew exactly how closely we worked together, they'd be appalled. Not only were we allied, but we shared almost everything and gathered ideas from each other — respected each other. Our long-range strategy had always been for each group to have an allied territory, which meant we all needed to have our respective areas under control.

"You know this shit with Caruso is just that — shit," he said when I stood straightening my jacket.

"You're not concerned?" I asked. Now that he'd brought Cora here and I was actually going to marry her, I wondered if it gave him pause … the things that Caruso said. That I was a *stain*. It still stung.

"Why would I be concerned? That little maggot knows feck all about what it took for us to get out and set things right. Don't you waste one-second thinking about that arsewipe."

I cleared my throat and shifted uncomfortably. "That means a lot to me. Thanks, Con," I paused. "Do you want to speak with Cora, or do you want me to?"

"I'll speak with her if you don't mind."

I didn't mind. I'd prefer. I was sure no woman liked to be told they had to marry someone.

"Tell her I'll pick her up tomorrow for dinner."

As I walked back through the silent hallways toward the exit, I couldn't shake the image of Cora standing there, green eyes sharp, assessing. She was no longer the little shadow who once hid behind her brother's leg.

She was something more now, something that would soon be mine, and the weight sat heavy and strange in my chest.

As I stepped outside into the sharp night air of New York, I wondered how she'd feel about this arrangement—if she'd resist it or accept it as inevitable.

Either way, there was no going back now.

CHAPTER SEVEN

cora

CONALL'S HEAVY FOOTSTEPS APPROACHED, each seeming to echo through the space as I waited in one of the guest rooms, still trying to process the man who had just left. Maxim Volkov. The name alone sounded dangerous, even if I hadn't felt the weight of his presence like an unspoken threat the moment I'd opened the door.

I'd bet he would be a good end-of-the-world partner. The guy probably wouldn't blink in the face of a zombie coming at him. These were things to consider. People could laugh if they wanted, but I had standards, and they all began with … could the guy knife a zombie? Yes or no. Maxim Volkov could with a smile on his face. No doubt.

I'd bet that Maxim Volkov would kill anything and dance in its blood. That'd be a picture worth taking.

I remembered him in pieces. He was one of my brother's friends from years ago, though I never saw much of him. A tall figure in shadows, a hard, unreadable expression. Even when he was younger, he looked angry. But now, that impression paled compared to the man who looked at me as if he were going to eat me alive.

He wasn't Irish. That much was obvious. Russian, through and through—those hard, unreadable eyes, the way he moved, the accent, and the sense of command he exuded without saying a word. I felt myself shiver, partly from that intense stare and partly from the realization that he must be tied to the same world Conall inhabited. Whatever Maxim Volkov was, he was no ordinary businessman.

He was hot, I had to admit. He was tall, at least six-four, broad, and muscular. He was not quite as stocky as Conall, but he was built like a god with dark brown eyes and hair. Tattoos peeked from his suit and covered even his hands. Maxim was sin and sex.

Probably would know where my clit was. I wondered if he could make me feel like those girls felt in those encounters I'd photographed

— the ones with glazed eyes. I wondered what sinking to my knees for him would be like. If he had a big cock. I'll bet he did. The thought made me all wet and warm.

Conall entered the room, his face set and serious, ruining my musings. He didn't sit down but watched me from where he stood. During their meeting, I'd set up camp on the king-sized bed with leftover snacks from my backpack and found a streaming channel with *The Walking Dead*. All that had been missing was pizza, and I could have died happy, but from the look on Conall's face, that wasn't going to happen.

"What was that about?" I asked, my voice coming out steadier than I felt. "Where is everyone? Brody and Paddy?"

He gave me that familiar, unreadable look before he spoke. "I'll be giving you the tour tomorrow. They don't know you're here yet, or they'd be banging on the door like the gobshites they are. There's something we need to discuss, Cora. Something I was going to wait on, but circumstances have changed."

The heaviness in his tone unsettled me. Conall had always been my rock, but now, he seemed hesitant enough to set me on edge. I frowned, but I nodded, waiting.

"Twenty-three years ago, our father made a

deal," he started. "It was between four rivals: the O'Kellys, the Volkovs, the Santellis, and the Anthakos. They decided to unite to help their interests and gain more power but didn't trust each other." He chuckled darkly, running a hand through his hair. "Mostly because they were all trafficking scumbags. So they came up with an idea. To prove that they'd be loyal, they signed a blood oath to seal the deal."

Trafficking. I remembered that part. Still, it made me sick to think that was what my father had been involved in, but I had never been surprised.

"What kind of deal was it?" I asked, but part of me already knew enough to dread the answer.

"To solidify the alliances, keep the bloodlines strong, protect the territories they agreed their sons and daughters would marry into each other's families."

The words hit me like a slap. My eyes widened, and I shook my head. "What? No. That's absurd, Conall. That kind of… agreement is archaic. Nobody does that anymore." Even as I spoke, I knew it wasn't true. It was common practice in mafia families. My heart raced. Was he saying what I thought he was saying? That I'd been sold off?

He didn't flinch. "We're not like other families, Cora. The mob, the mafia, bratva. In our world, these alliances mean stability, loyalty, and power. Promises aren't taken lightly—especially not blood oaths. Blood oaths are inescapable. The O'Kellys, the Santellis, the Volkovs, and the Anthakos have been allies for generations. The oath was to anchor those alliances."

I recognized what I was feeling. Panic.

My heart pounded as I tried to make sense of it, a jumbled mess of anger and disbelief clawing its way to the surface. "You can't be serious. You expect me to marry someone I don't even know?"

He sighed, running a hand through his hair. "I understand this is hard to accept. But this isn't just any man, Cora. His bratva and our crew—together, we can create something bigger than we've ever had. Maxim is powerful, and he's willing to honor the oath. He's a *good* man and my friend. He will treat you right. He will protect you."

"He's willing?" I echoed, incredulous. "What about me, Conall? Don't I get a choice in this? Did you ask if I'm willing?"

Maxim. I'd be marrying the sexy, hot stranger who had walked in the door.

My brother springing a marriage on me was not on my bingo card this year. Sure, in the back of my mind, I knew that the expectation was to make an advantageous match, but I'd been out of everything to do with my brothers and the mob or whatever they had going on here for over a decade. Living with Uncle Tommy in basic isolation meant I'd not met anyone serious. He may have been an inept guardian, but he wasn't that careless. Sure, I'd had a few meetups at the pub, but they'd been casual and unsatisfying. I'd not even dated. Maybe that was a mistake — I should have taken time to make friends instead of being lost in my camera.

Conall's expression softened, but only slightly. "I know it feels unfair, but we don't have the luxury of choice. This isn't just about you or me—it's about our people, our family. I will have to do the same thing very soon — marry someone I don't know." He looked down at his shoes and rocked a little, looking uncertain. "Angelo's sister."

I shook my head again, feeling the desperation rising. "But I don't want to marry him. I don't even *know* him."

Conall stepped closer, putting a hand on my shoulder. "You'll get to know him, and he'll get to know you. Maxim's a man of his word, and he respects tradition. He understands what's at stake as well as I do."

I pushed his hand away, barely able to contain the frustration bubbling inside me. "But what if I say no? What if I refuse to go along with this?"

He gave me a stern look, all traces of brotherly softness gone. "The O'Kellys honor their word, Cora. That's how our family became what it is, which means you will marry Maxim Volkov."

We stared at each other for a long, painful moment, a quiet clash of wills. I wanted to yell, scream, or do something that might change his mind, but I saw the resolve in his face. He wouldn't back down, and I didn't know if I could fight him on this or I'd even begin to.

The thought of becoming someone's bargaining chip, of having my life mapped out without my say, felt like a betrayal I'd never forget or forgive.

"Fine," I whispered, though I could barely hear myself. "But don't expect me to be happy about it."

Conall's face softened just a little. "In time, you might see the wisdom in it."

I didn't respond; instead, I looked away and focused on anything but him. I could run, I guessed, but what would my family do? If what Conall said was true, then there was a signed oath thingy, and the O'Kellys would be in breach of contract. There were no other girls in the family. I was it.

We'd barely been in New York a few hours, and I hadn't had a moment to think since I got off that plane. Every part of me ached with exhaustion, which had become permanent in my bones. I had hoped that finally being here, in Conall's fortress of security, would let me relax—give me space to process the whirlwind of the last twenty-four hours. But that feeling of safety I'd expected seemed farther away than ever.

Conall was still watching me, his gaze steady but weary. He looked just as exhausted as I felt, yet somehow, he stood as if he was the only one holding the weight of our family's fate.

"Cora," he said quietly, his voice softened now. "I know this is hard to accept, but trust me. I wouldn't do this if it weren't necessary. Maxim is ... well, he's the best possible option."

"You think so?" I asked, unable to keep the bitterness from creeping into my tone. "You think he's the best possible option for *me*?" I almost asked him how he'd even know since Conall himself was a stranger to me, but I kept the words inside, swallowing them down like acid on my tongue.

Conall's jaw clenched, but he didn't rise to the bait. "He's not just a man, Cora. He's an alliance. And one who can be trusted. If I have to see you wed to someone, I would rather it be someone like Maxim than a stranger with no ties or respect for our family."

"A stranger?" I laughed, a hollow sound that didn't feel like it was coming from me. "He *is* a stranger, Conall. Just because our fathers made some ancient promise doesn't make him less of one."

Conall's face turned to stone, and it was as if a rod was suddenly inserted into his ass. "You are an O'Kelly. An alliance would have been sought no matter what. That is our duty to each other." The words were practically spit at me. "I have bled my fingers to the bone for us without complaint, *princess*. I will continue to do so. You will do your part and quit being a brat."

I cringed. My brother had hit me where it hurt with that comment, effectively ending all my arguments.

My brother suffered for our tiny family. I wouldn't disagree that he was the only reason we had a roof over our heads and food on the table. Conall sacrificed. Would this be such a big price to pay?

I was being both of those things: a brat and a princess. My life had been free and easy so far. Nothing had been asked of me before. It was a bitter pill to swallow, but that didn't mean I wouldn't do it.

"Cora, we aren't a regular family. You

realize that, right? Just because you had time to spread your wings a little didn't mean your place wasn't always here. We all have a duty to fulfill."

The anger flared again, hot and stubborn. I wanted to scream at him that I didn't make this oath and shouldn't have to pay for something done in the past. But I knew that even if I shouted or cried, Conall would still stand there with that same resolute expression, unmoved by my protests. I reminded myself of his words — don't be a brat.

I closed my eyes, willing myself to breathe. To think past the rage. I'd only been back a few hours. We were exhausted, and I couldn't shake the feeling that Conall was keeping something else from me. Something darker, something that weighed on him as much as this arrangement.

"Maxim will pick you up tomorrow for dinner."

"Great," I said with no enthusiasm whatsoever.

Without another word, he turned and left the room, and I felt a hollow ache settle into my bones.

MORNING LIGHT SPILLED through the tall windows, golden and warm, as I wandered into the kitchen, still bleary from sleep. I barely had the energy to change last night, let alone try to make sense of everything Conall dumped on me. My mind still spun with questions, arguments I should have made, and the hollow ache of knowing my life was no longer my own.

"About time, sleepyhead."

I turned toward the voice and found Paddy grinning at me, leaning against the counter with a coffee mug in hand. Next to him stood Brody, the more serious of the two. He was already dressed sharply as a tack, as if he were heading to a meeting instead of breakfast. Seeing them both in person filled me with relief and irritation in equal measure.

I was the only O'Kelly with dark hair. The rest of them were all light-haired, and seeing them together reminded me of how I felt when I was little. I was always the odd one out.

"You're late," Paddy added, giving me his signature smirk. "What happened to that early bird energy you used to have?"

"Guess I left it in Dublin," I muttered, grabbing a mug and pouring some coffee. I was in a foul mood already. "Or I grew up," I mumbled into my coffee. I had to get over the bitterness that I felt seeing them now. I enjoyed my time in

Dublin and the freedom that I had. I needed to remember that, but somehow, I'd just felt abandoned there. That feeling hadn't ever gone away.

"Come here. We missed you." Brody was the first to come forward and hug me before passing me over to Paddy.

"Look at you all grown up. Barely recognize you since we last saw you," Paddy curled his hands around my shoulders, tipping my chin up so my eyes met his.

"Missed you too, Paddy," I said instead of what I wanted to say. *Whose fault was that?*

"Conall will be available in a minute." Brody shoved a phone into his pocket. "He's going to take you around and meet the guys. He'll meet us downstairs.

In the daylight, it was easy to see that the apartment was spectacular and the opposite of that shitty place we had hidden in when we were little. It was modern and open, with views of the river.

"Let me just grab a little cereal, maybe?" I looked around the kitchen, wondering if I was lucky enough that Lucky Charms would be in the cabinets.

"There's a kitchen downstairs. We'll show you where. Conall is like a miser with food up here," Paddy complained. "Fucking neat freak."

"So, did Conall drag you into this ridiculous marriage business, too?"

Paddy snorted. "Oh, we know about it." Paddy had the grace to look guilty.

Brody cut in, his tone measured but firm. "We don't love it either, Cora. But he's right—this isn't negotiable. Conall is going to marry, too."

The weight of their words sat heavy on my chest, but I pushed it aside. "I heard. You two going to show me around, or what?" The words came out sulky, but they seemed to take it on the chin. Conall probably warned them I wasn't happy about the arrangement being dumped on me.

Paddy grinned again. "Now that's the spirit. Come on, little sis."

The building was impressive—I'd give Conall that. Its polished wood floors and soaring glass windows with sleek modern touches made it feel more like a tech startup than an Irish mob headquarters. Paddy led the way, pointing out different floors, and Brody occasionally chimed in with more practical details.

"That's where Conall holds his 'boring meetings,'" Paddy said, nodding toward a large conference room. "Don't ever let him drag you in there. He'll bore you to tears."

"And that floor," Brody added, ignoring

Paddy, "is the weapons storage. Locked down tighter than Fort Knox, so don't get any ideas. Your print won't access that."

"Please." I rolled my eyes. "Like I'd ever need to break into your precious armory," I drawled. I was curious, though.

We turned a corner, and I was surprised when Conall appeared, flanked by a tall, broad-shouldered man with dark hair and a cold, sharp gaze. He moved like a shark, controlled and deliberate, and the moment his eyes met mine, I wasn't sure I would like him.

"Cora," Conall said, his voice calm but firm. "This is your new guard, Finn O'Donoghue. He'll be sticking close."

"Excuse me?" I stared at him, then at Finn. "I don't need a guard."

"It's not optional," Conall replied, his tone leaving no room for argument. "Finn's one of our best, and you'll be safe with him."

"Safe from what?" I demanded. "I've been here less than a day. What kind of trouble do you think I'm already in?"

Conall's gaze hardened. "I don't know, midget. You won't tell me, but in the end, it's not about what you've done, Cora. It's about the people around us. The world we're in. You're a target, whether you like it or not." He frowned. "Although you haven't told me what was so urgent." Conall shook a finger in my direction. "Don't think I've forgotten."

"I don't like it," I snapped. "And I don't need a babysitter."

Finn stepped forward then, his expression unreadable. "I'm not here to babysit. I'm here to make sure no one gets to you. That's all."

"Wonderful," I muttered, crossing my arms. "Just what every girl dreams of—a shadow."

Paddy snickered from behind me, and I shot him a glare. Conall didn't flinch, and Finn didn't so much as blink. I wanted to kick them all. Maybe I would get into that armory so I could shoot them.

"Fine," I finally said, though it felt like admitting defeat. "But don't expect me to make this easy."

Didn't I just say that yesterday? So now I had a marriage set up and a bodyguard.

Awesome.

Finn's face set, and he stepped back, but just barely.

On the second floor was a cafeteria that was out of my dreams, with cereal dispensers that even had Lucky Charms. Yeah, I was Irish and liked Lucky Charms. The irony wasn't lost.

"Well, I'll leave you to it. Don't forget that Maxim is picking you up at seven," Conall said as someone whispered in his ear. "Your print will give you access to the areas you need. The building, the elevator, this floor, and mine. You have your card, right?"

I nodded.

"Good. Finn will take care of you." His head inclined to Finn.

"I will, boss. With my life."

"You better."

CHAPTER EIGHT

maxim

AGE *15*

SPITTLE FLEW from my father's mouth as he screamed at me in Russian. The belt flew across my back, the buckle cutting deep into my skin. I'd learned long ago that the best defense was to keep my mouth shut, to hold as still as possible. His rage burned hot, but his stamina was shit.

"Those whores were meant for the Albanians. You had one job. One," he shouted in heavily accented English as he swung the belt again.

Unfortunately for my father, his container had caught on fire. The bodies burnt beyond recognition. If he were smarter, he'd realize that the bodies weren't all young women, but they were mixed with older women, too. He might catch on that they were already dead before the container caught fire, but he was stupid.

Lev, one of my father's vors, kept his face towards the floor as I was beaten. His face was wiped clean of emotion, even though I knew it killed him to watch me be hurt. He'd helped me haul the bodies from four morgues and relocate the trafficking victims before lighting the container on fire.

"I'm sorry, pakhan," I said clearly.

I couldn't always intervene, but this time, the path had been clear and relatively easy.

"You were supposed to be there a day earlier, mudak."

Another blow, but his strength was failing, and it glanced off my back. He threw the belt to the floor.

"Clean it up. Next time you better not fuck up, Maxim," he threatened. "This is your inheritance, too. Next time, I will beat that brother you love so much."

"Yes, pakhan."

THE AIR WAS cold enough to burn when you breathed it in. It was frosty in the early evening, but Manhattan was still alive, with the hum of traffic and distant sirens weaving through the rhythmic pulse of the city. But here, in the dim glow of a lone streetlight, the world felt smaller, more intimate—the kind of place where violence could unfold without interruption.

I leaned against the black SUV, the cold metal biting through my tailored coat. Lev stood a calculated distance away, a shadow against the brick walls. His presence was a warning—silent, immovable.

Across the narrow strip of cracked pavement, Dante Caruso emerged from the other side. His swagger was unmistakable, his sharp features set in a sneer that hadn't changed in decades. His disdain hit me like the stale stench of garbage that clung to the air.

Dante had been making noise for months now, whispering threats, making phone calls that ended in silence, and confronting my operations one too many times. Tonight, that noise would end. Dante was going to stop his yapping.

"You're bold, showing your face here," he said, stepping forward.

"You think so?" My voice was calm but was

laced with a warning. "We both know how this ends, Caruso."

Dante stopped a few feet away, his hand on the grip of a pistol tucked into his waistband. He didn't pull it, not yet. His smile was venomous, curling up like smoke from a dying fire.

"This ends with your blood on the pavement, Maxim," he spat, his voice thick with his Bronx accent. "You think you're untouchable? You're just a scumbag in a nicer suit."

I took another step, my men mirroring me without a word. "You've been running your mouth, Dante. Let's not pretend this is about business."

Dante's face twisted with something darker, his bravado slipping into something raw. "Business? You think this is about fucking *business*? This is about what your father did—what *you* let him do. Girls, Maxim. Trafficked like cattle. And you—" He jabbed a finger toward me, his voice rising. "You stood by. You didn't stop him."

The accusation hung between us, heavy as lead. For a moment, the city seemed to go quiet, the noise of the world muffled under the weight of what he'd said.

Shame spread like tar. This was something that I carried with me.

I'd done my fucking best for those lost girls. Bled to the bone for them.

I clenched my fists, my jaw tight. "I was a boy," I said, each word deliberate, cold. "A boy with no power. And my father? He paid for his sins."

"Not enough," Dante snarled. His hand twitched toward the gun, but he didn't draw. "You think I give a shit about your excuses? You're just like him, Maxim. A fucking monster hiding like a coward."

I didn't move, didn't blink. "Be very careful, Dante."

He laughed, a bitter, humorless sound. "Careful? No, you don't get to play righteous. You're filth. And filth gets cleaned up."

That was it. The leash snapped.

Before Dante could pull his weapon, I surged forward, slamming my fist into his jaw. The crack of bone meeting bone echoed through the alley as he staggered back, blood spraying from his mouth.

He recovered quickly, drawing his pistol, but I was faster. A well-placed shot struck Dante's hand, sending the gun clattering to the ground. He screamed, clutching his mangled fingers, his curses falling into incoherent snarls.

I grabbed him by the collar, slamming him against the brick wall. My forearm pressed into his throat as he gasped for air, his good hand clawing uselessly at my coat.

"You think you know me?" I hissed, my face inches from his. "You think you know what it was like?"

Dante laughed, blood trickling from the corner of his mouth. "I know enough… you were *there*."

I drew my knife—a sleek, black blade honed to perfection—and pressed it against his cheek. "Well, Dante. You've stepped into the darkness. You think I'm a monster. You have no idea. You want the monster, Dante? Now you'll get him."

His eyes widened, and for the first time, there was fear. Real, tangible fear.

"Maxim," he croaked, his bravado crumbling. "Wait—"

I didn't let him finish. With a swift motion, I slashed the knife across his face, leaving a deep, jagged gash that would scar him for life if he lived.

Dante screamed, collapsing to the ground as I let him go. He writhed on the pavement, his blood pooling beneath him, a stark contrast against the grimy concrete.

I crouched beside him, wiping the blade clean on his coat. "This is me sparing you," I said, my voice low and steady. "You speak my name again, and I'll bury you alongside any family you have left. That's a fucking promise. From me to you." I pressed my fingers into the wound until he screamed. "I'll tell you a secret, mudak. I never break a promise."

Standing, I motioned to Lev. He stepped forward, delivering a swift kick to Dante's ribs before dragging him out of the alley.

The silence that followed was heavy, broken only by the distant wail of a siren. I turned back toward the SUV and slipped the knife into its sheath.

Dante's words lingered in my mind, sharp as the blade in my hand. But his judgment didn't matter. Only one truth remained.

The sins of my father were not my own, but the man I was now? I damn well made sure no one forgot the name, *Maxim Volkov.*

* * *

I SAT in the back of the black SUV, the city blurring past in a kaleidoscope of lights and movement. New York felt charged with an energy that matched my mood. I was still keyed up from my confrontation with Dante. Dumb little fucker. I'd even had to change my shirt and jacket because of that asswipe.

Now, I could turn to the enjoyable part of my evening, not that I hadn't enjoyed cutting up

Dante's face. The thought that he'd be scarred forever by my blade did make me happy. However, enemies walking around weren't good to have. Caruso would have to go sooner rather than later, especially with my upcoming nuptials.

I tugged at the cuff of my tailored suit, the motion habit more than anything, as I mentally replayed my last conversation with Conall.

We'd agreed that I'd go first; I had not been too concerned at first. Many men in our line of work were in such marriages. They gave their wives an allowance and set them up in their own homes. I could have my life, and she could have hers. Hell, I could even put her on the other side of the country. Stick her over on the West Coast. I'd had my cousin Natasha draw up the contract when Conall had initially had us draw names — made it official that we could dwell in separate spaces.

But I didn't think that was going to work. Cora was nothing like I'd imagined. She wasn't the sort of woman that you put somewhere. She was the sort of woman you came home to. I knew just from the one encounter I'd had with her.

I couldn't wait to find out how she took the news of our nuptials. I grinned as the car pulled up to Conall's building, and I stepped out into the cool winter air. Two of my men fell into step behind me, as always, sharp-eyed and ready.

Finn O'Donoghue, Conall's assigned shadow for Cora, was waiting near the apartment door. He straightened when he saw me, his expression already set in defiance and colored with disapproval. The four of us had set our alliance, but that didn't mean our men had set aside their prejudices. Conall was out for the evening, something he had to do on the docks, so I was on my own tonight with Cora and her bodyguard.

"Evening," Finn greeted me, his Irish lilt sharper than usual. "I'll be joining you tonight."

I stopped, meeting his gaze squarely. "You're not."

I doubted it would work, but I thought I'd try it.

Finn took a step forward, his shoulders stiff. "She's my responsibility."

"And now she's mine," I replied smoothly, my tone leaving no room for argument. "You're not needed."

Finn hesitated, clearly itching to argue. "My orders are clear. I go where she goes. It's non-negotiable. Once she's your wife, she's your responsibility, but until then, she's still an O'Kelly."

I could feel Lev at my shoulder, just itching

to put a bullet in him, but Finn was Conall's man and under his orders. They weren't unreasonable.

"Understood." I jerked my head towards the door, ready to be done with this little chat. Finn curled his lip but knocked on the door and moved to the side, which I'd take as a win.

The sight of her was like a punch to the gut. Seeing her today was different than yesterday now that I knew this was the woman I'd be sharing my life with. Her dark hair was swept up into a ponytail, exposing her neck, and those green eyes—sharp, unflinching—met mine fearlessly. I loved that she was unafraid. Most people dropped their eyes, but not her. She was still dressed like an urchin. Either she didn't have proper clothes for dinner, or she was protesting.

Still, in her torn jeans and rubber rain boots, she was stunning with her full breasts that pushed against the t-shirt she was wearing that said, '*Zombies Eat Brains, Don't Worry You're Safe.*'

"You ready to go? Do you have a jacket? It's cold out."

She tilted her head at me as if waiting for me to complain about her clothes, but she would be waiting a long time if that was the case. I didn't give a fuck what she wore. If other people didn't like what she had on, that was too bad. Cora could wear what she wanted. People like my father would have wanted to dress her up like a fancy doll, but I wasn't going to be that man who made my wife into a Barbie doll.

"Yes." She frowned and gave a half-hearted shrug.

"Get it so we can go then. I'm starved."

She hesitated, then stepped almost out of the apartment, looking at me before returning to the interior.

"What is it, zayka?" She did look like a little rabbit hesitating. Like *prey*, but the endearment slid out of my mouth like I'd known her for years. It felt easy and right. The lines between her forehead wrinkled slightly like she was thinking. Those lips of hers made me think all sorts of tempting thoughts.

"Can I bring my camera?" she asked.

Camera. Why would she bring a camera?

"I haven't been in New York yet — into the city today. I might see something that I want to take a picture of?" Her cheeks pinkened. "Never mind."

"Of course, you can bring your camera."

It was a terrible idea. There was no scenario where I wanted a camera around me, but her face lit up, and she darted off.

"Pakhan," Lev started, probably thinking the same thing I was thinking.

My glare silenced him, and his mouth straightened in a thin line. He should know better than to speak out of turn. I would decide what I allowed or didn't allow. Cora practically skipped back into view with a camera over her shoulder. It was one of those fancy ones that you saw the paps using.

I was intrigued.

Cora bounced lightly on her toes as she slung the camera strap across her body, clearly pleased with my agreement. Her enthusiasm starkly contrasted with the tension radiating from Lev, who was undoubtedly biting his tongue so hard it bled. The thought pleased me. Still lingering by the door, Finn looked equally unimpressed but kept his comments to himself.

"Shall we?" I gestured to the door, and she brushed past me, her ponytail swinging. There was something magnetic about her energy. I could see how she looked at me from under her lashes that she was just as interested in me, so I'd take that as a positive sign.

The car was waiting, and Lev and Finn checked the area as we exited. It didn't keep me from placing my palm on her back and guiding her close to me. She jumped slightly but didn't complain as we moved to the car. I kept my head on a swivel. Our positions meant that we had enemies. My guys were good, but I could protect her if someone were foolish enough to try.

Cora slid into the armored SUV without hesitation, settling into the plush leather seat with ease, telling me she was no stranger to comfort, even if she tried to play the rebellious street kid. I followed, the door closing with a soft thud as Lev took his place up front.

The SUV moved smoothly into the traffic flow, and the city blurred around us, a symphony of lights and motion. Cora fiddled with her camera, adjusting the lens and checking the settings, focusing entirely on the device. Although I guessed she used it more as a shield so she didn't have to talk to me.

She raised it and framed me in the lens, snapping a few photos. Lounging against the bench seat of the SUV, I stretched my arm over the back close enough to feel her hair brush the back of my hand.

"You always take that thing everywhere?" I asked, genuinely curious.

She glanced up, smirking. "Not everywhere. Just places that might be interesting."

"And you think dinner with me qualifies?"

"Let's not get carried away," she shot back,

her eyes sparkling. "The city is interesting. You're just… an extra."

I chuckled, charmed despite myself. Shaking my head, I said, "Careful, zayka. You might hurt my feelings."

"Oh, I'm sure a man like you has feelings to spare," she teased, her tone light but cutting.

I laughed again, genuinely amused. "Touché."

The banter felt easy and natural, but beneath it, I was recalibrating. She was quick, perceptive, and unafraid to challenge me. If I wanted this marriage to work—and it must work—it wouldn't be on my terms alone. I'd have to find a balance, which I wasn't used to.

"What are you hungry for?"

"Pizza? I'm dying for pizza." She blushed. "If you wanted to go somewhere fancy, that's cool. I just don't have clothes for that. So you'll have to take me as I am."

I stared at her impassively, and I struggled to hold my temper. What the fuck did she mean she didn't have clothes?

"Doesn't seem like Conall to be cheap with his sister," I said carefully. I was close with Conall, but Cora was a topic not discussed, and honestly, I never asked about her. I had always had other things to worry about. "But of course,

102

we can have pizza. And I'll definitely take you any way I can get you."

Her eyes widened.

Speaking in Russian to Lev, I told him to take us to our favorite pizza joint in Brooklyn but to take the long way. It was in Angelo's territory, but that wouldn't be an issue. I still wanted more time to talk to her without Finn. He was in the second vehicle with our other guards, which probably pissed him off.

"Conall's not cheap. I have a credit card, but I've been in Dublin." She shrugged. "I wasn't going to fancy dinners and stuff there. No reason to waste money."

"Makes sense." I nodded, but I liked hearing that she hadn't been going to fancy dinners. "So, what did you do in Dublin all this time?"

"Went to school. Took pictures. I'm not very interesting." She shrugged and snapped a few more pictures out the window.

"Oh, I disagree." I didn't move from my spot on the other side of the car, but she raised her camera again and snapped a photo. "Did you have a guy? In Dublin?" I tried to ask nonchalantly, but I wasn't sure I managed as she cocked her head at me.

"A guy? She looked up, her camera poised mid-frame.

"Conall told you about our fathers? Their agreement with each other?"

"Yeah." Her gorgeous green eyes narrowed as she pivoted towards me, giving me her full attention.

"This arrangement, as unorthodox as it may be, doesn't have to be unpleasant."

Her eyebrows lifted in surprise, and she lowered the camera. "Unpleasant? That's a low bar."

"It's a starting point," I countered. "We'll build from there."

She tilted her head, studying me. "You think we can make this work? Two strangers thrown together for the sake of… what? Power? Money?"

"And survival," I added, my voice firm. "This isn't just about us, Cora. It's about our families and their futures. That kind of responsibility doesn't leave room for personal whims."

Her expression hardened, and she leaned back against the seat. "So, I'm just a tool in the grand scheme of things for you. Good to know. What would it matter if I had a guy then?" She waved her free hand, and those eyes sparked with anger. "Maybe more than one guy."

The thought made me irrationally angry, and I leaned into her space, crowding her back against the window the camera smashed between us. Her breath hitched.

"I guess it *doesn't* matter." I caged her throat with my hand so I could feel her pulse under my thumb — caressed the skin there as I squeezed just hard enough that she could feel it. "You're mine now," I growled.

I waited a beat until I saw her pupils blown wide and eased back to my side.

She scoffed, shaking her head. "Spoken like a true bratva boss. That's what you are, right? bratva?" Her voice was thready, and her fingers were shaking as she fiddled with the settings on her camera.

"Yes."

"Great. A criminal."

I wasn't ashamed of who I was, but I didn't like that she might be. She stared out the window for a few minutes, watching the lights of the city pass us by, leaving me to contemplate how I'd fucked the conversation up. Maybe I shouldn't have taken the tactic of saying that it was about the alliance. I should have leaned harder into the idea that I wanted it to work because she intrigued me. I thought she and I could be a good couple together. Why were women so complicated?

"Do you think you could kill a zombie?" she

asked suddenly with all seriousness, biting her bottom lip in a way that made my cock hard.

"A zombie?" I asked, confused.

"Yeah. Like if there were zombies. Like the *Walking Dead* kind. Could you kill one?"

I considered the gorgeous beauty across from me with those rosebud lips and sparkling green eyes.

"A thousand percent, zayka." She smiled at me and raised her camera again, and I felt like I passed some kind of test. Of course, she was crazy as a loon, but I'd kill all the zombies if that's what she wanted.

CHAPTER NINE

cora

"THIS MARRIAGE BENEFITS US BOTH, Cora. You might not see it now, but you will."

I laughed, short and humorless. "Wow. You must be a hit with the ladies."

His smirk returned, slow and deliberate. "More than you'd think."

The worst part was I believed him. Maxim Volkov was the kind of man women fell for despite knowing better, and I hated that part of me wasn't immune. That moment when he'd pushed me against the door and held my throat? Maxim was all power and control. My panties were still damp, and I'd bet everything he knew it.

His expression didn't change, but I could see

the flicker of something in his eyes. Amusement? Annoyance? I couldn't tell.

"What's there to say?" I shot back. "You've already decided everything," I bit out.

When I'd opened the door, and Maxim had stood there, flanked by two of his men who looked like they'd never smiled, my heart had stopped. He was so beautiful. There had been something almost lazy about his stance, but it was deceptive. He was not relaxed—he seemed always to be assessing everything, including me. His tailored suit clung to his broad shoulders, every line screaming money and power. His sharp cheekbones and piercing eyes made him look like he'd stepped out of a dark fairy tale— the kind where the prince was also the villain.

My stomach had twisted, with a mixture of nerves and something else I didn't want to name. I'd always hated being told what to do, and Conall knew that. But when I opened the door, my girlie bits didn't seem to get the message.

Then he let me bring my camera.

Now he looked at me with those eyes of his, gaze lingering, and I couldn't help but wonder what he saw. A reluctant bride? A means to an end? I folded my arms, determined to meet his gaze head-on, but it was harder than I wanted it to be.

His presence felt like a weight, heavy and inescapable.

I snuck another glance at Maxim. He was so put together and composed that it was almost irritating. His dark hair was perfectly styled, and his tie was impeccably knotted. Everything about him screamed control, yet something was raw beneath the surface—something dangerous.

"Well, you're right about one thing." He pulled something from his pocket, and I could immediately see what it was.

A ring.

"Some things have been decided." Capturing my hand, he slid it on my finger just as the car reached the curb.

"Are you ready?" His voice was smooth, but there was an edge to it, a quiet authority that made it clear he was not asking. "There are rules when we get in and out of vehicles."

"Rules?" I echoed, trying not to look at the ring already heavy on my finger but helpless not to. It was stunning—platinum with a large rectangular East-West set diamond.

"The men are here for your protection. To keep you safe. Don't get out unless they open the door. Always wait for them." He waited for me to nod. "Promise me."

"Promise." There wasn't any reason not to agree. What he said made sense.

"Alright. Let's get some pizza."

I rolled my eyes but pulled my jacket tighter around me and hitched the camera strap over my shoulder. When I stepped out, his men fell into position, one ahead and one behind, like we were heading to some covert operation instead of dinner. Maxim shifted slightly. His hand resting casually at his side, where I was sure there was a weapon. Lev loomed bulkily off to one of our sides, scanning the sidewalk like he expected trouble.

"Do you always travel with an entourage?" I asked, my tone sharper than I intended.

Maxim smirked, the corner of his mouth lifting in an infuriatingly charming way. "Occupational hazard."

It should repulse me. It didn't.

The air smelled like pizza and exhaust, a combination that shouldn't be appetizing but was. The pizzeria's sign was modest, with faded red lettering: Donna's Pizzeria.

Maxim moved beside me with an ease that made my stomach flip. He was casual, with one hand in his pockets and one lightly on one of my elbows, but there was a tension in his posture, a readiness. His men fanned out, their movements practiced. I glanced at the bulky one closest to me and caught the glint of something under his jacket. He was definitely armed.

"Do you ever relax?" I asked, tilting my head up to look at him.

He chuckled softly, a low sound that made me feel unsteady. "Not in my line of work. You'll get used to it."

I doubted it, but I didn't say that. Instead, I focused on the pizzeria as we stepped inside. It was warm and bustling, the kind of place where you had to shout to be heard. The walls were covered in black-and-white photos, mostly old snapshots of Brooklyn families and faded newspaper clippings. The smell of fresh dough and melted cheese was intoxicating. God, I'd missed New York pizza.

Maxim leaned down slightly, his voice low. "Pick a table, zayka."

I bristled at the nickname. "I don't need your permission to pick a table." He grinned, not even remotely fazed. "No, but I'll give it to you anyway."

Rolling my eyes, I chose a booth near the back, away from the door and the constant stream of customers. Maxim slid across from me, his broad shoulders taking up more space than should be physically possible. One of his men positioned himself by the door while the other took up a spot near the counter.

I'd never felt so conspicuous in my life. "Do you *always* make everything a production?"

His lips twitched like he was fighting a smile. "You're marrying me, Cora. Get used to it."

The reminder of our impending nuptials soured my mood instantly. I crossed my arms and glared at him. "I'm not some accessory you can parade around, Maxim."

He leaned forward, resting his elbows on the table, his expression suddenly serious. "You're not an accessory."

I snorted. "Oh, sure. Because nothing says 'partnership' like being forced into a marriage."

His jaw tightened, and for a moment, I thought I'd hit a nerve. But then he exhaled and shook his head, a small smile tugging at the corners of his mouth. "You're exhausting, you know that?"

"Good," I shot back. "I'd hate to be boring. I'm hungry," I grumbled, suddenly tired. Lifting the camera, I snapped a shot of the counter with its colorful chalkboard menu and pizzas sliding out. It looked like the place did a steady slice business from the street. They had a box on the counter displaying 'pizza by the slice.'

"Do you always use that as a shield?" he asked, nodding toward the camera.

"Do you always deflect with questions?" I countered.

The waiter arrived, cutting off whatever retort Maxim was about to make.

"What kind of pizza do you want?"

"Sausage and olive." Already, my mouth was watering. I was hoping that my husband-to-be wasn't one of those psychos who ate Hawaiian pizza. That'd be a real downer.

He ordered two sausage and olive pizzas and four other combinations without looking at the menu. He surprised me by ordering us both a beer.

"That's a lot of pizza. Who's going to eat it all?"

"Well, the guys will eat it, and something tells me it won't be wasted." He gave me a wink, his gaze softening. "This isn't what you wanted," he said quietly. "I get that. But this marriage isn't just for me. It's for you, too."

I raised an eyebrow. "Oh, really? And what exactly am I getting out of this deal?"

"Protection," he said simply. "Power. Independence."

"Independence?" I laughed bitterly. "I had that," I muttered bitterly under my breath, but luckily, Maxim didn't seem to hear because his attention was diverted by a group that rolled into the restaurant and right up to our table. I had to take a few moments to collect myself and remember that it was me who texted

Conall to come home. I had it good in Dublin, but I changed the dynamic. I was kicking myself, but there wasn't much I could do about it unless I wanted to go on the run and never speak to my brothers again. Even then, I wasn't sure that I'd be able to get away. Maxim didn't seem the type to let go of his toys.

"What's this, Maxim?" The man who spoke was sinfully good-looking but a little too cocky for my taste. He obviously knew he was pretty.

The men looked as dangerous as the one I was with, but I recognized the leader. This was another of Conall's band of merry men.

"Angelo," Maxim said easily. I was starting to realize he didn't get ruffled by much. "Here for a slice?"

"Maybe I want what you're having." He grinned wickedly at me. "She looks delicious. Want to share?"

"Careful, Angelo." Maxim's voice was low and smooth, but there was steel underneath. "You know that some lines don't get crossed."

Angelo raised his hands in mock surrender, his grin widening. "Relax, Maxim. Just making conversation." His tone was teasing, but the weight in his gaze said otherwise. He was sizing me up and testing boundaries, which I disliked. "Sharing is caring. You're here at Donna's.

Don't be so uptight. We're practically family now, aren't we?"

"Practically family. That's right," Maxim agreed. His tone was so even that it sent a shiver down my spine. He didn't look away from Angelo, and the tension at the table thickened.

I shifted in my seat, uncomfortable with how they circled each other verbally. "Is this going to be one of those turf wars, or are we going to eat?" I asked, injecting a little sarcasm into my voice to break the tension.

Angelo's eyes snapped to mine, his grin turning sharp. "Feisty. I like her."

Maxim didn't miss a beat. "She's mine," he said, his voice quiet but carrying enough weight to make Angelo's smile falter for a fraction of a second as his eyes moved to the ring on my finger.

"Damn it, Maxim." Angelo's whole face went through an entire host of emotions that I couldn't understand. I could sense anger and frustration. "Cora O'Kelly, I presume?"

"That's right," I confirmed, raising my camera and taking a picture of his startled face. "Nice to meet you.

Angelo shrugged. "See you around." He stepped back, glancing at his men.

I watched as he and his crew settled at a booth across the room, their laughter and conversation blending into the noise of the pizzeria. Maxim's gaze followed them until he was satisfied. Only then did he turn his attention back to me.

Leaning back in my seat and folding my arms, I said, "Do you always have to mark your territory like that?"

Maxim smirked, but there was no humor in his eyes. "In this world, Cora, hesitation can be dangerous. You show weakness. You get eaten alive."

"Lovely. Sounds like a great way to live," I said, watching him.

Confrontation had never been my thing, but I could see the appeal. Men. I mentally rolled my eyes. I suppose when you were a man, things were different. There could be an appealing energy in taking what you wanted. I wondered what it was like—what the pictures looked like.

"It's been how I've survived," he countered, his tone matter-of-fact. "And now, how I'll make sure you survive. Strength."

I was about to argue when the pizzas arrived, the waiter balancing two trays loaded with pies. The smell was divine, and my stomach growled despite the tension still lingering. Maxim thanked the waiter with a curt nod, and I couldn't help but notice how the man practically scurried away.

"So," I said, grabbing a slice. "What's Angelo's deal? Is he always so... charming?"

Maxim took a slice as well, his movements precise and controlled. "Angelo is a good friend and is normally very charming. He's also upset," he added. "About this situation. He'll do his part but hasn't been very agreeable."

The first bite of pizza was a revelation—crispy crust, gooey cheese, and just the right amount of tangy sauce. God, I'd missed real pizza. For a moment, I forgot I was supposed to be annoyed. Maxim's words rolled around, and I tried to make sense of them. So, they all four had to get married, then?

Maxim leaned back in his seat. "Do you always ask so many questions?"

"Do you always give so few answers?" I countered, raising an eyebrow.

His smirk widened. "Fair enough."

The intensity between us faded for a brief moment, replaced by something lighter. I could almost pretend we were just two people sharing a pizza in Brooklyn. But then his gaze flicked toward Angelo's table, and I was reminded of exactly who and what he was.

* * *

THE CAR RIDE back to Conall's apartment felt heavier than the one to the pizzeria. Maybe it was the sheer amount of food I consumed, but I knew better. Maxim was sitting too close in the confined space, his presence taking up all the oxygen.

"So," I said, breaking the silence, "is this how it's going to be? You giving vague answers, me asking too many questions, and your guys looking like they want to murder everyone who breathes wrong?"

Maxim's lips curved into that maddening smirk of his. "You forgot the part where you pretend not to enjoy it."

I scoffed, crossing my arms. "You're insufferable."

"Maybe." He leaned back, the leather of the seat creaking under his weight. "But you'll get used to it, zayka."

There's that nickname again. I bristled, though a tiny part of me enjoyed how it rolled off his tongue. "What does that even mean?"

"Little bunny," he said smoothly, his gaze flicking to mine. "It suits you."

My cheeks heated, and liquid pooled between my thighs. "I'm not some *helpless* thing. Don't call me that."

"I didn't say you were," he replied, his tone

maddeningly calm. "But you are quick, clever, and a little skittish."

I gaped at him, trying to decide whether to be insulted or flattered. "You've got a lot of nerve, you know that?"

He chuckled, the sound low and rough. "It's part of my charm."

"Charm isn't the word I'd use."

"Yet here you are," he murmured, his voice dropping just enough to make the space between us feel smaller. "Sitting beside me, wearing my ring."

My hand automatically went to the ring, its weight already a reminder of everything I'd been roped into. "This is just a formality," I shot back. "A deal. Nothing more."

I'd looked at the ring he'd chosen — the ring suited me. It surprised me how much. The stone was overly large, but I was sure that everything the man beside me did was done on a big scale.

His eyes darkened, and the tension in the car shifted. "If you say so."

I turned away, staring out the window at the blur of Brooklyn's streets. "So, what's the plan for this 'wedding' of ours?"

Maxim hummed thoughtfully. "Conall mentioned it would be an Irish wedding. Big. Traditional."

I glanced back at him. "Traditional, huh? What does that mean? You're going to wear a kilt?"

His laugh surprised me, rich and genuine. "That's Scottish, zayka. But if you want to see me in one, I can arrange it."

I rolled my eyes, though the image of him in a kilt—broad shoulders, muscular legs— lingered a little too long in my mind. "Spare me."

"I've already spared you a lot," he said, his tone turning serious. "But this wedding isn't just for us. It's for our families, our alliances."

I narrowed my eyes at him. "You mean for your business."

"Our business," he corrected, his gaze locking with mine. "Whether you like it or not, Cora, you're a part of this now."

I hated how his words sent a shiver down my spine. "Great. Can't wait to be a pawn in a bunch of old men's power games."

"You're not a pawn," he said, leaning closer. His voice softened, but there was an edge to it, a promise. "You'll be my queen. Start acting like it. And I'm not old," he grumbled.

I swallowed hard, the intensity of his gaze pinning me in place. There was something electric in the air between us, something that made it hard to think straight. "You're unbelievable."

I could feel the heat rising to my cheeks again, and I hated that he was right. Before I could respond, the car stopped in front of Conall's apartment. Lev opened the door, and Maxim stepped out first, extending a hand to me.

"You're going to be Mrs. Volkova," he said, his voice low enough that only I could hear. "A queen."

I ignored his hand, brushing past him as I climbed out of the car. But even as I stomped toward the building, I could feel his eyes on me, burning into my back. And damn it all, a part of me liked it.

The O'Kelly men watched every move-ment as we headed back into the building, and more than ever, I was aware of the flat-line smirks or the lip curls they gave Maxim and his men. Even if it didn't bother him, I was finding that it bothered me, and I moved a little closer to him and wrapped my hand around his arm, ignoring the possessive smirk he gave me.

Maxim held up a hand when Lev and Finn moved to get into the elevator with us. "Nyet," he said to Lev. "I'll take her up and see her inside."

I could see that they both wanted to protest, but neither did, and butterflies started as soon as the elevator doors closed, locking me in with Maxim in the small space.

"What was that about?" I asked, breaking the silence. My voice came out sharper than I intended. "You sending Lev and Finn away."

"I wanted a moment alone with my bride-to-be." His tone was calm, but his eyes glinted with something darker, more deliberate.

I let out a mocking laugh, though it sounded too forced even to my ears. "Bride-to-be. You're really leaning into this role, aren't you?"

He shifted closer, not enough to touch me but enough to make me feel him everywhere. "You think I'm playing a role, zayka?" His voice dropped, smooth as silk, and I hated how it made my pulse race.

I swallowed, leaning back against the cold metal of the elevator wall. "I think you're enjoying this too much."

His smirk returned, slow and dangerous. "Why wouldn't I? You're fiery, clever, stunning. You'll make a perfect queen."

"Stop calling me that," I snapped, though my voice lacked conviction. "I'm not your queen."

Maxim moved closer, and this time, there was no avoiding him. He was too tall and broad, and his presence was overwhelming in the confined space. He placed one hand on the wall beside my head, caging me in. "Not yet," he murmured. "But you will be."

I hated how his words made my stomach flip and how the sheer heat of him made me feel lightheaded. "You're awfully confident for someone forcing a woman into a marriage."

"Let's not pretend you're being dragged kicking and screaming, Cora," he said, his breath warm against my skin. "You agreed to this."

"I agreed to this for my family," I shot back. "Not for you."

"Ah." He leaned forward so his breath was a whisper against my cheek. I wondered for a moment if he was going to kiss me. "But soon, zayka, we will be family." One hand trailed against my neck, and no matter how hard I pressed against the wall, I couldn't get any further from the hard press of his body against mine and the evidence that he wanted me. I wondered if I should feel ashamed of myself and fight harder against the feelings of want that I was having.

I moaned.

"Feel how hard I am for you? You're making me crazy."

He slid his hand over the edge of my breast, cupping it before bending down to nip at my bottom lip.

Desire unfurled in hot, heavy waves.

Ding

Quick as lightning, he moved away just as the door slid open. Finn was waiting, face redder than a hot skillet. He must have taken the other elevator but looked madder than a hornet.

"Come on, gel." Finn gestured me towards him, all the while glaring daggers.

I sprinted to the door as if Maxim would run after me, but he didn't move a muscle as Finn hustled me away and down the hallway to Conall's door.

"You alright? That fecker tried to be fresh with you?" Finn looked me over carefully.

"I'm okay."

The last thing I wanted was to escalate some kind of feud between the O'Kellys and the Volkovs. Finn said nothing, but I knew he wanted to ask more questions.

"Text me if you want to go somewhere tomorrow."

I nodded and, with relief, shut the door behind me.

CHAPTER TEN

maxim

A-HOLE **Chat**

Angelo: Dude

Maxim: What the fuck you want

Angelo: You're getting married?! 🤯

Ilias: So you're doing it

Maxim: I don't say things I don't mean

Ilias: 💀

Maxim: So yes. I'm doing it.

Angelo: Fucker

Conall: That's my sister asshole. Be respectful.

20 MINUTES *later*

Conall: Meet for a drink at Fortune?

Ilias: I can do 7

Angelo: I can swing that

Me: Same

Conall: See you eejits there

Angelo: Not if I see you there first, you eejit

* * *

THE DIM LIGHTING in *Fortune* gave the lounge a certain mystique that men like us seemed to appreciate. Heavy with the scent of cigar smoke and whiskey, leather chairs circled a low table bearing crystal glasses and a bottle of Angelo's finest scotch. Angelo leaned back in his seat, his tie undone, the epitome of relaxed menace. Ilias sat to his left, drumming his fingers against the arm of his chair, his dark eyes sharp as ever but impatient. Conall was across from me, his expression unreadable but for the occasional twitch in his jaw.

"Any sign of Vladimir slinking back?" Conall asked.

Since my bratva had kicked Slavsky out of his territory and taken over his alliances, we'd had a smooth takeover. If I were him, I wouldn't have taken it lying down, but then I had ripped it apart at the seams and turned him inside out — dismantled any sort of support systems he could turn to.

"There were one or two attempts to reach out, but he got turned away." The satisfaction I felt when his men came to me with the report probably was wrong. To ruin a man like I had and then get visceral satisfaction from his continued helplessness wasn't normal. Then again, I never said I was a good person. "He wasn't well-liked by his men. They were glad when he was swept out. There was some grumbling about the prostitution ring."

The men stirred restlessly. The skin trade was something we all felt strongly about. That was a no-go for us. We would always put a stop to forced prostitution or any flesh trading. The foundation of the blood oath our fathers made had been to further their trafficking ties, but we had worked for years.

Literally.

To take them fucking apart at the seams.

To this day, we were uncovering additional contacts or routes that were still someone continuing under the auspices of our last names. Those weren't the legacies we wanted.

Caruso's words still burned like poison in my gut.

"I've replaced it with a better system of checks and balances. Increased the protection to make sure the participants are willing." I shrugged. We weren't going to put a stop to women who wanted to make a living, but we would be damned sure that they weren't forced into something.

"Sounds like things are going well," Ilias said, swirling his drink.

"Vladimir might have had an unfortunate accident in Jersey," I admitted. "Loose end."

Conall chuckled. "You're not wrong. I was thinking along the same lines."

Angelo poured another glass of scotch, lifting it toward me with a smirk. "So, Maxim," he began, his voice all easy charm, "how's your fiancée settling into her new role? Or should I say, her new leash?"

I narrowed my eyes at the jab, though Angelo's tone was more teasing than hostile. "Cora will adjust," I replied, swirling the amber liquid in my glass. "Not that it's any of your concern."

Angelo's smirk widened. "Oh, I'm concerned. She's fiery. Irish girls usually are." He gave me another sly grin. "She's a beauty, though."

Conall stiffened in his chair, his hand curling into a fist on the armrest. "Careful, Angelo," he warned, his voice low and even. "You're talking about my sister."

Angelo raised his hands in mock surrender, though the gleam in his eyes said he was enjoying this far too much. "Relax, Con. I'm just saying she's not what I expected for our Volkov friend here. I imagined someone more… docile."

"Cora's not your concern," I snapped before Conall could. My voice cut through the tension like a blade. "She will be an asset to both our families."

Conall's gaze flicked to me, a hint of surprise softening his sharp features. But Angelo and Ilias exchanged a glance, something unspoken passing between them.

"An asset," Ilias echoed, his tone flat. "Is that what you're calling this arrangement now? An asset?"

I didn't miss the bitterness in his voice or how he leaned forward, his elbows on his knees. "You know as well as I do," I replied, meeting his gaze head-on, "that this is about more than just alliances. This is about ensuring our future. For all of us. Stability."

"Stability," Angelo muttered, knocking back his drink. "You mean dragging us all back into a blood oath none of us wanted to uphold in the first place. Making our family members targets?"

I let the silence hang for a moment, the weight of their resentment palpable. They weren't wrong, not entirely. If I had sided with them months ago, we could have ignored the contract and charted our own paths. But that wasn't who I was. A promise was made. It hadn't been a secret among other crews or organizations. I wouldn't make it my legacy that I broke a blood oath. That wasn't how the Volkovs operated.

I wasn't a liar.

"I didn't make the oath," I said quietly, my voice carrying the weight of finality. "My father did, but my signature and blood were on it, too. And I will not be the one to break it. I will take Cora into my family and under my protection. She will be the queen of the Volkov Bratva. I will honor that." I pinned Angelo with a stare.

"Angelo, our family members are targets now. It isn't a secret who they are. An unmarried female is at risk. You know that. You both know that." I looked to Ilias. "Marrying into a family provides them extra security, extra protection. Yes, we get an alliance, but we have that now, too. This way, we uphold our promise and give each other something."

Angelo and Ilias shared another look, but neither challenged me further. It was not resignation—it was acceptance. Conall's stare was nothing but interest as if he didn't know I had it in me.

Angelo shouldn't antagonize Conall so much since he would be marrying into his family. If I were Angelo, I'd be more than a little curious about Conall's approach to the institution of marriage. Angelo's sister Francesca had been quite the party princess for a while, but she'd been working as a nurse, if I wasn't mistaken. I wondered how long it'd be before Conall locked that down.

"When's the wedding?" I asked, shifting my focus to Conall.

His posture straightened, and he took a deliberate sip of his drink before answering. "Soon. A couple of weeks."

My brows rose, though I kept my expression neutral. "That's fast, even by our standards."

Conall shrugged. "If we're going to do this, we're doing it right. A proper Irish wedding, in a church. None of this courthouse nonsense."

I suppressed a groan. Of course, he wanted a traditional church wedding. "A church," I repeated, letting the word hang between us.

"Problem, Maxim?" Conall's tone was casual, but there was a challenge in his eyes.

"Not at all," I replied smoothly. "Just wondering if your sister agrees with your plans. If she'll even wear a dress. She doesn't seem much for dresses. More of the jeans and zombie t-shirt type."

Angelo laughed. "God, my pops would be rolling in his grave if I brought home a girl who dressed like that. It would have been worth it just to piss him off. Was she wearing rain boots yesterday?"

"Yeah." I chuckled. My zayka was an enigma.

"What was the camera about?"

"She likes to take pictures." I shrugged.

"Great idea," Ilias said, the words holding all the sarcasm he could imbue them with.

"She's always loved to take pictures. Tommy said that was how she spent her time," Conall admitted. "I didn't see much harm."

We all knew plenty of harm could come

from running around taking pictures, but I wouldn't stop her.

I finished my drink, setting the glass down with a soft clink. "Then it's settled. A traditional Irish wedding in a couple of weeks."

The conversation drifted afterward, but the tension remained, a silent undercurrent beneath the surface. As I watched Angelo and Ilias brooding over their drinks and Conall's carefully guarded expression, I couldn't help but feel the weight of what was coming.

I hadn't told them yet that I had found my half-sister. Well, found wasn't the right term. I'd known where she was all along.

CHAPTER ELEVEN

cora

> Unknown Number: Thinking about me?

Me: No

> Unknown Number: Lie to yourself all you want when you touch yourself at night, zayka.

* * *

A FEW DAYS LATER, I'd settled into living at Conall's and learned how to sneak around the building without too much interaction with others. I'd found that most of the staff in the building used the elevators, which left the stairwells free. Even the men stuck to the elevators, which surprised me. I thought they'd be looking for extra exercise. It made it easier for me, so I wouldn't complain. Conveniently, my prints were coded for the doors so I could pop out into the alleyway and back in. It seemed awfully sloppy of my brothers.

They were hard to pin down. Paddy and Brody seemed busy all the time, and I hadn't even seen where they lived. I knew it was in the building, but that was it. I wouldn't lie and say it didn't hurt my feelings that they seemed to have so little time for me. It wasn't as if I wasn't used to being alone, but in this big building, it seemed I was even more alone than ever. Everyone but me had a place to be or a job to do.

Heading down to the cafeteria this morning, I had to admit that even this was a gorgeous space. The smell of baked goods, coffee, and bacon lingered in the air, and I was suddenly starving. I scanned the room, balancing a tray with toast, Lucky Charms, and a steaming mug of tea. It was mostly empty, except for a few of Conall's men seated in the corner, heads bowed over their plates as they shoveled food into their mouths.

They didn't seem to like me much or were afraid of Conall.

Or Maxim.

I spotted Finn at a table near the back, flipping through a dog-eared paperback, a half-eaten scone, and a mug of tea in front of him. I headed his way, my boots echoing on the floor.

"Mind if I join you?" I asked, setting my tray down without waiting for an answer. If I touched base with him for a few hours a day, I'd found that he would stay out of my way the rest of the time. He seemed to think I was a good girl if I let him follow me around for a while.

Finn glanced up, giving me a faint smile. "Be my guest."

I sat, tearing a piece of toast in half. "Do you always eat alone, or am I just lucky?"

He chuckled, closing his book. "Not everyone's up for conversation this early. Especially not in this place."

I glanced toward the corner where the men were sitting. One of them looked over, his gaze sliding past me to Finn before he leaned in to whisper something to his companion. Finn didn't react, but I caught the subtle stiffening of his shoulders.

"Looks like they've got something to say," I muttered, taking a bite of my cereal — fishing for a blue horseshoe.

Finn shrugged, his expression neutral. "They've always got something to say."

Another man approached a lean figure with

sharp features and an unshaven face. He gave Finn a respectful nod, murmured something in his ear, and then walked off without glancing at me.

"Friendly," I remarked, raising an eyebrow.

Finn smirked. "They're not ignoring you on purpose."

"Oh, really?" I leaned back in my chair, looking at him with disbelief. "Care to explain, then? Or is it because I'm marrying Volkov?"

Finn hesitated, his gaze flicking toward the men. "It's not like that, Cora."

"Of course it's not," I said, rolling my eyes.

Like I had a choice. I was grumpy and wouldn't begin to admit that it was because Maxim hadn't come to see me in days. I was itchy, not understanding what I should expect from this relationship. If only we had defined how we were going to move forward … what marriage would *be* like.

We lapsed into silence, the clatter of dishes and low hum of conversation filling the space. I finished my breakfast quickly, the tension pressing against my chest.

"I'm going out," I announced, standing and grabbing my camera bag.

Finn arched a brow. "Out where?"

"Outside," I said, slinging the strap over my

shoulder. "Into the neighborhood. I want to take some pictures."

He sighed and stood, brushing crumbs from his lap. "Okay. I'm coming with you."

Finn disapproved of my picture-taking. I suppose I didn't blame him since this was essentially a criminal organization. They probably were allergic to the thought of people photographing them.

I already regretted my decision. "You don't have to babysit me, Finn."

"Not up for debate," he replied, his tone firm. "Bring a jacket and a hat. It's cold out there."

His orders grated on me. Everyone was always trying to get me to bundle up for winter. I wasn't a moron or three years old. I knew it was cold.

We left the building, stepping into the winter air. Vinegar Hill's streets starkly contrasted with Conall's world's cold sterility. Brick townhouses lined the cobblestone streets, their facades worn but charming. Some were polished up like Conall's, but the neighborhood was still full of character. I loved the architecture of the older buildings. I hadn't been able to get a firm handle on the layout of the streets yet. I was still learning them block by block.

I pulled out my camera, adjusting the

settings as I wandered down the sidewalk. Finn trailed a few steps behind, his hands shoved into his jacket pockets, his eyes scanning the surroundings. He obviously wasn't a fan of me walking around, but that wasn't my problem.

It was nice to have Finn with me because I could take pictures of whatever I wanted, but I made sure to keep it tame with him here.

Click. The camera captured a window. Click. A man working. I saw the looming Brooklyn Bridge in the distance, so I headed in that direction.

Finn's shadow fell over me as I crouched to snap a shot of a stray cat perched on a stoop. "You always take pictures of cats, or is this a new hobby?"

I glanced up, giving him a wry smile. "I take pictures of anything that catches my eye. Cats included."

He chuckled, stepping back to give me space.

Like always, I could let myself go when I was taking pictures.

Point.

Shoot.

Point.

Shoot.

Each frame told a story.

I couldn't stop my mind from wandering to

Maxim. His gaze felt like a touch, the low timbre of his voice when he called me zayka. My reaction to him frustrated me. It wasn't like I hadn't been around men who were confident— or arrogant, for that matter—but Maxim was different.

He was in my head, under my skin, and it was infuriating.

I stopped in front of a crumbling townhouse, its windows boarded up and ivy vines withered by winter creeping up the bricks. Late morning light filtered through the dead leaves, casting a golden glow over the scene. I lifted my camera and framed the shot.

"Do you hear that?" Finn asked.

I did. It sounded like an animal. Faint. Finn was already moving toward the edges of the building as he bent over.

It was cold today. Winter was creeping up in New York; even my puffer coat wasn't enough to keep out the chill. Huddled back in a pile of scraps was what had to be the scruffiest kitten I'd ever seen. I couldn't even tell what color it was. I'm not sure how Finn even heard its cries. They were so faint.

It was alive, but barely. It looked like it'd already had a rough start to things — half frozen, and its ear looked like it had been chewed on.

I removed my beanie, picked the kitten up, cradled it inside, carefully wrapped it, and put it close to my puffer coat to protect it from the elements.

"What are you doing?" Finn sputtered.

"Keeping it. It's cold."

"Cora," Finn had begun to protest. "Conall won't like it …"

I couldn't give two fucks what Conall would like, and I turned to tell him when —

Bang.

The sharp crack of gunfire.

I froze, my heart lurching in my chest. Another shot followed, and shouts echoed down the street.

Bang.

The sound reverberated off the buildings, loud and close enough to make my ears ring. My first instinct was to drop to the ground, but the tiny bundle in my hands stopped me. Instead, I spun around, clutching the kitten against my chest like it was my lifeline.

Finn's body collided with mine, pushing me down behind a parked car. His hand was firm on my shoulder, his other already reaching for the gun tucked under his jacket.

"Stay down," he hissed, his voice low and sharp.

I didn't argue. My heart pounded so hard I

thought it might burst out of my chest. The kitten squirmed weakly, a faint, pitiful mewl escaping its tiny mouth.

"Who the hell is shooting at us?" I whispered, glancing around the car to catch a glimpse of the street.

Finn pressed me back, his weight pinning me to the cold metal of the car. "I said stay down."

Shouting erupted in the distance. The words were indistinct and filled with panic. Another gunshot rang out, then another, the sound bouncing off the brick walls of Vinegar Hill's narrow streets.

Finn peeked over the edge of the car, his eyes scanning the street ahead. His movements were quick and deliberate, as if this were second nature to him.

"Finn," I started, but he cut me off.

"Not now, Cora. Just keep quiet and don't move."

The sharp edge in his voice silenced me, though it didn't stop my pulse from racing or my mind from spinning in a dozen directions. Who was shooting? Was it random, or did this have something to do with Conall? With Maxim?

God, I was terrible in a crisis. If some virus

broke out and there were zombies, I was totally fucked.

I clutched the kitten closer, its frail body trembling against me. My camera dug into my side, but I didn't dare shift.

Finn ducked back behind the car, his jaw tight. "We need to move. Now."

I didn't hesitate as he grabbed my arm and pulled me to my feet. My legs wobbled, but I followed his lead, clutching the kitten and my bag as we darted toward an alley, running even as I expected the sharp sting of a bullet to hit.

The world around us blurred—brick walls, iron fences, shattered glass glittering on the sidewalk. Finn's grip on my arm was unrelenting as he guided me through the labyrinth of streets, every corner feeling like it could be our last.

Finally, we ducked into a narrow passage, the noise of the gunfire fading behind us. Finn pressed me against the wall, his breathing harsh but controlled.

"Are you okay?" he asked, his voice low but urgent.

I nodded, unable to form words.

His gaze dropped to the bundle in my arms. "You still have that mangy kitten?"

"Don't be a dick. Yeah, I still have it. I wasn't going to leave it behind," I whispered.

Finn shook his head, muttering something under his breath that I couldn't catch.

"Finn, what the hell just happened?" I demanded, my voice trembling despite my best efforts to sound steady.

He looked at me, his expression grim. "Trouble. Conall is going to be pissed."

I opened my mouth to argue, but the distant sound of sirens stopped me.

"Come on," Finn said, his tone leaving no room for debate. "We need to get you back. Now."

I followed him, the kitten in my arms grounding me even as my mind raced. Trouble. That word felt too small for whatever this was, but I knew one thing for sure.

If Conall was going to be pissed, I was positive that it would pale in comparison to what Maxim would be.

CHAPTER TWELVE

maxim

THE DOOR SLAMMED against the wall as I stormed into Conall's apartment, my stride eating up the distance to the main sitting room. A decorative vase wobbled dangerously on its pedestal from the force of my arrival, but I didn't care. My focus was singular, my anger hot and unrelenting.

Conall looked up from where he sat perched on the edge of an armchair. His face tightened at the sight of me. "Maxim."

"Why the hell am I hearing about this from *my* contacts?" I snapped, my voice sharp enough to cut steel. "A shooting on the streets where your sister was wandering around? And no one thought to inform me?"

Before Conall could answer, Cora appeared in the hallway, a bundle of towels cradled in her arms. She looked exhausted, her hair tied back in a messy bun, and streaks of something dark were on her sleeve. She still looked like an angel. My anger softened just slightly, replaced by a deeper, more primal emotion: worry. Today, she wore a t-shirt that said, '*The First Rule of Zombieland: Cardio.*'

"Maxim," she said softly, stepping forward.

I turned to her, my brow furrowing. The storm raging inside me shifted focus entirely. In two long strides, I was in front of her, my hands grasping her shoulders. I struggled to beat back the sticky feeling of anxiety that was strangling my heart — the worry that had blanketed me at the thought that she'd been hurt—the irrational fury.

"You're okay?" I asked, my voice lowering as my eyes searched hers for confirmation.

"I'm fine," she said firmly, her tone calm and steady. "It wasn't as close as you're imagining. Finn got me out before—"

"You shouldn't have been out at all," I interrupted, my grip tightening but careful not to hurt her. My eyes scanned her again, looking for injuries I prayed I wouldn't find. "You should have been here. Somewhere safe."

"I can't live in a bubble." Her lips pressed into a thin line, but instead of arguing, she rested her hand against my chest. "I'm fine," she repeated, her voice softening. "Really."

My forehead nearly touched hers for a moment, and I exhaled deeply, letting some of the tension bleed out. My hand cradled her cheek, my thumb brushing gently against her skin. "You could have been hurt, zayka," I murmured.

A faint smile curved her lips. "But I wasn't."

The moment hung between us, fragile but grounding until a small sound—a high-pitched squeak—shattered the quiet.

I froze, my hand dropping as my eyes shifted to the bundle in her arms. "What is that?" I asked warily. My voice edged with suspicion.

Cora lifted the towels slightly, revealing the ugliest kitten I had ever seen. Its pale grayish-white fur was alarmingly small. Its eyes were narrowed at me as it let out a little hiss.

"It's a kitten," she said as if I should have already known. "I think he likes you."

I took a step back, frowning deeply. "Why is it in here?"

She raised an eyebrow. "Because I wasn't going to leave it to die on the street. What kind of monster do you think I am?"

"A practical one," I muttered, staring at the

tiny creature as though it might spring out of her arms and attack. "That thing is… fragile. And unpredictable."

"It's a kitten, not a grenade," she said, her eyes sparkling with laughter.

Conall, who had been watching the exchange from his chair with a smug grin, leaned back casually. "He's afraid of cats," he said, his tone filled with mockery.

I glared at him. "I am not afraid. I just don't… trust them. They carry diseases."

Cora laughed softly, the sound tugging at something in my chest despite myself. She adjusted the kitten, cradling it closer to her chest. "Well, you'll have to get over it because this one needs my help. I'm keeping it."

Fuck. I hated cats. I eyed the little beast. Was it missing an ear? It also looked like it had a patch of fur missing.

I stayed at a distance, my arms crossed tightly over my chest. "You're really keeping it?"

Cora didn't even look up, her focus entirely on the kitten. "Of course I am. It needs me."

I exhaled sharply, muttering under my breath in Russian. "You already have me worried about you constantly. Now I have to worry about this… thing?"

She glanced up then, her eyes sparkling with

amusement. "You don't have to worry about the kitten, Maxim. Just let me handle it. And yes — I'm keeping it. This kitten and I are a package deal."

My jaw tightened, but I didn't argue. Instead, I stalked to the far end of the room, putting as much distance as possible between myself and the kitten and Conall's irritatingly smug grin.

"You're lucky she's so soft on you," Conall said, his voice thick with amusement.

I shot him a dark look. "And you're lucky I don't throw you out the window for not telling me about the shooting."

Cora's quiet laughter filled the room, and despite myself, the sound eased some of the tension coiling in my chest. Still, I kept my distance from the kitten. I could handle shootouts and rival factions. I'd even handle zombies or betrayal—but kittens? That was pushing it.

I turned my attention back to Conall, though the tiny bundle in Cora's arms was still in my peripheral vision, a soft distraction I didn't need. "Tell me everything," I demanded, my voice like ice. "Who fired the shots, and what the hell were they doing so close to her?"

Conall's smirk disappeared as he straightened, brushing invisible dust from his shirt.

"We're still working on it. It wasn't random, though. Too precise. A drive-by on Vinegar Hill doesn't happen without intent."

"That's not good enough," I snapped, stepping closer. "What are you doing to find them? I want names."

"My men are combing through surveillance footage," he said evenly, meeting my glare without flinching. "And questioning locals. The neighborhood's tight-knit—they'll talk eventually. But it's not instant, Maxim." Conall's jaw tightened. "This isn't your territory," he reminded me.

"No, but it's my fiancée's safety at stake," I shot back. "Or have you forgotten that she's marrying into *my* family?"

"Enough," Cora said firmly, her voice cutting through the tension like a blade. She hadn't looked up from the kitten, but her tone left no room for argument.

I exhaled sharply, forcing myself to ease back a step. "Cora," I began, turning to her, "did you see anything? Recognize anyone?"

She shook her head. Her gaze still focused on the kitten as she tickled it and rubbed it with the towel. "I didn't see much. It all happened so fast. I heard the shots, and Finn grabbed me before I could even turn around."

Finn. That man deserved a raise—or at least a drink.

"Was it one car? Multiple? Anything that stood out?" I pressed, trying to piece together any scraps of information.

Cora finally looked at me, her expression tired but thoughtful. "I didn't see anything." She paused, frowning.

It wasn't her fault. I sighed, "Conall, I want every scrap of information by the end of the day."

Conall inclined his head, his expression neutral. "Understood. We'll team up on this."

I took a steadying breath, trying to temper my frustration. Losing control wouldn't help. "I want to be kept informed, Conall. No more surprises."

"Fine," he muttered, though his tone suggested he wasn't thrilled about it.

"Good." I glanced back at Cora. She had settled into the sofa, the kitten tucked securely against her chest. She was calm—too calm. I realized it was her way of coping, but it still unsettled me.

"You're sure you're all right?" I asked again, softer this time.

She looked up at me, her eyes steady and reassuring. "I'm fine, Maxim. Really."

I didn't believe her entirely, but I let it go. Instead, I took another step closer, crouching beside the sofa. My hand found hers, resting gently against her knee. "I'll make sure this doesn't happen again, zayka. You're safe with me."

"I know," she murmured, her free hand brushing against mine.

The kitten squeaked again, a pitiful, wheezing sound, and I instinctively pulled back. Cora's lips twitched in amusement.

"Still afraid of it?" she teased.

I glared at the tiny creature, which seemed smaller and more fragile now that it was nestled against her warmth. "I'm not afraid," I said defensively.

"Uh-huh," she said, her tone light but her eyes soft.

I stood, adjusting the cuffs of my jacket. "I'll leave you to... whatever this is." I gestured vaguely at the kitten.

Conall snorted from his chair, but I ignored him. As I moved toward the door, I turned back to Cora. "Call me if you need anything."

"I will," she promised, though I wasn't sure I believed her.

As I stepped into the hallway, the kitten's faint cries followed me, and for a moment, I considered asking someone to take it far, far away. But then I thought of how Cora's face softened when she looked at it, and I knew it wasn't going anywhere.

For better or worse, the kitten was here to stay.

Just as I reached the door, Cora's voice stopped me. "Wait," she said, sitting up straighter on the sofa, her brows furrowing in thought.

I turned, already on edge. "What is it?"

She looked at me, then down at the kitten cradled against her as if gathering her thoughts. "My camera," she said slowly, the realization dawning on her. "I was taking pictures before it happened. I might have caught something."

I stared at her for a beat, the tension in my chest shifting. "Where is it?"

"Finn had it," she said. "He took it when everything started. It should still be in the bag I left by the door."

I nodded sharply and stepped back into the apartment. Finn was standing near the window, speaking in low tones with one of Conall's men, but when I approached, he immediately shifted his attention.

"Cora says her camera might have caught something," I told him. "Where is it?"

Finn frowned, his gaze darting toward the entryway. "In her bag, by the coat rack. I didn't think to check it."

"I'll get it," I said, brushing past him and heading for the door. The bag was precisely where Cora said it would be, and I retrieved the camera, its weight reassuring in my hand.

When I returned to the living room, Cora was already setting the kitten down gently in a small basket someone had lined with soft towels. She reached for the camera as I approached, her fingers brushing mine as she took it.

"Thanks," she murmured, powering it on and scrolling through the images.

I leaned over her shoulder, watching as photo after photo of Vinegar Hill's streets appeared on the screen. Brick facades, the Brooklyn Bridge, the stray cat before she'd found the kitten—each image felt painfully beautiful, but I stayed silent, letting her work.

Then she froze.

"There," she said, her voice tight.

I followed her gaze to the screen. The image was blurry, snapped in motion, but there was no mistaking it: a dark sedan with tinted windows, the license plate partially visible.

"You caught it," I said, my pulse quickening.

Cora nodded, her grip tightening on the camera. "It was driving away. I didn't even realize I'd taken the picture."

I straightened, already calculating my next move. "Can you send that to me? I could get this to my people. They'll pull everything they can from it—plate numbers, details, anything that connects it to the shooters."

"Sure," Cora nodded.

"We'll work on it together. Remember," Conall complained. "Don't be a hog."

"Fine," I conceded.

Her hand shot out, grabbing my sleeve. "Be careful, Maxim."

I looked down at her, her worry etched into every line of her face. "Always," I said softly.

She released me, and as I turned to leave again, I glanced back at her, still sitting on the sofa, her focus shifting briefly to the kitten now curled in its makeshift bed.

Whoever had targeted her had made a mistake—a grave one. And I intended to make sure they knew it.

CHAPTER THIRTEEN

cora

I LET the stairwell door close quietly, holding on just long enough that the latch let out a low hiss instead of the clang you'd usually get. I paused on the landing, listening. Nothing. The guards who usually prowled the upper floors of Conall's building must have been distracted, or maybe I was getting good at slipping past them. Either way, the thrill of escape sent an intoxicating shiver down my spine.

I adjusted the camera bag strap across my shoulder and started down the stairs. Conall consistently underestimated me and thought I was still the quiet, obedient little sister he'd raised to be unseen and unheard. But there was a fire in me, a restlessness that grew while I'd been away. Since I'd been sent to Dublin, I'd only become less house-trained, not more so.

My methods for filling my loneliness weren't exact, but my photography had helped.

I'd planned this outing carefully, memorizing his men's shift changes and routines. The shooting a few blocks away last week had rattled them and made them more vigilant. It should've scared me, too, but it didn't. If anything, it made each of these moments sweeter.

I was invisible when I reached the back exit —a shadow slipping into the night. The cool air hit my face as I stepped onto the sidewalk, and I smiled a small, defiant thing.

Tonight, I had a destination in mind. The area had been calling me since I first glimpsed it from the car window weeks ago. Its industrial charm mingled with the grit of the city. It was raw, imperfect, and alive.

I kept my head low as I walked, the camera in my hands like an extension of myself. Every step brought me closer to freedom and the world I craved to capture.

The streets around Vinegar Hill were quiet except for the occasional car hum or distant subway rumble. I ducked into an alleyway, and the faint glow of a flickering neon sign cast fractured light onto the damp pavement.

Perfect.

I crouched down, adjusting the settings on

my camera. The lens focused on how the light hit the puddles, creating a kaleidoscope of colors against the worn brick walls. Snap. Another angle, this time catching the silhouette of a lone figure in a window, their face obscured by shadow.

Click. The curtain moved. *Click.*

The adrenaline surged again. Being out here, vulnerable and unseen, was dangerous, but it made me feel alive. It wasn't just about the pictures—it was about the *moment*, the risk, the beauty of finding art where no one else looked.

I wandered further, weaving through the maze of narrow streets. Near the bridge, I found my next shot. The looming structure was framed against the night sky, its lights reflected in the inky waters below. A rusted chain-link fence in the foreground gave it a gritty edge, a reminder of the city's roughness beneath its polished surface.

Click.

I climbed a few steps onto a low railing to get a better angle. My balance was precarious but steady enough. The skyline beyond was a study in contrasts, its clean lines softened by the haze of the city's light. Behind an alley, I caught an incredible shot. A restaurant worker coming outside to yell and scream their frustrations at the sky. The woman shook her fist and kicked at the wall before her shoulders slumped as she lost heart — exhausted. Finally, she took a disconsolate look at the stars and returned inside.

The click of the camera shutter was like music. Each shot a note in the symphony I was composing.

I lost track of time, as I always did when I was behind the lens, but the sound of footsteps snapping against the pavement behind me jolted me back to reality. My heart leapt into my throat, and I turned quickly, clutching my camera.

A man stood at the end of the alley, his figure silhouetted against the streetlight. My pulse raced, but I forced myself to stay calm. He didn't move. He just stood there, watching.

I stepped down from the railing, my fingers tightening around my camera strap. "Can I help you?" I called, my voice steady despite the knot forming in my stomach.

The man didn't answer, but after a moment, he turned and disappeared into the night.

I exhaled, the tension draining from my body. Maybe it was nothing. Or maybe Conall had caught wind of my little adventure and sent someone to watch me. Either way, it was time to go.

I slipped the camera into my bag and

returned to the building. My steps were quicker now, the exhilaration of the night tempered by a new wariness.

The shots I'd taken tonight were worth the risk. Each frame was a piece of the city's soul, raw and unfiltered, a reminder that there was beauty even in the darkest corners.

And in those moments, behind the lens, I was free.

Even as I climbed the stairs back to my room, avoiding the elevator and the prying eyes of Conall's men, a small smile played on my lips. The stairwell was empty as I hurried up the landings, a spring in my step just as I whipped around the last corner.

Wham.

Straight into a wall of muscle.

"Hello, zayka. Where has my naughty little girl been?"

I'd been thinking about the images I'd managed to grab and hadn't been as careful as I should have been. My head had been down, and I'd run smack into Maxim. He steadied me with both hands as I wobbled. *Naughty* … my cheeks flushed.

"Just here and there. None of your business," I deflected. He wouldn't be happy if I were out by myself. For that matter, my brother wouldn't be happy either.

"You don't think so?" His eyes sparked dangerously. "You're not wearing your ring."

"So?"

"Don't sass me." His hands tightened imperceptibly on my biceps, and I felt a thrill. For once, he wasn't wearing a suit, and I could see the tempting display of tattoos spread even further.

"Will you punish me then?"

His eyes lit up, and my core pulsed. God, he was sexy.

"Yes. You'll be punished. Where were you?"

I thought about it for about a minute. Did I want to go down this road? He wasn't stupid. I was sure he knew exactly where I was and what I had been doing. Just as sure as he knew that I had slipped my guard, which was undoubtedly why he was here. If I provoked him, there was one outcome.

Did I want a real relationship with my soon-to-be husband? Looking at his fiery eyes and heated gaze, the decision was easy.

"Outside. All. By. My. Lonesome," I sang out.

His jaw ticked, and he spun me around as he dragged me up the stairs towards the apartment.

"I can't decide if I'm going to spank you or murder you," he ground out.

"I vote for the spanking," I said under my

breath just as he hauled me by my wrist through the hallway furiously to the door.

"It's really too bad that Conall is upstairs right now wondering where you are, zayka. Finn went to the cafeteria to look for you. I should tell him that you escaped. I wish we had time for that spanking." His eyes were hot on mine. "I promise that you'll get one soon."

"Can't wait," I taunted before ducking under his arm and dashing for the apartment door. I wasn't lying, either. The thought of it turned me on so much that I hoped it would happen. I wasn't sure if that made me fucked up or just a little … naughty.

CHAPTER FOURTEEN

cora

MY PHONE DINGED.

Maxim: how's your new pet

Me: he's good - eats a lot

Maxim: Conall said you have a dress fitting today

Me: 😠

Maxim: Don't be like that, zayka - you're going to look beautiful. You've been a good girl, haven't you?

Me: I'm getting a black dress

Me: Yes, I've been good.

Maxim: If that's what you want
to wear, I don't give a fuck.
Wear whatever you want as
long as you meet me at the end
of the aisle.

The text made me almost dizzy. Did he mean that? He didn't care what I wore? I'd been having some irrational anxiety about walking down the aisle in some frou-frou number.

Me: Really?

Maxim: Really

I flopped back on the couch, letting the phone lay on my stomach for a moment. I wasn't looking forward to going dress shopping. I wasn't a fan of wedding dresses in general, but I especially wasn't a fan of lace or extra feminine things. It was probably because I'd not had girly friends — or friends … to shop with. I didn't have any idea of what to buy. Conall had informed me that I had an appointment at a shop and that Finn would take me. It depressed me more than anything, but if Maxim didn't care, then I'd buy something that I liked.

It couldn't be that hard.

* * *

THE SHOP SMELLED like roses and satin—overwhelming, delicate, and expensive. It wasn't a scent I was used to, and I wasn't sure I liked it. The weight of it seemed to settle on my chest as I followed Finn through the door, already feeling out of place.

I tugged at the hem of my t-shirt, scanning the space. Racks of pristine white gowns lined the walls like a parade of frothy, overpriced ghosts, and I had no idea where to start.

"This is awkward," I muttered under my breath.

"What is?" Finn asked, his voice low as he glanced around.

"Everything about this," I admitted. "I don't belong in a place like this. And you don't belong here either."

Finn grinned. "Fair point. But I'm the one who drew the short straw."

I rolled my eyes. "You're getting paid."

He chuckled and gestured for me to go ahead. "Come on. Might as well get it over with."

I sighed and stepped inside, trying to ignore how small I felt. I didn't have girlfriends to bring along for this, and I wished I had. Growing up in Dublin, I'd never really had those kinds of friendships—not with my family's life looming over me. My brothers had always been enough, but now they were out hunting the shooter, and Finn was the only one left to take me.

Finn wasn't exactly a friend. I barely knew him; having him here only made the whole thing feel more awkward.

A petite woman with sleek black hair and a tape measure draped around her neck approached me, smiling brightly and practiced. "You must be Cora," she said, her gaze flicking to Finn. "And you must be—"

"Not the fiancée," Finn cut in with a grin. "Just the chauffeur."

I looked at the woman with an apologetic expression. "The fiancée couldn't make it," I said. He's… busy.

The woman, whose name turned out to be Elise, nodded sympathetically. "Let's get started, then."

The next hour felt endless. Elise and her team brought out gown after gown, each more elaborate than the last. I stood before a gilded mirror as they zipped, clipped, and cinched me into a rotating collection of satin, lace, and tulle.

"Too much," I said, eyeing one dress that seemed to have swallowed me whole.

Elise chuckled. "We'll find the right one. Sometimes, it just takes a little patience."

Patience wasn't my strong suit.

Finn lounged in a corner, looking far too amused by the entire process. He offered occasional commentary—"That one's not bad" or "You look like a cupcake in that"—but mostly, he kept quiet.

I sighed, staring at my reflection in the mirror. I wasn't used to being on display like this, and the loneliness of it pressed against my ribs. My life was filled with men—brothers and bodyguards—and in this moment, I missed the kind of easy support I'd seen other women have. I even missed those early days in that crappy apartment when we were hiding out, and it felt like my brothers and I were close. Now, they seemed far away.

The door chimed, and I glanced toward the sound.

My heart lurched as Maxim strode into the shop, looking sharp and impossibly confident. He wasn't supposed to be here, and his sudden presence stole the air from the room.

"Maxim," I said, startled. "What are you doing here?"

His eyes softened as they found mine, his lips curving into a faint smile. "I had some time," he said, as though that explained everything.

Finn straightened, muttering something

under his breath before leaving the shop. "Cora, text me when you're done. Yeah? I'm going to go get a smoke."

"Okay."

Elise looked delighted, her professional demeanor never faltering. "Mr. Volkov, we were just trying some options. Would you like to see?"

Maxim nodded, stepping closer to me. His gaze swept over my gown, lingering in a way that made my cheeks heat.

"It's... fine," he said, his voice warm but firm. "But it's not you."

I blinked. "Not me?"

He tilted his head, studying me. "You need something simpler. Classic. Something that fits who you are."

I didn't know whether to be flattered or annoyed, but his confidence was disarming.

"Classic, huh?" I said, crossing my arms. "And you think you know what that looks like?"

He smirked, leaning in slightly. "That doesn't matter. She does."

Elise didn't miss a beat. She disappeared into the back and returned with a sleek satin gown, minimalist and striking.

"Let's try that on." Maxim gestured to the changing room.

Nodding, I followed Elise and let her assistants help me out of the dress I'd been laced into. The one thing I'd discovered about wedding dresses was that they were heavy, cumbersome affairs.

"I'll take over." Maxim stood in the doorway as if he had every right to be there, staring at me in my underwear.

Elise handed the gown to him without complaint, shooing her staff from the large changing area as if it wasn't out of order for a tattooed man to order them around, but what did I know? Maybe it wasn't. "Of course, Mr. Volkov." She practically curtsied.

"What do you think you're doing?" I hissed.

I wasn't ashamed of my body exactly. Even in this 360-degree mirror with every flaw on display, every divot and mark, I wasn't going to hide or cower. If he didn't like my curves, then that was too bad, but thank God I'd worn my nicest set of underwear. Elise had already taken my measurements and set aside wedding lingerie for me, saying what I had wasn't acceptable. She'd frowned at my practical cotton like it was a personal affront.

"Helping you into your dress, of course."

He came close, pooling the material around my feet, so I had to set a hand on his shoulders to step into it. He paused for a moment, kneeling at my feet, his dark eyes looking up at me — wicked.

"You're so beautiful, Cora. I like to be on my knees for you."

I liked that thought, too.

He raised the dress, his fingers grazing the sides of my legs as he went. I couldn't take my eyes off him even as he pulled the dress higher, gathering the fabric at the waist as he stood behind me and yanked me to him.

I looked flushed in the mirror, and he loomed behind me, his hands locked at my hips, crushing the fabric. His fingers were digging into my hip bones, and I could see one creeping toward my panty line. My breath came out in a harsh exhale. Please let him touch me. I might even beg. I'd been thinking about him since last week.

"Max."

"Do you want me to touch you?" he asked silkily.

"Yes." The admission broke from me as he bent to kiss the nape of my neck. I desperately wanted his hands on me.

"I've been thinking about you, zayka." His voice was guttural as he slid his fingers into my panties with a groan, sliding between my folds. "You're so wet." He rocked against me, and I realized with satisfaction that he was as turned on as I was, if the giant cock against my ass was any indication.

"Look in the mirror," he commanded.

I'd let my eyes fall shut as I concentrated on the feelings that he was pulling from my body as he circled my clit and gently thrust a finger inside my entrance, but I did as he asked. We looked — sinful and right.

Those tattooed hands did something to me.

I groaned and ground up into his palm.

"That's right, I'm going to give you what you need. Watch." My chest was flushed red. My lips parted as he thrust another finger into me. "I can't wait to fuck you. To taste you. Slide my tongue inside you. Spank you like I promised. I will, zayka. You'll be naughty, won't you?"

I nodded. I felt hazy and warm, and it was surreal as he pumped, flicked, and nibbled at my ear.

"You feel so swollen and ripe for me, zayka. Is that how you feel inside? Like you're ready for my cock?"

He rocked against me in motion to my hand, gripping me to him like a lifeline. The feeling burst over me in a crescendo of sensation, and I threw my head back onto his shoulders with a sigh as it rushed over me. I'd not known it could be like that. I'd been missing out.

He cupped my pussy protectively for a few more moments and kissed my temple.

"Soon, my cock will be here. I'd take you now, but you'll scream too loud. I'm going to *ruin* you," he promised.

He slid his fingers from me and raised them to his mouth. I watched in fascination when he licked them clean. "Delicious." He sent me a smirk. "Soon, I'll be able to spread you out on our bed and bury my head in that sweet little pussy of yours. Make you come over and over."

The thought of him between my legs sent a wave of heat through me. I wished it could happen now.

"Be good, zayka."

Pulling the straps up over my shoulders, he slid the zipper up.

Maxim's expression softened as his gaze met mine in the mirror. "Now this," he said, his voice like a caress, "is you."

The dress didn't try to turn me into someone else—it just let me *be*. It was extraordinarily simple, with no sleeves, no lace, or jewels. The skirt was full and generous, the fabric luxurious, the neck square, and it was white but plain. And — it had pockets. I loved it.

Maybe this wasn't so bad after all.

"Isn't it bad luck for you to see the wedding gown?"

"I make my own luck, zayka."

Figures he would say that.

Turning me, he set his mouth on mine and proceeded to rock my world. I'd been kissed a few times by inept boys, once in school and once down by the pub, but they were sloppy, and it seemed like they didn't know what to do with their tongues. But like everything else, Maxim made it feel like everything was as natural as my heart beating. His fingers threaded through my hair until they met my scalp, grabbing hold of the roots as he deepened the kiss, delving into my mouth, biting and tasting — exploring. Each taste seemed like another opportunity to show his dominance over me.

When he finally pulled away, I was breathless, my cheeks flushed, and my lips swollen. I wouldn't deny I looked thoroughly kissed, but Elise was professional, and her staff rallied.

She hadn't liked our choice of gowns, declaring it too simple for such a grand affair, but Maxim had shut that down right away after seeing my face, even after she'd argued against the practicality of such a gown for a winter wedding.

I left the shop with my gown ordered and a veil made of the most gossamer of Chantilly laces. If, for one day, I'd be wearing a dress, I was happy that I'd be wearing that one.

Later, when I sat in the back of the SUV, I ignored Finn to hang onto the feelings that Maxim had left me with. I wanted to savor the heady sensation of falling hard into the whirlpool that Maxim seemed to bring with him. He was sucking me further and further into this vortex of desperate desire. Suddenly, it didn't seem so bad that I was stuck marrying him.

CHAPTER FIFTEEN

maxim

THE WHEELS of my black SUV crunched over loose gravel as Lev pulled us into the abandoned warehouse lot. The place was a relic of some bygone industry—crumbling walls streaked with graffiti and broken windows. A few rusting steel drums sat haphazardly near a pile of debris, and the faint smell of oil and decay lingered in the cold air.

"Charming," Lev muttered from the driver's seat, his tone dry as he shifted into park.

I smirked. "What, not up to your standards?"

"Let's just say I wouldn't put this place on the sightseeing tour." He cut the engine and turned to me. "You want me to stick around?"

I shook my head. "Stay close but out of sight. If things go sideways, I'll let you know."

Lev nodded, his expression sharpening into something more serious, and I stepped out of the car. The air hit my face, crisp and biting, the faint hum of the city far in the background. Conall's SUV was already parked near the building, its dark bulk blending into the shadows.

As I approached, I saw him leaning against the hood, a cigarette dangling from his fingers. His expression was as relaxed as always, but a tightness in his shoulders gave him away.

"Maxim," Conall greeted me, flicking ash onto the ground. "Thought you might be late."

I raised an eyebrow. "I'm not the one who's so old they need an extra half hour to get out of bed."

He smirked, taking a long drag. "Touché."

Behind him, Angelo stepped out of his car, smoothing down the lapels of his coat like he was about to attend a gala, not inspect an abandoned car.

"Gentlemen," Angelo said, his voice soft but sharp as a blade. "I see we're slumming it today. Nobody thought to give me a text message. Had to hear through the grapevine. What the fuck?"

"Your invitation must've gotten lost in the mail," Conall replied with a grin. "Although I'm not sure why you eejits all decided to show up for this. Not like we all needed to be here — or any of us. Could have sent one of the boys." He frowned.

"Some things should be done in person," I growled.

I wasn't delegating shit when it came to some fucker shooting at Cora. If there were evidence to find, I would do it in person, not delegate it to one of my soldiers or one of Conall's.

"Like we wouldn't come in person. Dick," Angelo said, shooting him a look of equal parts amusement and irritation before turning his attention to the old sedan parked near the warehouse.

The car was unremarkable at first glance—an old, battered model with mud caked along the sides and a crack in the rear windshield. But the partial plate matched the one we'd been looking for, making it worth our time.

"You find anything?" I asked Conall as we approached the car.

"Not much yet," he admitted, gesturing toward the vehicle. "I was waiting for the experts to arrive." He rolled his eyes at us.

I crouched near the driver's side door, running my gloved hand along the frame. Then, I opened the door to lean in and opened the glove box.

"Amateur?" Angelo muttered. "Or do you think this was professional?"

"This is an interesting choice of a vehicle," I commented. "Either because it was convenient or because it wasn't traceable.

"All the information is still in the glove," Conall said, crossing his arms as he leaned against the car. "They ditched it. So that tells me that they didn't want to get caught. We know it wasn't some random shite. It was targeted. We just don't know why."

Before we could speculate further, another car pulled up, its sleek, dark profile unmistakable.

Ilias stepped out with his usual air of calm authority, his coat flaring slightly in the breeze. He was the only one of us who never seemed to rush, but a weight to his presence commanded attention.

"Late to the party, I see," Conall called out, his grin widening.

Ilias raised an eyebrow. "Some of us have real work to do. At least I'm at the party."

"Real work or more secrets?" Angelo quipped, his tone sharp but not unkind.

Ilias ignored him, striding over to the car. "The plates are a match," he said without preamble. "But more importantly, I know who it belongs to—or who it did."

We all fell silent, waiting for him to continue.

"The car was reported stolen two days ago," Ilias explained. "The owner is clean, and the theft was reported. Print was from the owner."

"You don't think the owner had anything to do with the shooting?" I asked.

Ilias shook his head. "I don't actually. The owner is just over eighty years old. He had the car in a garage. He hasn't driven for years."

Angelo frowned, tilting his head. "Do we have fucking anything?"

Ilias reached into his coat pocket and pulled out a printed still image. "I pulled surveillance footage from the garage where the car was stolen."

He handed me the photo. It showed a young, scruffy man with a lean frame caught mid-motion near the stolen vehicle. My stomach tightened as I studied the image. Who the fuck was this asshole?

I glanced at Conall. "We need to get back to your building. I want to talk to Finn. See if he has anything to add."

"Agreed," Conall said. "Let's move."

Angelo folded his arms. "Think we'll get more than we did here?"

"If we don't, it's your turn to pay for

drinks," Conall quipped, already walking back to his car.

I wanted the 'who' … and the 'why.' I'd be calling my cousin Ronnie in Arizona. Maybe she could work some magic and turn some dirt up on this fucker.

CHAPTER SIXTEEN

cora

I WAS STRETCHED out on the sofa in the apartment, halfheartedly watching an episode of *The Last of Us*. The kitten, Clyde, was curled up on my chest. Conall had had a vet swing by to check him out and give him an exam and his first round of shots. He was in remarkably good shape for being on the streets on his own. He was a little scruffy, but I was already in love with him.

When the knock came at the door, I knew exactly who it was. No one else knocked with that mix of determination and restraint—like they had to remind themselves not to kick the door down.

It had been a few days since the bridal shop encounter, and I'd wondered when I'd see him again — I ached for it.

"Come in, Max," I called, not bothering to get up.

When the door opened, he was tall and commanding, wearing a dark coat that made the apartment feel smaller. His eyes went straight to me, then narrowed at the kitten as if it were going to leap at him any second.

"You still have that thing?" he asked, stepping inside and shutting the door behind him.

"His name is Clyde," I corrected with a smirk. "And yes, I still have him. What did you think I'd do, toss him out on the street?"

"I wouldn't put it past you." His tone was dry, but I could see how his jaw tightened, his focus shifting warily between me and the kitten.

"You're scared of him, aren't you?" I teased, sitting up. "You know he's still a baby. He can't hurt you."

Maxim didn't answer, but he didn't deny it either. Instead, he crossed his arms and gave me a look. "I came to check on you, not to be interrogated about your furry menace."

I rolled my eyes, grinning. "I'm fine, Max. Really. You're more shaken about the shooting than I am."

His expression darkened, and he took a step closer. "You were almost killed, Cora. Forgive me for being a little… invested in your survival."

"I appreciate the concern," I said lightly, "but you should know something about me. It'll take more than a stray bullet to scare me." I wasn't lying about that.

The shooting hadn't left any lasting damage. Finn was quick at covering me. The experience had only shown me that Conall was right about assigning me protection.

He huffed a breath, clearly not amused, and his eyes lingered on me a moment longer. There was something different in his gaze—something deeper, heavier as if he was seeing me in a way that unsettled even him.

"What?" I asked, suddenly self-conscious.

"Nothing," he said quickly, though his voice had softened. "Just… you're amazing, you know that?"

His lips quirked into a faint smile, but the intensity didn't leave his eyes. He moved to sit on the armchair opposite me, his broad frame making the modest furniture seem smaller.

Maxim's gaze flicked to the kitten, then back to me. "I have family coming in soon."

I raised an eyebrow. "Oh? Should I be worried?"

"Not unless you're afraid of strong-willed women."

I laughed. "I think I can handle it. Who's coming?"

"Ronnie and Natasha, my cousins," he said, a hint of pride creeping into his tone. "You'll like them. Natasha's a lawyer—sharp as anything—and Ronnie's... well, let's say amazing. Like you. My brother will be coming also with his wife and their daughter."

I couldn't help but smile. There was something warm in how he talked about them, a rare softness in his usually hard-edged demeanor.

"And they're coming for the wedding?" I asked, tilting my head.

"Partly. But also to meet you."

I blinked, taken aback. "Me?"

He leaned forward, his elbows resting on his knees, his gaze locked onto mine. "You're important to me, Cora. That means you're important to them."

My heart did a little flip, but I forced myself to keep my expression neutral. "Well, no pressure then."

He smirked, but it didn't quite reach his eyes. "They'll love you. ... maybe don't bring up the kitten."

I laughed again, and for a moment, the tension eased. But as Maxim sat back, his gaze lingering on me, I couldn't shake the feeling that something deeper was at play.

"Max," I said softly, "what are you worried about?"

He hesitated, then shook his head, his jaw tightening. "Just want to make sure you're safe. That's all."

I knew he wasn't telling me the truth, but I let it go for now.

"What are you watching?" he asked, plopping down on the sofa next to me, slinging an arm over the back so it rested on my shoulders. "This one of those zombie things you like?"

"Don't tell me you are so out of touch you haven't seen this?" I said, aghast. "We need to get you up to speed."

Maxim raised a brow, clearly unimpressed. "If I wanted to watch a show about the end of the world, I'd just check the news."

I smirked, leaning into the cushions, my shoulder brushing his arm. "This is art, Max. It's about survival, humanity, love, loss… zombies are just a bonus."

He glanced at the screen, where a tense standoff between survivors was unfolding. "Doesn't look very romantic."

"Not everything has to be romantic," I shot back. "But since you're here, we could change that. You could woo me with your deep, profound thoughts about society's collapse."

His lips twitched in amusement. "Deep and

profound, huh? All right. Here's one: if people had more sense, they wouldn't let a kitten into their house when the world's falling apart."

I gasped, pretending to be scandalized. "Clyde is the very reason I *would* survive the apocalypse. He's adorable. No one would shoot me while I was holding him."

"Or they'd shoot both of you for being a nuisance."

I playfully shoved his shoulder, and he chuckled, a rare and quiet sound that sent warmth through my chest. His arm slipped from the back of the sofa, resting lightly against my shoulders, and the teasing energy shifted.

"Tell me something, Cora," he said, his voice lower now, his eyes locked on mine. Those cinnamon eyes were searching my face for something — answers?

I swallowed, suddenly hyper-aware of the inches between us. "What?"

"How are you this calm?" He tilted his head slightly, studying me as though he couldn't figure me out. "After everything that's happened? The shooting, the wedding, my… job? I would have thought you'd be freaking out. Putting up a bit more of a fight." He angled himself closer to me, and my nipples pebbled in response.

I shrugged, trying to downplay the question.

"I guess I'm just good at compartmentalizing, or maybe I know when to let things go."

His hand moved, brushing the curve of my shoulder as he pulled back slightly. "Let things go, huh? Like fear? Or do you just pretend it's not there?"

The weight of his words hung between us, and for a moment, I didn't know how to respond. Maxim wasn't someone who wasted time with small talk—he had a knack for cutting straight to the heart of things, and I wasn't sure if I liked it or hated it.

"Maybe fear is a luxury," I said finally, my voice quieter than intended. "If I let it in, it'll swallow me whole. Should I be afraid?"

He didn't answer right away, but the intensity in his gaze deepened, his usual armor slipping just a fraction. "It's not a weakness to be afraid, Cora. It's human."

"Are you afraid?" I asked before I could stop myself.

His lips pressed into a thin line, and for a moment, I thought he wouldn't answer. Then, he reached out, brushing a strand of hair from my face.

"Yes. This is all new to me."

I nodded, leaning over to lay my lips on his.

"That's okay, Max," I murmured. "I've got you."

Maxim froze at first, his lips still under mine as if caught off guard by the gesture. Then, slowly, he responded, his hand cupping my jaw, his thumb brushing the curve of my cheek. The kiss deepened, a blend of caution and hunger, as though he was testing the waters and staking his claim all at once.

For a moment, the world outside ceased to exist. There were no shootings, no family expectations, no shadows lurking on the horizon. It was just us, the kitten's faint snuffles and the soft flicker of the TV casting muted light over the room.

When we broke apart, his forehead rested against mine, his breath warm on my lips. His thumb traced an absent pattern along my jawline, and I saw something raw in his eyes—something that made my heart ache.

"You're dangerous, Cora," he murmured, his voice a hoarse whisper.

I smirked, though my chest was still tight. "Pot, meet kettle."

Maxim chuckled softly but didn't pull away. "You make me want to believe in things I shouldn't."

"And what's wrong with believing?" I asked, my fingers brushing the fabric of his coat.

"Nothing, as long as it doesn't get you killed."

The weight of his words settled between us, and I knew this wasn't just about me. Maxim carried a burden I couldn't fully see, but I wanted to understand and share it.

I leaned back, giving us both a little space, though his hand lingered on my leg. "Speaking of danger... have you discovered anything about the shooter?"

His expression hardened, and he sat back, the softness giving way to his usual edge. "Not enough. Conall and Finn have been working on it, but whoever they were, they knew what they were doing. Professional. Stole a car. Left no prints. "

My stomach churned at the thought, but I forced myself to stay composed. "Any leads? Something to go on?"

Maxim nodded slowly. "We have a photo, and we were able to get a bullet casing. The bullet matched a specific kind of ammunition used by a small group of assassins tied to a South American cartel. They're efficient, but they rarely operate this far north. It's... unusual."

"Unusual enough to worry about?" I asked, my fingers tightening fractionally around the small body that stretched on my chest.

"Unusual enough that we're not ruling out the possibility of a bigger connection. A message, maybe."

"To you?"

"To all of us," he admitted, his tone grim. "The timing is too precise to be a coincidence, especially with the wedding coming up."

The knot in my stomach tightened, but I kept my voice steady. "So what do we do?"

He looked at me for a long moment, then reached out to trace the curve of my cheek. "We stay vigilant, and I keep you safe. I guess I'll have to keep the little beast safe, too." He narrowed his eyes at Clyde as if personally offended by the tiny thing.

It wasn't a question or a request—it was a promise. One I hoped he could keep.

The door swung open with a bang, and I was startled back away from his heat as my brother stalked in, his eyes bouncing from me to Maxim.

"What are you doing here?" Conall asked, frowning.

"Seeing my fiancée."

"You'll see her at the end of the aisle in just a few days."

"That's right. Then she'll be moving in," Maxim needled Conall.

The thought sent another frisson of awareness through me. Me in his space. I hadn't even thought about it and everything that would entail. I'd been so unsettled recently coming from my uncle's house that even Conall's didn't feel like home yet.

"You arse," Conall growled, swinging away from us and stalking off to his office.

Once he was out of earshot, Maxim leaned close to kiss me, biting my bottom lip hard enough that the coppery taste of blood hit my mouth. "I can't wait to have you all to myself, zayka. The things I'm going to do to you." His words were filled with dark promise.

"Will I see you before the wedding?" I asked as he pulled back.

"Probably not. I've got business, but I'll be the one at the end of the aisle."

He got up abruptly, his fists clenched and his jaw working as he looked at me. I wanted to ask him to stay, but he was out the door before I could tell him I wasn't afraid. I wanted him to ruin me. I couldn't wait.

CHAPTER SEVENTEEN

maxim

THE DOORBELL RANG, sharp and impatient, followed by Pike's voice booming through the door. "You're dragging your feet, Volkov. Get to it!"

I set my glass of vodka on the bar and walked to the entrance, already bracing myself. "Don't break my door, Pike," I called before swinging it open.

The moment the door to my townhouse opened, laughter spilled into the entryway. Dimitri's deep chuckle was unmistakable as he strode in, his arm slung casually around Hollis's shoulders. Natasha followed close behind, her eyes scanning the place with practiced precision. Pike looked like he'd stepped off the set of a crime drama, all leather, and swagger, while Ronnie trailed behind, dragging Eli by the hand.

"Come on in. Let me hug my cousins."

Natasha and Ronnie were the ones I was closest to, even more than my brother. He'd left when he was fifteen, and while we had reestablished a relationship recently, the girls had been a steady presence in my life.

"You couldn't have picked something bigger, Maxim?" Natasha teased as she surveyed the foyer. "It's not like you're on a budget."

I smirked. "It's New York. Space is at a premium, even for me."

Pike whistled, glancing around. "Still swanky enough for the likes of us. Fancy digs," Pike said, brushing past me. "Where's the booze?"

"It's a townhouse, not a bar," I shot back.

"Same thing," Dimitri added, smirking.

Ronnie rolled her eyes, plopping onto the sofa like she owned the place. "Swanky doesn't even begin to cover it. This place looks nice. A little bit Bond and a little bit old-school librarian."

"You can all make yourselves comfortable," I told them, though my tone was more *don't touch anything expensive*.

Natasha looked around, lingering on the high ceilings and carved wood. "This is beautiful, Maxim."

"It'll do," I replied with a shrug. The townhome had been a find that I'd snapped up as soon as the realtor had shown it to me. Three stories of prime real estate that had been well-kept with private entrances, a basement, and a courtyard. After extensive renovations and additional safety measures, it would be an excellent home for us.

Ronnie nudged Eli as they stepped into the living room. "I bet you're already picking apart the security."

Eli's lips barely twitched, his version of a smile. "Already did."

"Well, if you think of anything I could improve," I said. "Please let me know." I would be foolish not to take Eli or Ronnie's advice if they saw something missing.

Hollis laughed softly, leaning into Dimitri. "This is going to be *fun*."

Dimitri raised an eyebrow. "Depends on your definition."

Once everyone settled in, Pike immediately made a beeline for the bar in the corner. "Finally, something I can get behind," he said, pouring himself a drink. "Flying doesn't suit me."

"You're worse than my men," I said, shaking my head. "And you had a private plane thanks to Eli."

"Hey, I'm good comedic relief. You know you love me," Pike shot back, raising his glass in a mock toast.

Well, I tolerated him because Natasha loved him, but I wouldn't say so. I turned to Natasha, Ronnie, and Hollis, who had clustered near the sofa. Natasha gave me a knowing look. "You look tense."

"Not every day I host a circus," I replied dryly.

Eli remained quiet, his gaze sharp as he observed his surroundings. He was always sizing things up, even when there was no apparent threat. It was a trait I respected—and one I could never entirely trust.

Dimitri pulled Hollis to the bar, pouring her a glass of wine. "So, big brother, is the bride nervous yet?"

I shrugged, leaning against the edge of the counter. "She's still at Conall's. Probably sneaking around to avoid her security detail."

Natasha frowned. "She's sneaking around *still*?"

I'd told Natasha about Cora's little photography expeditions into the city. Natasha had been equal parts horrified and impressed.

"She's stubborn," I said, a hint of amusement in my voice. "And she hates being cooped up. She thinks I don't know, but I'm aware of every time she slips out."

"You let her?" Hollis asked, surprised.

"She's alive, isn't she?" I replied dryly. "I trust her to handle herself—mostly. I send men to trail her."

"She's got guts," Pike said. "Sounds like my kind of woman."

Natasha swatted his arm. "Watch it."

"Relax," Pike drawled. "I'm a happily married man."

"Speaking of marriage," Natasha said, settling onto the sofa. "Cora doesn't have friends here, does she?"

"She doesn't have friends anywhere," I admitted. "She keeps to herself."

It was something that I'd noticed about her — that edge of loneliness that she carried around her. I wasn't sure that her brothers had picked up on the fact that Cora was desperate for connection.

Ronnie's eyes lit up. "Well, that's unacceptable. She's getting a proper bachelorette party."

"Agreed," Natasha said firmly. "Hollis, you're in, right?"

Hollis grinned. "Of course. Someone's got to make sure you two don't end up in jail."

"And who will make sure *you* don't?" Pike muttered.

"I heard that," Hollis shot back, smirking.

I loved that Hollis was more comfortable in groups now. There had been a time that she hadn't been, but it seemed like she had settled into the little family that Dimitri had created in Arizona for himself. If anyone knew what it was like to be alone it was Hollis.

The women were already plotting as they moved into the living room, leaving the rest of us standing around the bar. I glanced at Dimitri, who shrugged, his grin as wide as ever.

"Looks like we're outnumbered," he said.

"Not for long," Pike chimed in. "If they're having their night, we're having ours."

"Careful," I warned. "You're not on home turf here."

Pike snorted. "Please. It's New York, not another planet."

"Doesn't matter," Dimitri said, his tone more serious now. "Maxim's right. We need to keep our heads down. Too many eyes on us."

The lighthearted mood shifted as we moved into my office. Once the door was shut, business took over. Dimitri leaned against the desk, arms crossed, his casual demeanor hiding the sharp mind that had become an asset to my operations on the West Coast.

"How are things running out there?" I asked him.

"Smooth," Dimitri said. "The shipments are on time, and we have things under control. There's been some chatter—small-time players thinking they can take a slice of the pie. I'm going to have Eli help me out with a few of those assholes."

I glanced at the hulking brute, who was head over heels for my delicate cousin Ronnie. Eli was a former underground fighter and fight promoter who had also proven that he would take things to the next level.

"Alright. Handle it," I said simply.

He nodded. "Already in motion."

Pike leaned back in his chair, his boots resting on the edge of the desk. "What about here? Anything we need to know?"

Pike wasn't overly involved in my business, but I was sure Dimitri had hauled him in on a few jobs since he and Dimitri's MC were in business together. Pike was the president of an MC and had previously handled some gun smuggling for my bratva. He was competent and smart.

"Nothing you can't already guess," I said. "The takeover went fairly smoothly. No big problems. The main player had an unfortunate accident."

Eli covered a chuckle. "I'll just bet he did. Stumble on the blunt end of someone's knife?"

"Something like that," I said.

"I've got this fuck face from one of the Italian families. The Olivetos. That is stirring the pot. Dante Caruso. I'll handle him. The biggest issue is someone took a shot at Cora the other day. I sent the picture to Ronnie."

"She worked on it," Eli confirmed. "We don't know much more. She's still trying to connect the hit — see if a contract was out on Cora."

Ronnie was an excellent hacker, and I'd used her in the past for all sorts of bratva business. She'd come into my life roughly nine years ago. Our families hadn't always been close, and Ronnie and Natasha's mother had hidden from my father for years—for good reason. I'm not sure Sasha had known how vile my father was, but she was smart enough to keep the girls hidden. It wasn't until Ronnie got sick that she came forward and asked for my help and protection to return to the family.

Ronnie's illness had been the scariest thing I'd ever experienced. At first, I'd tried hard to keep her at arm's length. She'd been so young, frail, and small when we first met but full of sunshine. It was hard not to admire her bravery in the face of everything. Just skin and bones as she lay on her sheets in the hospital.

Childhood leukemia.

I wasn't prepared.

I was still terrified that she'd get sick again. Loving Ronnie and having her in my life made it much richer. I was so grateful for her, but the dichotomy of potentially losing her made me ache. I couldn't imagine how Eli felt. She'd been in remission for years, but I knew life was fragile.

Natasha, her sister, once told me that I was a fool—a stupid one at that.

"Max," she looked at me with love then. "Death waits for us all. You, more than anyone else, know that. We live with courage and love with courage. That's all we can do now. Face each moment with dignity."

The girls' devotion to each other had inspired me for years. I'd been missing my brother when they came to me, and they filled my heart with joy in his absence. It seemed only right that when Dimitri finally called for help, I had sent Natasha to him. In the end, both Natasha and Ronnie had found their own love stories.

The room fell silent for a moment until Pike broke it with a grin. "All right, boys. Enough doom and gloom. Let's figure out where we're going tonight."

CHAPTER EIGHTEEN

cora

THE KNOCK STARTLED me as I was halfway through organizing my camera gear. I wasn't expecting anyone, and Conall hadn't mentioned visitors. I hesitated before pressing the intercom.

"Yes?" I asked cautiously.

Last week, Finn and I had decided on an uneasy truce. He buzzed up if someone was coming to the apartment, but otherwise, he didn't hover outside. The arrangement was exactly what I needed for my little excursions.

"It's Natasha," a confident voice replied, followed by a giggle and another voice chiming in, "And Hollis. And Ronnie! Open up!"

Confusion tugged at me. Who? How'd they get past Finn?

The intercom buzzed again, this time with a cheerful urgency.

"Maxim sent us!" one of them called. "Well, kind of. Just open the door. We're not axe murderers, I promise."

Against my better judgment—or perhaps because their energy was infectious—I opened the door to reveal three women who could not have been more different from one another.

The tall one with lush dark hair that cascaded down her back and grey eyes stepped forward, a broad smile on her face. "You must be Cora. I'm Natasha, Maxim's cousin." She had the air of someone who could charm someone into submission.

The one beside her, shorter with a carefree vibe, grinned. "I'm Hollis, Dimitri's wife. Don't worry, we're not as intimidating as we look."

"And I'm Ronnie," said the youngest, her eyes sparkling with mischief. "Also Maxim's cousin and his biggest headache."

They were all beautiful in their own way. Ronnie was delicate and petite, and the other women almost dwarfed her. Her hair and skin were nearly translucent, but her eyes were gray-blue like Natasha's. She resembled a little fairy.

I blinked, taking them in. "Uh, hi. What are you all doing here?"

"Rescuing you," Hollis said with a wink,

brushing past me into the apartment. Natasha and Ronnie followed without hesitation.

"From what?" I asked, still standing in the doorway, baffled. "How'd you get past the guard dog?"

"Pff. Easy peasy," Ronnie said as she let herself in. "Oooh. Is that a kitten?" She squealed as she saw Clyde.

Natasha started to laugh.

"Oh my God. Is Max having an absolute conniption? He is terrified of cats."

I grinned back at them as I shut the door.

"He does seem unnaturally tense around the little guy," I chuckled. "So you're rescuing me?"

"Of course, you can't just stay home the night before your wedding, for one," Natasha said, her tone brisk. "Maxim told us you don't have any girlfriends in the city."

"Well, or anywhere," Ronnie added bluntly. Natasha shot her a look and then returned to giving Clyde little kisses.

"Ronnie," Hollis scolded gently, but then she turned to me with a soft smile. "We're here to fix that. Girls' night out. What do you say?"

I stared at them. I wasn't used to this—people showing up, wanting to include me in their world. It felt foreign but also... nice.

"I don't know," I said hesitantly. "I've never really done anything like that."

"That's why we're here," Natasha said, taking my hands firmly in hers. "Trust me, by the end of tonight, you'll be glad you did. We're going to have so much fun."

"We need drinks. Let's raid the bar. Max has a car for us, and Finn is bringing us pizza," Natasha scouted around the apartment.

Conall had a very nice liquor assortment, and before long, we were well on our way to whatever fresh hell the trio had planned. I was a little afraid to ask, but I did text my fiancé.

Me: What is this chaos?

Maxim: They say they have a plan but don't trust them.

Me: ☺

Maxim: jk - I'm sure you'll have a good time.

ME: What are you doing? Strippers?

Irrationally, jealousy flared at the thought

that he might touch another woman or another woman might touch him.

Maxim: Of course, not

Me: Good

"SO, we were banned from clubs since our last time," Natasha's eyes shot to Ronnie. "We went to a club thing there were issues."

"Hey," Ronnie said indignantly. "That really wasn't my fault that someone tried to kill me."

Color me interested.

"I'd love to hear all about this," I admitted.

"It's boring," Ronnie's mouth set in a frown. She looked adorable, glaring at her sister with the froth of all that hair around her. Ronnie had a goth girl vibe going on that I sort of envied, and it really worked with her coloring. She grinned evilly. "I lived. The end. You could ask Max. He was there."

"You can text him in the car," Hollis said, looking at her phone. Out of the three of them, she was the quietest one. "Pizza is here. Finn texted."

"You have Finn's number?" My eyes widened.

"Shush. I just got it right now for exactly

this. Dima would murder him if it were for anything else."

"Seems to run in the family — the murdering." The way the others looked nervously at each other, I knew I wasn't far off.

* * *

THE CAR RIDE was alive with chatter and laughter as Natasha, Ronnie, Hollis, and I exited the city. Ronnie was laughing so hard that she had to get out her inhaler after she started coughing. The others hadn't been alarmed, but it had scared me when she began huffing and wheezing like she couldn't breathe. Natasha had just calmly pulled Ronnie's purse close, riffled through it, and found an inhaler.

After a few moments, she was fine, but I watched her warily for a few minutes.

Finn sat in the front seat with the driver, visibly on edge, but the four of us were wrapped up in our world of chaos. We had a follow car with a ridiculous group of another four other bodyguards, which seemed unwarranted, but Natasha said they were non-negotiable. She had pizza boxes stacked beside her, and the faint scent of tequila still lingered from the earlier shots.

"Where are we going?" I asked, leaning

forward and taking another slice of pizza. "And why are we leaving Manhattan?"

"You'll see," Natasha said with a mysterious smile.

"Don't worry, it's nothing illegal," Hollis added, then paused. "Well, probably not illegal."

"Why don't I believe you," I said, raising an eyebrow.

"It's legal-ish," Ronnie chimed in. "You're going to love it. Trust us."

"I'm not sure I have much of a choice," I replied, though I couldn't help but smile at their infectious energy.

When we crossed the bridge into Jersey, I wondered what they had planned. Eventually, the car pulled into a brightly lit go-kart venue surrounded by high fences and neon lights.

"A go-kart track?" I asked, my surprise evident.

"Not just *any* go-kart track," Natasha said, hopping out of the car. "Max rented the whole place for us. No crowds, no lines. Just us and the track. Supposedly, you can drive about 40 miles an hour on the track. Should be fun."

"I can't believe Maxim signed off on this," Finn said as we walked toward the entrance. "You eejits are scattered."

Ronnie's nose wrinkled as she peered at him.

"Drunk. He's saying we're drunk," I clarified.

"Don't be a party pooper, Finnster."

"Don't worry about him, Ronnie." Natasha slung an arm over her sister's shoulder, and Ronnie grabbed my hand. "We're going to have so much fun. Oh, and Max wasn't happy about the whole thing," Natasha replied with a mischievous grin. "We told him it was for his peace of mind. You know, fewer strangers, tighter security. It was for him, really."

Ronnie snorted. "Yeah, I'm sure he bought that."

"We did say that we could hire some male strippers instead," Hollis said wickedly, taking my other arm. "Come on. Let's drive some cars."

Inside, the staff handed out helmets and directed us toward the track. I wondered if I should tell them I'd never driven a car, but I figured winging it seemed like a good plan.

"I've never done this before," I admitted as I adjusted the strap on my helmet, settling on a vague half-truth.

"Well, you're in for a treat," Hollis said, her eyes sparkling excitedly. "But fair warning—I'm competitive."

"So am I," Natasha added, cracking her knuckles. "Don't expect me to go easy on you just because you're the bride."

"Noted," I said with a laugh.

Strapping into her kart, Ronnie said, "You guys can fight for second place. I'm winning this."

"She is kind of a bad driver," Natasha admitted. "Eli even says she's terrible."

The first race was pure chaos. Natasha took the lead early, weaving expertly around the curves, while Hollis and I battled it out for last place. True to her word, Ronnie zipped through the course like she was born to it, laughing maniacally every time she overtook one of us.

"Watch out, rookie!" Natasha yelled as she sped past me, her kart nearly clipping mine.

"Oh, it's on now!" I shouted back, gripping the wheel tighter and leaning into the next turn. The whole driving thing wasn't that hard. I kind of liked it.

Hollis, hot on my tail, shouted, "No fair! I was about to pass her!"

By the time the race ended, my cheeks hurt from smiling. Ronnie took first place, of course, with Natasha close behind. Hollis and I finished neck and neck, arguing good-naturedly over who crossed the line first.

"Let's call it a tie," Hollis said, clapping me

on the back. "You held your own out there. That bump game of yours was on point."

Between races, we sat at a small table near the track, devouring slices of pizza and gulping down water. The atmosphere was electric, filled with teasing banter and the occasional outburst of laughter.

"So, Cora," Natasha said, leaning back in her chair, "what's it like marrying into our chaos?"

I smiled, wiping my hands on a napkin. "A little overwhelming, honestly, but also, it's kind of amazing. My brother moved me to Ireland when I was young, and I never made friends there. I've been on my own. I felt like it, anyway. I've never had anything like this before," I admitted.

"Well, get used to it," Hollis said warmly. "You've got us now. No backing out."

Ronnie raised her water bottle in a mock toast. "To Cora. Welcome to the madhouse."

I laughed, clinking my bottle against hers. "Happy to be here."

"When I met Dimitri, my daughter and I didn't have any family either. I know how you feel," Hollis said softly.

Throughout the evening, she'd confided some of her story of how she'd met Maxim's brother — how he'd saved her when she was trafficked. My heart nearly beat from my chest when she explained everything that had happened. I knew she was safe now, but it sounded so scary.

"Thanks, Hollis. I had family, but sometimes they felt farther than the ocean separating us, if that makes sense."

"It does."

By the time we wrapped up, the track lights were dimming, signaling the end of the night. As we piled back into the car, exhausted but exhilarated, I couldn't help but feel a warmth in my chest.

For the first time in years, I felt like I belonged—not just to Maxim but to these incredible women who had welcomed me into their world without hesitation.

Tomorrow would bring the wedding, the vows, and the whirlwind of a new life. But tonight? Tonight, I was just Cora—laughing, racing, and loving every minute.

maxim

THE PRIVATE LOUNGE in *Fortune* was thick with cigar smoke and the low hum of conversation. Dimitri poured another glass of vodka, leaning back in his chair with a smirk. Pike was sprawled out like he owned the place and was in rare form, tossing out stories about their younger days that I didn't care to know about but couldn't help laughing at.

Lev, ever the enigma, sat quietly, nursing his drink. Eli, on the other hand, had barely touched his glass. His sharp eyes scanned the room like a predator, waiting for the right moment to strike.

Conall, Angelo, and Ilias lounged indolently around the area, watching the others. They hadn't interacted much with my brother and had never met the Walters brothers. Pike and Eli were their own interesting tales of tragedy.

It was a miracle that they had found each other again after such a long time apart, but that they had fallen in love with sisters was fascinating.

This was supposed to be a celebration—a night to mark the end of one chapter of my life and the beginning of another. Yet, I couldn't help but feel the weight of the room, the unspoken tension that seemed to follow us wherever we went.

"To Maxim," Dimitri said, raising his glass. His voice carried that lighthearted charm that always managed to mask the steel underneath. "For finally letting someone tie him down. Though I'm still not convinced, it'll last."

Conall growled, shooting Dimitri a dark look, but I didn't bother rebuking him. The arrangement wasn't one I'd appraised my brother of, and Conall knew this already, even if he didn't like it. Somehow, I still couldn't stop sheltering my brother from the knowledge of how depraved my father was.

The table laughed, and the weight of responsibility lifted for a moment. These men were powerful in their own right—kings of their respective kingdoms. But tonight, we weren't rivals or allies bound by uneasy truces. Tonight, we were simply men celebrating life, even if that life was built on blood and shadow.

"So," Angelo began, swirling the whiskey in his glass, "what's next for you, Maxim? Settling down? Building a nice little garden in the suburbs?"

I smirked. "I'll leave the gardening to you, Angelo. I have an empire to run."

Ilias raised an eyebrow, his deep voice rumbling with amusement. "Empire, yes. But don't let the empire ruin the home. A man needs balance."

"Spoken like someone who's never had a day off," Pike interjected, grinning. "Gardening. That's funny. Right, Dimitri?" He jostled my brother with his arm. My brother's wife had a garden at their Arizona bungalow, so Pike was throwing him some serious shade for all the garden boxes he'd had to build, but I didn't think my brother minded so much.

Ilias shrugged, unbothered. "Perhaps, but I've learned the value of keeping the right balance of fear and loyalty."

A murmur of approval went around the table, but Lev broke the moment, leaning forward with a sly smile. "And what's a proper celebration without a little entertainment?"

I shot him a look. "No strippers, Lev. I told you that already."

Lev's expression didn't falter. If anything,

his grin widened. "Who said anything about strippers? I've got something much better."

"Really?" My interest was already piqued. I set my glass down. The night was looking up. I knew the sorts of gifts Lev gave. They typically came bloody — my favorite.

* * *

AN HOUR LATER, we arrived at the same warehouse Lev had set up for our darker dealings. The air was damp, and the faint sound of dripping water echoed through the cavernous space. Conall, Angelo, and Ilias followed in measured steps, their curiosity hidden behind unreadable expressions.

In the center of the room, under a harsh spotlight, was a man hung up on a hook. His face was swollen and bloodied, his dark eyes glaring up at us with defiance.

"Marco Sánchez," Lev announced, gesturing grandly. "Cartel operative with the Mancebos. He also hired the man who took a shot at your sister." He sent a sly grin to Conall, who went red with rage.

My insides went volcanic as I thought of Cora hiding behind a car while she was being shot at — hurt because some fuck put out a hit on her. Thank God this guy hired someone so inept. If he'd hoped for an easy death, that ship had sailed. Between Conall and me, his death was going to be ugly and slow.

I stepped closer, meeting the man's gaze. His lip curled into a sneer despite his condition. "You hired someone to shoot at Cora O'Kelly? Why?"

Marco spat blood onto the floor.

The air in the room shifted, a tangible tension crackling like a live wire. Dimitri moved closer, his jaw tightening. Pike exchanged glances with Conall, who schooled his expression, folded his arms, and waited.

Lev, of course, looked delighted. "He's got spirit. I thought you'd appreciate that, Maxim."

"So, this is my present?" I said, leaning to Marco.

I stepped forward, my voice calm but cutting through the silence like a blade. "I do like your style, Lev."

Taking the knife Lev offered, I turned back to Marco. The man's bravado faltered, replaced by a flicker of fear.

"You think you're going to outlast this?" I asked, my voice low but steady. "You're wrong, but if your cartel wants to test me. *Test us.* You're welcome to try."

The blade gleamed in the spotlight as I raised it, the weight of my choices settling over me. This was who I was. I'd long ago come to grips with the joy I took in killing. For a long time, I wondered if it made me like my father — like the scum he was. He took exceptional joy in butchering his victims. I was careful to keep myself to men who deserved their deaths, but I would never say I was merciful.

"You know I saw Maxim once skin a man. It was impressive," Angelo said conversationally.

Marco's eyes widened even further, darting from man to man.

"What the fuck is wrong with you? *Dios mío*." Frantically, he started saying a Hail Mary in Spanish. I could tell him that wouldn't help, but I let him babble on.

"That what you're going to do?" Eli asked, stepping out of the shadows. "It's always hard work. I don't mind helping." He grinned as if the thought of it would make his day. Probably would. He stepped behind Marco and poked a knife right at his ass. "I always start right here. Skin them from the ass out."

"Really? I like to do the face first. Start at the ear." I watched Marco as we talked. His mouth quivered, but he locked his jaw as if determining that he wouldn't scream. That was funny. The fucker would be screaming in just a few minutes.

He was quivering now, practically vibrating with it as he tried to pull himself away from Eli even though Eli was moving into his space with a knife poking him a little here and there. I did not doubt that Eli had done precisely what he'd said. I wanted information more than anything at this point.

Well, that was a lie.

A little fun — maybe.

"Was it your cartel that put the hit on my sister?" Conall asked, pushing the man so he swung a little on the hook."Give me something. I'm more reasonable than he is."

Well, that was a fucking lie if I ever heard one, but Marco seemed to think it was a lifeline because he stopped his Hail Marys and said feverishly, "We didn't put the hit out. Not us."

"What are you doing in New York? Why Cora?" I asked.

Eli poked him again with his knife, a bored expression on his face.

"Nothing. I know nothing," he screeched with desperation.

"Nothing, huh? Okay," Ilias said, doubt lacing his voice.

He nodded frantically as we chuckled. Maybe

he thought we believed him, but we weren't that stupid. If he were in the cartel game, he should know his orders, at the very least. There was no way that I'd ever believe he didn't know anything.

I'd had my hands behind my back as I walked around Marco before I grabbed one of his hands viciously, and with the pruning shears that I'd been holding, I yanked one of his fingers at an angle and cut it off.

Marco began to howl, snot bubbling from his nose. If he thought that hurt, he'd love the next bit.

"Conall?"

The small stump bled dramatically, dripping satisfactorily onto the floor.

I threw the finger at Marco's feet as Conall moved behind him menacingly. I was happy that Pike wasn't upset by our little interrogation. Eli, I'd had some experience with, but I'd never worked with Pike.

The whoosh of the blowtorch filled the room, and that set Marco trying again to swing himself as he screamed while Conall cauterized the wound.

"Let's try again," I began. "What were your orders when you came to the city?"

I snipped off another finger.

"We were paid!"

And so it began. Bit by bit, information came.

When it was done, the room was silent except for the dripping corpse. Marco hadn't gone easy, so I'd give him that.

Conall exhaled slowly, breaking the tension. "Well, that was... educational."

Angelo tipped his glass in my direction, his smile sharp. "Efficient, as always."

We'd learned that there had been a hit put out on Cora, but not much else if I were being honest. The Mancebos had accepted the hit, but only because they were down on some cash for a gun transaction with some other cartel. Marco was their best shot, which wasn't saying much since he obviously sucked so badly that he tried to hire some other yahoo — who also sucked. It was like a Three Stooges episode.

"What do you want done with the body?" Lev asked. "Displayed? Shipped?"

"Where are they based out of?"

"La Paz."

"Nah. Let's not be sloppy. I don't want to have any reason for sloppy work or trace evidence that could end us up in jail," I replied. Some things had to be weighed out as not worth it.

"No joke," Pike said.

I knew he got that. Pike had done some

serious jail time and had narrowly escaped doing more for some serial killings. Only Natasha coming to Arizona and acting as his lawyer had allowed him to escape that mess.

"Push through an encrypted picture of the body. I want them to know what happens to the men they send here," I added, glancing at what was left of Marco. "And call the cleaners."

"Let's hope the message is received," Ilias added, his tone neutral.

As we left the warehouse, Dimitri clapped a hand on my shoulder. "You've got a good woman waiting for you, Max. Don't let all this —" he gestured vaguely to the warehouse "— get in the way."

I nodded, my thoughts already drifting to Cora. She was a beautiful surprise, and as much as the night had reminded me of the darkness in our world, it also made one thing clear: I'd do whatever it took to keep her safe, and I didn't mind dipping my fingers in blood to do it.

One of the things my brother had never understood about me was that I was okay in the dark.

"So, we still don't know who ordered the hit?" Conall said with concern as we closed the door.

"No, but I have Ronnie on that. Hopefully,

we'll figure it out because that is key," I answered.

That piece of information was ultimately the lynchpin. One minor inept shooter was one thing … but that didn't mean another wouldn't follow that wouldn't be more skilled than the first.

CHAPTER TWENTY

cora

THE BELLS OF ST. Patrick's Cathedral rang, their deep, solemn sound echoing straight through me. The cathedral's grandeur was overwhelming when we'd pulled up, its soaring spires piercing the crisp grey sky. Inside, the air was thick with reverence and the soft hum of conversation.

I'd never been one for churches once I'd moved to Ireland, which would have made Conall have an absolute fit. I still wasn't sure how he'd gotten the priest to perform the service without all the required meetings or whatever they needed. Probably bribed them, I guessed.

I stood in the bridal suite just off the main sanctuary, staring at my reflection in an antique mirror framed in gilded gold. The gown still felt right to me. Maxim was right —classic fit me best. Though the old cathedral was drafty, I didn't even regret that it was sleeveless. Conall had a makeup artist and stylist come and arrange my hair. I probably looked nicer today than ever. I never could get the hang of the cat-eye look, but the girl who came had whipped it out with no problem. I peered at myself as the stylist set my veil.

"Say cheese."

Ronnie had been taking nonstop pictures all morning. She discovered that Conall had not hired a photographer and had gone bananas. Honestly, I hadn't considered any wedding details and hadn't thought I'd care, but now I was having second thoughts about the small things like commemorative photos. I was glad Ronnie had decided to do it for me. This morning, I'd photographed my dress and veil hanging up. It had given me a nostalgic longing for my mother, who had died when I was a toddler.

The girls had somehow designed color-coordinated dresses and showed up to be bridesmaids. I had so many feelings about it that I wasn't even sure how to express them.

"You're like the prettiest bride I've ever seen," Natasha said.

"We all look gorgeous," I admitted.

The girls looked fantastic today in their burgundy ankle-length dresses. Each was slightly different to suit their tastes but worked cohesively together. Ronnie said yesterday that Natasha loved high fashion, and that showed today. She'd pulled out a magic trick at the last minute.

"Thank you so much. You worked miracles."

A knock at the door broke through my thoughts, and Conall stepped in. He looked powerful and dangerous, his tuxedo perfectly tailored, but his expression drew my attention. His eyes, always so sharp and calculating, were softened with a rare vulnerability.

"You look so beautiful, Cora," he said, his voice low and thick with emotion. "So grown up. I'm sorry Ma isn't here to see it."

"Me too," I answered. I didn't remember her, but I didn't bother saying that to Conall. I knew that he missed her, too. I smiled, though my stomach churned with nerves. "I feel like I might faint."

There were equal parts of me that seemed fraught with anxiety and excitement. Yes, I'd made my peace with this arrangement, and I would admit that I was wildly thrilled by the thought of sex with Max.

But.

I wasn't sure if I was even ready for marriage.

To be a wife.

I didn't even know much about him.

Conall stepped closer, his hands settling on my shoulders. "You won't. You're stronger than you know. Remember that. And if you do need me, I'll be right there. I'll catch you if you fall. You can always come to me if you need to."

The reassurance steadied me, and I nodded. Taking his offered arm, I drew a deep breath.

OK then.

I didn't have much choice anyway. Did I?

THE SANCTUARY WAS a breathtaking mix of power and history. On one side, the Irish —my family—filled the pews. Men and women whose bloodlines traced centuries of rebellion and loyalty sat alongside our allies: Angelo, his brother, and what had to be his sister, and Ilias, whose huge Greek family took up several pews.

On the other side, the Bratva occupied the pews with military precision. Maxim's men, each one sharp and severe, stood in rows with their shoulders squared and chests tall. Their stoicism only highlighted the presence of a few women in the front.

Security was thick, almost suffocating. Well-armed men in dark suits with earpieces lined the walls, stationed at every entrance and alcove.

As the music began—the hauntingly beautiful strains of a Celtic harp—I clutched Conall's arm tightly as I followed Ronnie down the aisle lined with white roses, their fragrance mixing with the scent of incense. The cathedral's vaulted ceilings seemed to stretch endlessly, and the stained glass cast vibrant patterns of color onto the polished marble floor.

Maxim stood at the altar, his figure commanding in a perfectly tailored black suit and what must be his brother Dimitri at his side. Even from this distance, I could see the tension in his jaw, the way his hands clenched and unclenched at his sides. His cinnamon-brown eyes locked onto mine — determined.

"Breathe," Conall whispered, his arm steady beneath my grip.

I took a step, then another. Each one felt monumental, the weight of expectations and alliances pressing down on me. But as I moved closer to Maxim, the pressure eased, replaced by a growing sense of clarity.

Conall leaned in, his voice low. "Almost there. Hold your head high. You're doing brilliantly."

The final steps were a blur. And then we were there. Conall placed my hand in Maxim's, his grip firm as he transferred me to the man who would now share my life. Maxim's fingers closed over mine, warm and steady.

Conall leaned into Maxim, his voice a low murmur only the three of us could hear. "You take care of her, or you'll answer to me."

Maxim's lips curved into a faint smile, but his tone was unwavering. "You have my word."

Conall stepped away, leaving me alone with the man I was about to marry.

"You look exquisite," Maxim said, his deep, accented voice carrying a note of sincerity that made my breath catch.

"You're not too bad yourself," I replied, surprising myself with a small smile.

The priest began the ceremony, his voice solemn as it filled the cathedral. I barely registered the words. My focus was on Maxim—the quiet power he radiated, the way his thumb traced gentle circles against my hand.

When it came time for the vows, his voice was steady, each word carrying the weight of a promise. "I will honor and protect you, zayka. Always." He slid the wedding band onto my finger, and a lump settled in my throat as I raised my eyes to his.

"You may kiss the bride," the priest said.

Maxim didn't hesitate and swept me to him, capturing my mouth in a kiss that was too long and too heated for the altar of St. Patrick's, but I couldn't find it in me to care.

As we turned to face the congregation, the applause was electric with expectation. Maxim leaned down, his breath warm against my ear.

"Let's make this reception fast, *da*?" He murmured, his voice low enough for only me to hear.

"If that means yes — I agree." I winked.

CHAPTER TWENTY-ONE

maxim

BY THE TIME Cora and I arrived, the wedding reception was already in full swing. The lavish ballroom at The Plaza had been transformed into a dream of silver and gold, with glittering chandeliers casting a warm glow over tables adorned with elegant centerpieces. Cora clutched my hand, her nervousness almost palpable beneath the radiant smile she wore as we entered.

She looked like a princess or an angel walking down the aisle. Her dark hair floated in dark waves around her face like a storm, and her eyes set on me like I was her destination.

I hadn't been in a church since … well, never. I was surprised that I didn't burst into flames on the altar where I stood.

I leaned down to whisper in her ear. "You look stunning, zayka."

Her cheeks flushed a delicate pink. "You don't clean up so bad yourself."

As we were announced, the room erupted into applause, a mix of familiar faces and powerful allies filling the space. Dimitri was the first to approach, and his wife, Hollis, was at his side. I'm sure to give me shit. He already had a mocking grin on his face.

"You made it," Dimitri said with mock surprise, clapping me on the back. "I thought Lev might have dragged you off to some interrogation chamber again."

"Not this time," I replied dryly.

Hollis hugged Cora, her energy infectious. "You look like a princess," she gushed. "Maxim, you're lucky she said yes."

I chuckled, giving Cora a grin. Hollis had no idea that Cora hadn't had a choice in the matter.

"I'm reminded every day," I said, earning a laugh from the group.

Pike and Natasha had joined us, Pike with a drink in hand and Natasha looking effortlessly regal in a deep burgundy gown splashed with flowers. It had been such a sweet gesture from the girls that they'd stepped in as bridesmaids for Cora.

"Maxim, I'm shocked," Pike drawled, his

grin devilish. "You're smiling. I'm not sure I've seen that expression on your face before."

"It's been known to appear," Natasha cut in, elbowing him lightly. "Not that often, but sometimes."

"Come on, let's get seated so they can get this dinner going," Conall said grumpily.

Cora shot Conall a dark look as I helped her into her chair, making it clear that she didn't appreciate her brother's high-handed attitude. He'd acted squirrely all day, stiff as a board, his shoulders all square, and grumpy as all get out. Neither Cora nor I had planned this wedding, so it wasn't as if we had a say, but we did as he asked, even as I sent him a glance that told him we needed to talk.

For now, I wanted to focus on my new wife.

I glanced down at the ring on my finger and then at the vision next to me.

A wife.

The night unfolded in a blur of laughter, food, and the kind of banter that only close family could manage. After much debate, the cake—a towering masterpiece of white and gold with sugar flowers cascading down the sides—was ceremoniously sliced. They'd set aside the cake topper for us, and Cora eyed it with discomfort.

"You cut it," Cora whispered, eyeing the knife like a weapon.

"No, we cut it," I corrected, guiding her hand with mine as we made the first slice.

"No smashing it in my face," Cora said as I picked up the small piece of cake in my fingers as my cousin had instructed me.

"I would never."

Her lips parted for me as I placed the bite in her mouth, her tongue darting forward to catch a few crumbs. Brushing the edge of her cheek with my thumb, I stood back while she picked up the slice she was supposed to feed me.

It was a weird tradition, the whole cake slice thing. I wasn't sure who had thought it up. As she turned to me, I caught her eye and saw the moment she decided — oh, my naughty little zayka. Bending to accept my bite, I wasn't surprised when she smashed the cake in my face full-on.

She spun away, laughing like a maniac, her dark hair swinging in a curtain around her and those eyes sparkling with mischief. What was a man to do? Grabbing her by the waist, I dug my hands into her hair and kissed her like she was the air I breathed, smashing my frosting-covered face into hers and licking vanilla into her mouth.

Servers were passing out the cake by the time we'd come up for air, but the cake wars had already begun because Ronnie was the first to grab a slice and smash it into Eli's face, causing an uproar of laughter.

"You're dead," Eli muttered, wiping frosting off his nose.

"Not if you can't catch me!" Ronnie darted off, leaving Eli to shake his head in exasperated fondness.

Cora laughed, leaning into me as the music shifted to a slow waltz. I held my hand, and she took it without hesitation, her fingers threading through mine. As we moved to the center of the dance floor, the crowd parted, and the band played the first notes of a soft melody.

Her gown flowed around her as I pulled her close, my hand on the small of her back, her eyes locked with mine. For a moment, the world faded away, and it was just us—two people tangled in a marriage built on duty but growing into something much more.

"You're a good dancer," she teased, her lips curving into a smile.

"I'm good at many things," I replied, earning a quiet laugh. "Just you wait. I'm going to show you."

The warmth of her laugh wrapped around me as I spun her, the chandeliers above casting a soft glow over her face. She tilted her head, studying me. "You're smiling again, Maxim. People will talk. Say you are losing your edge."

"Let them."

I pulled her closer as the song reached its crescendo, my lips brushing her temple.

* * *

"I'VE GOT to talk with your brother," I murmured to Cora, kissing her forehead. "Stay with Hollis and my cousins. I won't be long." Gesturing to Lev and Kolya, I beckoned them forward. We had invited some of our partners to the wedding, and especially in such a crowd, I didn't want any mistakes to be made.

There were still too many unknowns about the shooter and who hired the hit. Ronnie hadn't found anything about where it originated. She said she scoured the usual places but had come up empty. Frustrating as it was, that left us on the defensive for now.

She nodded, understanding. As I stepped away, I noticed Hollis dragging her onto the dance floor, Natasha and Ronnie joining in with matching grins.

The four of them spun and laughed, Cora's initial tension melting away as Ronnie twirled her dramatically, earning cheers from the nearby crowd. I couldn't help but glance back again before joining Conall and the others in a private lounge off the main ballroom.

* * *

THE RECEPTION WAS a blur of laughter and music when I caught Conall slipping away from the ballroom. His shoulders were stiff, his stride deliberate, but something in the way he moved set me on edge.

I glanced at Angelo, who was nursing a drink at the edge of the crowd. "Conall's ducked out. Let's follow."

Angelo's jaw tightened, but he gave a short nod. Ilias joined us as we moved toward the discreet exit Conall had taken.

We found him in the lounge, pacing like a caged animal. A glass of whiskey sat untouched on the table, the ice melting into a watery mess.

"Care to explain what's eating you, Conall?" Angelo asked, leaning against the doorframe. His voice carried its usual calm, but a heat was simmering underneath.

"Not here for small talk, Angelo," Conall shot back, his brogue sharper than usual.

"That's fine. I'm here for answers," Angelo replied, his voice suddenly cutting. His shoulders squared, and his spine stiffened. "What's going on with you and my sister?"

Conall froze mid-stride, his back to us. Slowly, he turned, his eyes dark with something between regret and defiance.

"This isn't the time," Conall said, his tone low. "And she's going to be my wife. That's what's going on."

"*I know*," Angelo snapped. "Francesca told me."

"I don't—" Conall stopped, shaking his head for a minute, his fists clenching at his sides. "I can't talk about her right now," he bit out, shaking his head. "Other things are going on right now that we need to discuss." Conall frowned at Angelo and crossed his arms the posture

Conall frowned at Angelo and crossed his arms, the posture one he rarely took with us and generally reserved for meetings with people he didn't like. I was sure I wasn't the only one baffled by the messages being thrown back and forth between Conall and Angelo about Francesca. It wasn't a secret that Conall and Francesca were getting married — probably soon if I were a betting man. If I knew Conall, the timeline would be fast and furious. Francesca was here. I had gotten a fleeting glance at her, but my attention wasn't exactly on the guests.

"Then enlighten us," Ilias interjected, stepping between them before Angelo's temper could fully ignite. "Clearly, something is weighing on you. Spit it out."

I wondered for a minute if Angelo would step back in, but he seemed to think better of it as he nodded and gulped his scotch, looking away from Conall.

"Some of my supply houses have been hit," he admitted finally, his voice tight. "Six in the past two months. High-value stock and they knew exactly where to strike."

"That's not small," I said, stepping forward. "And it's not random."

"No," Conall agreed. "Whoever it is, they're coordinated. This isn't some street-level gang taking potshots."

Angelo crossed his arms, his anger shifting into something colder. "Why didn't you come to us sooner?"

"I wanted to keep it contained," Conall said, his jaw tightening. "Bringing it to the Commission risks making it a bigger target."

"You waited until Maxim's wedding to mention this?" Ilias asked, incredulous.

"It's escalating," Conall said grimly. "The latest hit was yesterday. They cleaned out the warehouse in Queens. My men barely got out alive."

"Queens?" I repeated. "That's dangerously close to the Oliveto territory."

"You have any idea who is behind this?" Ilias asked, his brows furrowed.

"It's possible it's the Olivetos," Conall admitted. "But if so, they're playing coy. I've had no direct confrontations, no warnings. Maybe it was some O'Gara boys, but I don't think so."

The O'Gara's were a small-time Irish crew that Conall had had some competition with, but my understanding was that it was all petty. Brody had been the one who had told me he'd been stamping out the threat and making sure they understood that they should keep themselves in Boston and out of New York.

"I've continued to have issues with Caruso," I said. "Since our last meeting, he hasn't popped out of the woodwork, but that doesn't mean he couldn't be helping whoever this is. This could be a coordinated effort against all of us."

"We need to bait them," I said. "Set a trap. Something they can't resist."

"Something they won't expect," Ilias added.

Conall frowned. "You want to use my supply line as bait? That's risky."

"No," Ilias said. "Not your line. We'll use something more enticing—a shipment from my side. Something high-profile enough to draw them out but contained enough that we control the fallout."

Ilias ran an interesting set of businesses that were always secretive. Sometimes, he'd let us in on a piece of the action so we could all profit, but most of the time, even we were out of the loop on what he was doing. His old man was a cagey son-of-a-bitch who had bartered each of his sons off with binding blood contracts to other crime families. Ilias's two older brothers, Vaso and Kostas, were intimidating and brooding. Both were tied to opposing families, which I bet made Thanksgiving a bit of a drag.

Angelo nodded slowly. "And when they bite, we close the net."

Ilias leaned back against the table, his expression thoughtful. "What about our recent moves on the East Coast? Maxim? Conall? Could that play a role in their aggression?"

"Possibly," I admitted. "But I've kept my expansion measured and contained to just Slavsky's organization. I haven't overreached into other territory. The opportunity exists since some neighborhoods in the Olivetos territory are poorly managed. They're sloppy. Same goes for the Scarpato territory. There are areas there that could be snatched away. It just felt prudent to wait."

"This feels more opportunistic—like someone's trying to capitalize or test the waters," Conall said, but he sounded unsure. "They're a bit like hit and runs. I've got the footage. I'm just stumped on why they're hitting and quitting." He rubbed a hand down the side of his slacks. "It's like the answer is right there. I just can't see it. It's a little like Cora's shooting."

"What do you mean?" I came to attention.

"It just doesn't make sense. There's an attempt, but it's half-assed."

That piqued our interest because I saw Angelo and Ilias look at each other knowingly. Perhaps some of this was just testing the waters. Or — a distraction?

"Send us the footage. We should see it. Let's double down on these and Cora's hit. Maybe this is an attack on the Commission," Illias considered. "Maybe we haven't been looking at all the pieces. We'll put some bait into play."

"Whatever you need, I'm in," Conall said, his voice steadier now.

"Great. If we're done, then." I jerked a thumb towards the reception, where Cora was laughing on the dance floor, her joy momentarily lifting the shadows from my chest. "I've got a celebration going on that I'd like to get to."

"Yeah, yeah. Go ahead." Ilias shooed me

with both hands, but I heard Angelo say under his breath to Conall as I was leaving …

"Maybe we can talk about my sister now, Conall?"

I should have stopped and helped, but the sight of Cora laughing with Natasha and Hollis immediately softened the edges of my mood. Ronnie was mid-spin, dragging Eli into the mix, much to his chagrin, though he couldn't seem to deny her anything.

Cora caught my eye and broke away from the group, walking toward me with a radiant smile. "Business handled?"

"For now." I pulled her close, resting my forehead against hers. "I told you, zayka. You're the only one who matters."

"Good," she said, her hands resting on my chest. "Because I was starting to miss you."

"I'm right here," I promised, leading her back to the dance floor.

And as we moved to the rhythm of the music, the weight of power and responsibility melted away, leaving only her warmth and the promise of a future we'd carve out together.

CHAPTER TWENTY-TWO

cora

AS WE PULLED up to the townhouse, my breath caught. Maxim's Manhattan home was precisely what I'd expected: grand, foreboding, and impeccably intimidating. The tall, brick façade loomed over the quiet Upper East Side street like a fortress, its windows glowing faintly with soft, golden light. Two guards stood by the front entrance, their expressions stoic, and the air seemed to hum with the subtle tension that followed Maxim wherever he went.

I clutched the lined cape tighter as Maxim stepped out, turning to offer me his hand. Although his tuxedo jacket was slightly rumpled after the reception's whirlwind, he still exuded the same commanding presence that always made me feel simultaneously safe and wary.

"Welcome home, zayka," he said, his voice

rough, though there was an undercurrent of something softer beneath.

"Home," I repeated, hesitating as I gathered the heavy skirts of the wedding dress and stepped onto the curb. My heels clicked against the stone, the sound unnervingly loud in the stillness of the night. I hadn't felt like I'd had one of those for a long time.

The guards nodded silently as we passed, and Maxim's hand remained firm on the small of my back, guiding me inside. The door clicked shut behind us, muffling the sounds of the city and plunging me into a world that was distinctly his. It even smelled like him — sandalwood and spice.

The interior was… unexpected. I'd braced myself for cold marble and sharp, modern furniture, but the townhouse was warm and inviting, with dark wood accents and deep jewel-toned furnishings. A grand staircase swept up to the second floor, and a crystal chandelier sparkled overhead, casting soft prisms of light onto the polished hardwood floor.

"You live here?" Unable to hide my surprise.

He smirked, loosening his tie and giving me that side eye that made me all hot and bothered. "What were you expecting? A dungeon?"

I raised an eyebrow. "Considering your whole vibe? Maybe."

Maxim chuckled, the sound low and rough. "I save the dungeon for special occasions."

I rolled my eyes, but my stomach fluttered at the way his gaze lingered on me as if he could see straight through my bravado.

Before I could respond, a sudden, faint meow broke the charged silence. I turned toward the sound, my heart leaping.

"You didn't," I said, a grin spreading across my face.

Maxim stiffened beside me, his head snapping toward the noise. "I certainly did not."

Sure enough, a familiar ball of fluff came bounding down the hallway, his tiny paws skidding on the sleek floor. It was my kitten, Clyde, his little tail held high as he darted straight for me.

"Clyde!" I exclaimed, dropping to my knees to scoop him up.

Maxim stepped back, his expression shifting from mild confusion to outright horror. "Who brought that here?"

"Maxim, he's not a rabid wolf." I cradled Clyde against my chest, scratching behind his ears as he purred loudly.

"He has claws," he muttered, his gaze wary. "Could be rapid."

I laughed, standing up with Clyde still in my arms. "You're still afraid?"

"I'm not afraid," he said sharply, though the way he kept his distance told a different story. "I just don't trust cats."

"Well, you'll have to get used to him," I said sweetly. "He's family now."

His scowl deepened. "Whose idea was this?"

"One of your men must have brought him," I said, shrugging. "They probably thought I'd want him here."

Maxim pinched the bridge of his nose. "Remind me to have a word with my staff about boundaries."

"You're just jealous because he's cuter than you," I teased, holding Clyde up so his tiny face was level with his.

He glared at the kitten as if he were a ticking time bomb. "Keep him away from me, Cora."

"Noted," I said with a smirk, setting Clyde down. He promptly darted off, his little paws barely making a sound as he disappeared into the shadows of the grand home.

Maxim sighed, running a hand through his hair. "Your things are upstairs," he said gruffly. "I had them brought over earlier today."

"All of them?" I raised an eyebrow.

He nodded. "You don't own much."

The comment stung, though I knew he didn't mean it maliciously. My worldly possessions could probably fit into a few suitcases, starkly contrasting the luxury around me.

"Well, I don't need much, really," I said, crossing my arms. "As long as I have my camera, things are good. I'd prefer that people weren't shooting at me, of course."

His gaze softened, but his reply was firm. "Well, we'll work on both of those things. Try to make your life safer, but you'll need to work with me on your nightly excursions."

"Your safe isn't the same as mine, Maxim," I said quietly, though I didn't push further. The weight of the day—and the reality of this new life—was pressing down on me, and I wasn't ready to battle tonight about how my life would change. I knew it wouldn't be easy, but if Maxim thought I'd let him steamroll me, he was in for a surprise.

"I'll meet you upstairs," he said, his tone gentler.

I nodded. "Okay."

As I turned to ascend the staircase, I couldn't shake the feeling of his eyes following me, their intensity burning into my back.

* * *

I HESITATED at the base of the staircase, my fingers trailing along the wood railing. Maxim's voice echoed faintly from downstairs, smooth and commanding as he gave last-minute instructions to someone I couldn't see. His townhouse felt cavernous, the weight of its silence pressing on me now that I was alone.

The steps under my bare feet were carpeted in a deep, plush fabric that muffled my movement. I gripped the railing tighter as if it could steady the whirl of emotions inside me. The heady scent of sandalwood intensified as I ascended, wrapping around me like a tangible reminder of him.

At the top, the hallway stretched wide, the gray walls softened by warm, golden light from ornate sconces. I paused in front of the door at the end of the corridor. It wasn't marked, but I knew it was his—ours, now, I supposed. The oak door was massive and unyielding, just like the man himself.

Pushing it open, I stepped inside and froze.

The room was larger than I'd expected, accentuated by the towering floor-to-ceiling windows that framed the glittering city skyline. Heavy midnight-blue drapes hung to the sides, half-pulled, their weight lending the room a sense of quiet intimacy.

The bed caught my eye first. It was massive,

with an intricate and elegant blackened iron frame—a piece of art as much as furniture. The bedding was simple yet luxurious, with deep charcoal-gray sheets and a black duvet that seemed too perfect to disturb.

I walked farther in, my bare feet sinking into the thick, soft rug that covered the dark wood floor. The room's scent enveloped me—him, distilled into this private space. To the left, a sitting area held two low, leather armchairs flanking a small table. On it sat a half-empty decanter of whiskey, an ashtray with a single stubbed-out cigar, and a stack of books.

I reached out, fingers brushing the spines. Tolstoy, business strategy, and—oddly—a tattered collection of poetry. It didn't seem like Maxim, but then again, I barely knew him beyond the layers he chose to reveal.

The walls were equally revealing. On one side, sleek shelves displayed books, files, and what I assumed were personal mementos— trophies of a life that straddled intellect and violence. On the opposite wall hung a single painting, its starkness drawing me in. It showed a wolf pack in a snowy forest, with the leader standing apart. The wolf's eyes burned with a fierce, lonely intensity, and I shivered despite myself.

In the corner, a black suit jacket hung casually on a coat rack near a perfectly neat desk. The desk was almost unnervingly tidy, with papers stacked in precise piles and a pen placed parallel to the edge. Everything was in its place, just like the man who owned it.

My gaze fell on a silver-framed photo sitting on the desk. Maxim, unmistakably, stood beside a younger boy with the same piercing eyes and rigid posture. His brother, I guessed. The boy's expression was guarded, almost defiant, a shadow of the man he'd become.

I turned away, my heart beating faster as my eyes landed on a door to the side of the room. A closet, maybe, or something else. My curiosity itched, but I stayed where I was. Tonight wasn't the time for trespassing, not in a space like this.

I caught sight of myself in the tall mirror near the bed, my reflection pale and uncertain against the rich darkness of the room. This was my new life now, wasn't it? A life that began tonight.

The sound of footsteps below pulled me back to the moment. Maxim would expect me ready—whatever that meant—and waiting. I pressed a hand to my chest, forcing myself to breathe evenly, and turned toward the en suite bathroom.

I was inexplicably nervous, staring at myself in the mirror.

"Mrs. Volkova." I tried it out. "Cora Volkova." For Russian women, an 'a' was added. Maxim was 'Volkov,' and I was 'Volkova' … it was interesting. The girl in the mirror looked unsure of the name. Pale and young. Reaching for the zipper on the back of my dress, I edged it down. Luckily, this was a simple affair.

Elise hadn't steered me wrong. She'd set me up with a tempting lingerie set. Scooping up the dress from the floor, I gathered it in my arms and moved towards the connecting closet.

The walls were lined with suits in a spectrum of blacks and greys, shiny shoes, ties, and crisp shirts. Whoever kept track of Maxim's clothes obviously had an eye for detail. Everything was organized and precise.

In contrast, space had been made for me, but most of it was empty.

My paltry jeans and tee shirts were literally hung up. *Le gasp*. Hung up. The shelves were backlit, so they looked even funnier. I wanted to snap a picture of my *Zombieland* t-shirt hanging next to Maxim's suit jacket, but instead, I took one of the covered wooden hangers and twisted it out on the wall hooks to hang up the gown. Sitting on the low bench in the middle of the room, I stared at the dress and everything it represented.

"It's a beautiful dress."

I startled. Maxim was framed in the door, his jacket off, tie gone, eyes smoky.

Hot.

I'd never seen him so disheveled.

"You're my wife now. Mine."

I tipped my chin up. There might be nervousness on my part, but none of it stemmed from what would happen in the bedroom. Getting to my feet, I walked to meet him, hyper-conscious that every flaw I had was on display. I felt brave and sexy. He liked what he saw. His tongue came out as he licked the bottom of his lip and then bit it as if stopping himself.

"That's right. I'm your wife now," I confirmed as I came closer. "You're my husband."

"Yes," he breathed. "That's right."

"If I'm yours, then you're mine."

I sank to my knees.

"Are you going to let me fuck that mouth that I've been fantasizing about?"

I nodded. Desire pooled as he pulled his belt from the loops with a snap.

"You look a vision on your knees," he groaned.

I wanted to see him in all his glory. He complied, pulling his cock out so I could stroke his length. It strained toward me. Hot, hard, and thick, the veins standing out on it like it was angry and hungry.

"Have you ever done this before?" he asked.

"No." I shook my head, my eyes rapt on his. He looked viciously pleased.

"We'll start slow, but I like it hard." He cautioned. "I'll help you."

I wanted to please him. Leaning forward, I licked the slit experimentally, lapping the milky-white pre-cum from the tip as he groaned. Encouraged by his response, I stroked him as I drew his cock partially into my mouth enthusi-astically as far as I could. Alternating between licking and sucking, I worked on pulling him into my mouth, watching him from under my lashes, the way he breathed as he looked down at me, struggling to let me control the move-ments and not thrust into my mouth as I got used to him.

"Just like that, zayka. Can you take a little more?" When I nodded, he began to stroke into my mouth, his hips flexing as my lips stretched around his cock, saliva pooling around the corners until he hit the back of my throat.

He was breathing hard now. Head thrown back. He'd clamped a hand to the back of my head, tangled it in my hair as he thrust into my mouth. There was an ache in my jaw as he pumped. The earthiness of his smell surrounded me — but I felt …

Powerful.

Sexy.

"Fuck. Fuck. Just like that. Suck harder."

Feeling like my goal was close at hand, I redoubled my efforts, cupping his balls, tugging on them just as he groaned and released into my mouth, salty and warm in a rush. Drinking him down, I licked him gently as he released my hair, and his eyes opened with renewed interest.

"I think this marriage thing is going to work out," he said.

CHAPTER TWENTY-THREE

maxim

SCOOPING HER OFF THE FLOOR, I strode to the bedroom and tossed her on the bed. She had been a vision walking down the aisle.

An angel. A princess — but on her knees for me with my cock in her mouth?

Fuck. She undid me completely.

Taking her mouth savagely, I delved into its corners, sliding my tongue against hers. Her mascara was smeared, and I rubbed my thumbs against it as I parted her thighs and pulled back to look at her. She was arched against the back-drop of my bed, her milky skin and the white of the lingerie a beacon in the moonlight.

Her tits were gorgeous, soft, and full with those rosy pink nipples that beckoned through the sheer lace as I popped the front clasp of the bra and set them bouncing free. Cradling each in my hands, they spilled over as I kneaded and licked, sucked each nipple to a hard point — bit as she moaned and writhed.

"Do you like that baby? I can't wait to figure out what turns you on."

She was so responsive. I loved it. I could play with her for hours. I had promised her a spanking and that was definitely in our future. My zayka wouldn't be a good girl for long. She'd earn that punishment all too soon. My cock couldn't wait.

Edging down her body, I traced the curve of her belly and the dip of her waist, allowing myself to linger at her belly button, licking around it and kissing her panties.

"Spread your legs wider," I ordered. She looked at me from under her lashes, those green eyes a beacon. "You won't need these." Gripping the edges of the thong with both hands, I tore it off. "Look at that pussy." The words were more for me than her.

She was beautiful. Dripping and swollen.

Spreading her folds, I looked at her even as she squeaked and tried to sit up.

"What are you doing?"

"Looking at what's mine. Lie still."

She lay back but continued to watch me with those malachite eyes as I settled between her legs and proceeded to lick her lazily. I shivered as I got my first actual taste. Every woman tasted different. This was just a fact. Cora tasted like pineapple and rain. Spreading her so I could take my time, I plunged my tongue into her, fucking her with it while I circled her clit with my fingers. God, she was heaven. No way would I let her come like this. Maybe later.

My cock was already hard as an iron as she bucked and ground against my mouth.

"Max. Max."

Fuck, I loved the way she screamed my name. I was almost tempted to let her come. I could feel her getting close, the way she fluttered and heaved as my tongue plunged.

Still, I sat up even as she protested. "You're coming on my cock, zayka. That's final."

Notching against her slit, I rubbed the head of my cock against her clit. It felt so good I almost felt my eyes roll back, but I pulled her close and rocked into her in a savage thrust even as her eyes widened.

All the way in, balls deep.

"Oh, God."

Then I stroked back and slammed forward, keeping my eyes on her. I was going to fuck her into oblivion.

Into the stars.

Into the darkness.

"Harder, Max. Harder."

Her breasts bounced as I wedged her leg onto my shoulder and obliged. I gave myself over to instinct and drove her mercilessly until we were covered in a fine sheen before I felt her flutter around me and gush over me. With one more savage thrust, I came hard.

Collapsing onto the pillow beside her, I watched as she gave me a lazy look.

"So, I agree. Married life will work out just fine," she said.

CHAPTER TWENTY-FOUR

maxim

THE MORNING LIGHT filtered through the heavy curtains of my bedroom, casting faint golden streaks across the charcoal-gray sheets. I lay on my back, staring at the ceiling, my mind already turning over the day's demands. A pakhan in the bratva didn't get to rest just because he took a wife. There was a whole organization to run.

Beside me, Cora stirred, her dark hair spread like ink against the pillow.

My wife.

The word felt foreign, almost unreal, but the sight of her in my bed made it undeniable. She shifted, her bare shoulder peeking out from the blanket, and for a brief moment, I allowed myself to marvel at the quiet strength in her. She didn't shy away from me, even when every reason to run was written in the vows she had spoken last night.

The thought had been unappealing to take a wife, but now I couldn't imagine her not being here in my space.

The vibration of my phone on the nightstand shattered the fragile peace. I reached for it, my chest tightening as I saw the name flashing on the screen: Conall.

What the fuck was he doing calling me today?

"What is it?" I asked, my voice rough from sleep but sharp with urgency.

"There's been a fire," he said without preamble. "*Fortune's* gone, Maxim. Burned to the ground."

The words hit like a physical blow, but I didn't react. Not outwardly. Years of training my expression into a mask of steel kept me composed. Inside, though, fury roared to life. *Fortune* wasn't just a club—it was a symbol of power, wealth, and control. An attack on it was an attack on each of us.

"I'll be there within the hour," I said, ending the call before he could say more.

I swung my legs out of bed, calculating my next moves, but Cora's voice stopped me.

"What happened?" she asked, sitting up, the

blanket clutched around her. Her eyes, still heavy with sleep, were full of worry.

"It doesn't concern you," I said automatically, pulling on my pants and then immediately regretted it as she flinched.

Her jaw tightened, and she threw the blanket off, stepping out of bed with more determination than I'd expected. "I'm your wife now, Maxim. If it concerns you, it concerns me."

I stared at her, torn between irritation and reluctant respect. She had spirit. I couldn't deny she belonged more than I'd anticipated in my world.

"Fine," I said, grabbing a shirt. "But you stay close to me. No wandering off, no questions unless I say otherwise."

She nodded, already heading to the bathroom. I could hear her rustling around before she emerged in what seemed to be her standard jeans and a T-shirt. This one said: 'The Hardest Part of the Zombie Apocalypse — To Act Like I'm Not Excited.'

I huffed. She was a laugh riot. She'd be dead meat if an apocalypse happened. Of course, I'd do my best to save her. She had her camera with her, but that was to be expected. Cora was Cora. I hadn't shown her my wedding present yet. I'd set her up with a studio here so she could work on her photography. I wasn't sure what she needed, but I wanted her to have space to do what she loved. I'd had it stocked with a couple of extra cameras, a desk, and a high-end computer loaded with editing software. I figured she'd like that better than any jewelry I'd get her.

Sending a text to Lev, I tried to focus on business as I got dressed instead of my gorgeous wife, who still had swollen lips and flushed cheeks as if she was reliving our escapades from last night.

Lev and Kolya were waiting downstairs, grim-faced but ready. As my two most trusted enforcers, their presence constantly reminded me of the volatility of my life. Without needing instructions, they walked beside us as we left for the club and got into the armored SUV.

I spoke to them both yesterday about Cora's security. Kolya had been assigned to her as a personal bodyguard, and there would be two more men when she left the property that would shadow her that he personally vetted. Her tendency to sneak out and take photos would have to be curtailed. I wasn't sure how she would handle the extra security, but she couldn't wander around without the additional safety measures. It wasn't safe.

The drive to *Fortune* was tense, the air thick with unspoken questions. Cora sat beside me, silent but watchful, her gaze flickering between the city rushing past and my face chomping on her baggie of dry Lucky Charms that she'd brought in her camera bag. I kept my eyes forward, already anticipating what I'd find when we arrived.

After all — the club had burnt down before.

The smell hit first—acrid, choking smoke that lingered even though the fire was long out. When we pulled up to what had once been *Fortune*, the devastation was absolute. Someone had been thorough. Charred beams jutted like broken bones from the wreckage, and the air was still heavy with ash.

Conall stood near the remains of the entrance, his hands shoved into his coat pockets. Angelo was beside him, his sharp features unreadable.

"We spoke to Oscar and reviewed the footage he sent. This wasn't an accident," Conall said the moment we approached.

"No," I agreed. It wasn't even a question. Whoever had done this wanted a message sent, and they wanted it loud.

Oscar was *Fortune's* manager. I could see him in rubble on the far side, sifting through what should be left of the office. He was a big man, built like a bear, with shoulders that intimidated and a voice that brooked no nonsense, but he had a keen mind for business and a streak of loyalty that wouldn't quit.

"Maxim," Angelo greeted, his voice low and measured. "Whoever did this is dead."

I glanced at Cora. She stood slightly behind me, her expression calm but her hands clenched at her sides. I didn't miss how her eyes darted to each of us, then to the wreckage, trying to piece together the politics of the scene.

"Lev, Kolya," I barked. "Go through what's left. Find anything that survived—documents, cameras, anything useful."

They nodded and moved off, stepping carefully over the debris.

Cora took a step forward, her gaze locked on the destruction. "Do you know who did this?"

Her voice was steady, but I could hear the undercurrent of fear—not for herself but for what this meant for us.

"I have suspicions," I admitted, glancing at Conall.

He met my gaze, a flicker of agreement in his eyes. Whoever did this would pay, but the why was what mattered now. *Fortune* wasn't just a club; it was our gathering place. Someone wanted to tear down more than just the walls.

I reached for Cora's hand, pulling her close. "Don't wander," I said, quieter this time. "I'm going to look around."

CHAPTER TWENTY-FIVE

cora

MY WEDDING NIGHT WAS ILLUMINATING. I hadn't known what to expect, but if someone had told me that I would feel like I was unraveling into the universe as my husband gathered me back up in pieces and put me back together, I would have told them that they were crazy.

I still didn't know anything about him — the details of his life, but I had explored as much of his body as he had allowed. He was tattooed across his back and front, but most intriguing were his scars, which crisscrossed his back. I'd wanted to ask what they were from but was afraid it was too soon.

The opportunity to watch him work was too good to pass up. Not to mention, I wanted to establish early where I would stand in our relationship.

I didn't want to be a woman who was left behind, so I was glad he'd conceded, even though I could tell he hadn't wanted to bring me. I promised myself the whole car ride that I'd behave.

The smoke had been visible from blocks away, rising above the frozen city in puffs like a ghostly mirage.

I assumed it was a property that Maxim owned with his business, so I was surprised to see Angelo here. I understood on some levels what kind of business Maxim did, but what confused me was how it meshed with my brother's and how that intermingled with Angelo's and then Ilias's.

My brother had told me about the deal our father had made—the deal all of the dons had made. I hadn't expected the way the new generation of men were friends. I was working out this in my head. I'd always been a good observer; even as a little girl, it was what I was best at.

As we exited the car, my brother gave me a careful nod but a warm smile, grasping my hand and squeezing it. "Good to see you, little sister."

"This looks a bit of a mess." I fiddled with my camera strap as Maxim spoke in low tones to his men before striding over through the smoking rubble.

I was already framing shots and deciding what to capture first. I had so many images in mind that I wasn't listening until Maxim gripped my hand to draw my attention.

"Cora." His voice was sharp as he tilted my face to his. "Don't wander. Watch where you step."

"I will," I said, meaning it — sort of.

He nodded and spoke sharply to Kolya in Russian before letting me go.

The angles were hauntingly beautiful—beams collapsed in strange symmetry, their burned edges sharp against the dull backdrop of ash. Embers still glowed faintly in some places, tiny reminders of the fire that had burned hot here just hours ago.

I lifted the camera, letting its weight settle in my hands. The first click of the shutter brought a strange kind of focus. Through the lens, the destruction transformed into a story waiting to be told.

Maxim's voice drifted faintly from somewhere behind me, but I couldn't make out his words. He and Conall were discussing who could be behind this, their tones grim and unyielding. It didn't matter; the fire had already spoken louder than any name they could pin to it.

I framed them in the shot and snapped a whirl of pictures.

Click.

The wreckage seemed endless. My feet carried me toward the back of the building, where the air was quieter, and the devastation was untouched by the men combing through the site. Here, the ruin felt more personal, and the destruction was less trampled by boots.

I knelt to capture a shot of a burnt beam leaning precariously against what was left of a wall, its surface blistered and raw. The angle was perfect—the contrast of jagged black against the pale morning sky.

The attack came so quickly that I didn't even register the sound.

A hand clamped over my mouth, yanking me backward with brutal force. The camera fell from my hands, landing with a sickening crack on the debris-strewn ground, but then the strap yanked against my neck as I struggled, my heart pounding as adrenaline surged through me.

The man's grip was iron, his other arm pinning mine against my side as he dragged me deeper into the wreckage and further back into misty winter shadows.

"Come on, ye scanger," he growled in my ear, his voice rough and unrecognizable.

Panic surged as I twisted against him,

kicking at the debris to gain some leverage. The Irish brogue was unmistakable, and the stupid female comment wasn't a good start in my favor. My foot caught the edge of a beam, and I heard a grunt of frustration as my resistance threw him off balance.

"Ye're coming with me. I want those pictures."

My feet dragged in the soot and ash, the weight of his grip leaving me no room to maneuver. I fought harder, panic sharpening every instinct. My mind raced.

My eyes were blown wide, my nostrils heaving behind the dirty scent of his palm. Everything stood out to me as my brain struggled to calibrate itself.

What pictures?

I took so many that it could be anything.

The realization hit me like a slap—Dublin. That afternoon, I'd wandered too far from the safety of my uncle's townhouse, camera in hand, chasing the allure of the city lights, and, on instinct, snapped those pictures. The pictures that had altered the course of my life forcing my hand to call Conall. I had never thought that marriage was waiting for me, but I also didn't think some alley-way murderer would follow me to the States.

The man had been relentless that day when

he'd run after me. I'd been scared enough to panic. Later on the plane, I'd wondered if I'd been hasty, but now I realized I'd been worse — I'd been stupid. I should have come clean to my brother about why I had called.

As the man dragged me further into the ruins, I realized how naive I'd been.

"You don't even know what ye've got, do ye?" he sneered, his fingers digging into my arms. "But it's enough to bring hell down on the wrong people, and I can't have that. When I saw ye get on that O'Kelly plane with that fecker. Well, O'Kelly sent spies into our territory. That was clear as day."

I struggled, but he was too strong, his grip unrelenting. My breaths came in ragged gasps, smoke mingling with the cold air to sting my lungs. "You're making a mistake," I managed to choke out, though my voice wavered.

"Oh, I don't think so." His lips twisted into a cruel smirk. "Ye shouldn't have been in that alley. But don't worry—ye won't have long to regret it. Where is the SD card? I know ye kept it."

He shoved me against a charred wall, his hand reaching for something at his side—a knife. My blood turned to ice as his hand struggled to clasp back over my mouth as I bit and twisted.

"My brother. Maxim—they'll kill you." I squeaked out between his fingers.

"Well, they don't even know ye're here, do they?" he cut me off, his brogue thick with mocking venom. "No one does. Ye're just a stupid girl who wandered where she didn't belong."

He drew the knife along my collarbone as I squirmed, parting my flesh like it was nothing, blood oozing and dripping down my shirt. Pain bloomed like a poppy under my skin, like the fire that took over the *Fortune*, raging through my chest. It felt like he had cut deep enough to hit bone, but I knew that wasn't true. His eyes and teeth gleamed as he leaned into me as if he relished the sight of me bleeding.

"I'll make it hurt. Tell me where to find what I want." The knife tip dug in as I whimpered.

Surely, they were already looking for me, but I wasn't about to wait around for a rescue. I kicked out again, my boot catching him in the shin. He cursed, his grip tightening as he raised the knife. I flinched, waiting for the worst, when a loud crack split the air, and he buckled away from me. His fingers grasped as he fell, the knife scrabbling against my skin, scratching, rending, and burning as it went pain-sparking in giant bursts.

The sound was unmistakable—gunfire.

The man froze, his eyes widening for the briefest moment before he crumpled backward as he was yanked to the ground.

"Cora!"

Maxim's voice thundered, and before I could process what had happened, he was there, his face etched with fury and something deeper —fear. Those toffee eyes were wide and wild, panicked.

His hands were on me, checking for injuries, his touch both gentle and frantic. "You're bleeding?"

The words were a roar. I shook my head, unable to speak as Kolya and Lev approached. His hands fluttered around me, peeling back my shirt from where it stuck wetly to my skin while I watched the man on the ground. Kolya nudged the man's body with his boot, his expression grim as he put his foot on the man's throat, pressing hard.

Maxim's jaw tightened as his gaze landed on the knife still clutched in the man's hand. "Who is this fucker?"

"I—" My voice cracked. "He's a man from Dublin. I accidentally… I took a picture. I didn't know—"

Maxim's expression darkened, his fury shifting to a cold, calculating focus. He turned to Kolya. "Search him. I want to know who he's working for. You're okay, baby." He ran a hand through my hair and wiped the tears from my cheeks. "I'm going to tear the flesh from his bones."

The words were visceral, bloody, but my hands clutched at Maxim, curling into him as I whispered, "Good." His automatic defense of me settled something deep inside that I didn't know I needed.

"I don't care two shits what pictures she took," he ground out towards the man struggling to breathe under Kolya's boot. "She can take all the pictures she wants. Nobody touches her and lives. *Nobody*. You'll die screaming. I promise."

Kolya crouched beside the body, rifling through the man's pockets. Meanwhile, Maxim pulled me closer, his hands firm on my shoulders. "You're okay, zayka. Let's get you home." Then, in Russian, he cursed as he shouted at Kolya, stabbing a finger at the man on the ground.

He examined me again as Conall roared around the corner, his boots scraping up the ashes in clouds that raised motes into the air like paper snowflakes. Angelo chased on his heels, their expressions frantic.

"Cora! Cora!" His face was stricken as he took me in. "Maxim, you were supposed to be watching her. Not two fucking seconds, and she's hurt." His words were thrown into the air like knives. Maxim flinched with each one. "Who is the fecker who thought they could put their hands on her? Who is he?" Conall demanded.

"He followed me here from Dublin," I told Conall as I tried to pull myself back together. "I don't know his name." My fingers still held fast to my husband, and I closed my eyes, letting my forehead rest against him for a second before opening them again. I wished I could close this episode away, teleport myself back to my kitten for a cuddle, lie in bed with Max, and watch a movie.

Kolya rose, holding a phone and a scrap of paper, as Conall descended on the man, dragging him to his feet and shaking him.

"He's connected to the O'Gara's," Kolya said, his tone heavy with meaning. "Joe O'Gara." Kolya shook a passport, waving it in the air.

Maxim's expression turned deadly. "Of course, he is."

The name didn't mean anything to me, but the man still glinted at me with ill intent.

"That hoor sister of yers was somewhere she wasn't supposed to be," the man growled.

"Whore?" Maxim's whole body stilled,

coming to attention. "She is my *wife*. You'll be an example to all the O'Gara's." The words were filled with meaning. If I were him, I'd be pissing myself.

"Feck ye," Joe hissed.

"We'll take him to the wet room," Conall gave the man a savage kick and pressed on the bullet hole in his leg. "You think you'll hold up," he scoffed. "You'll see. I'll get a turn." He grinned evilly. "But that guy right there with my sister? That guy is your worst nightmare."

Joe O'Gara shrunk on the concrete as Kolya yanked him up before clocking him over the head with the butt of his gun.

"Just don't start until I get there. He's mine." Maxim swung me up into his arms. "Come on, baby. Let's get you home, and I'll call a doctor. We need to get you looked at."

"I'll send Doc O'Flannery to your town-house. He's been on my payroll for years. He's trustworthy. Unless you have someone."

"Thanks. That'd be great. I haven't had time to get established with someone yet."

I let myself relax in Maxim's arms as he took purposeful strides away from my brother, Kolya, and Joe O'Gara, who slumped drunkenly between them.

CHAPTER TWENTY-SIX

maxim

THE BASTARD HAD HAD A KNIFE.

He had planned to kill her.

My wife.

I wasn't sure when it had happened that I began to care so much.

I couldn't stop the red haze clouding my vision as I watched Cora tremble in my arms, her breaths shallow and quick. Her cheek was smeared with soot, her skin torn where the blade had dug into the flesh. My hands itched for violence, for a reckoning that would wipe the O'Gara name from the face of the earth.

Instead, I focused on her.

"Cora," I murmured, trying to keep my voice steady though it felt like gravel in my throat. Her wide eyes darted to mine, glassy with shock. "It's over. You're safe now."

Kolya would have his own reckoning for letting her out of his sight. It never should have happened. I had told him to search the debris, but … fuck.

Her lip quivered, and for a moment, I thought she might cry. Instead, she swallowed hard and nodded, her bravery a sharp pang in my chest. She trembled as I lifted her, her weight light against me, though the tension in her frame told me she wasn't used to being carried.

"Let me—" she began, but I silenced her with a look.

"Not now," I said firmly. "You're hurt, and I'm not negotiating with you about this."

She fell silent, but I could feel her frustration radiating. That was good. Anger was better than fear.

Joe O'Gara was the kind of thug who thought his family's name would protect him. A parasite feeding off the scraps of power handed down by better men. He was wrong.

I focused back on Cora. Her breathing was steadier, but she was clutching her chest, blood seeping through her fingers. Rage flared again. She needed me calm, not murderous.

At the townhouse, Lev held the door open, his gaze flicking to the blood on her coat. "Conall is sending O'Flannery," he said.

I nodded, carrying her upstairs and laying her gently on the couch in the sitting room. She tried to sit up, but I knelt beside her, catching her hand.

"Stay still," I ordered.

"Maxim, I—"

"Cora," I interrupted, brushing a strand of hair from her face. "Please."

The word slipped out before I could stop it, soft and unguarded. Her eyes widened slightly, but she obeyed, leaning back against the cushions. I wanted to vomit apologies, toss the head of the man who did this at her feet, devour her in his blood — all of those things — any of them to beg her forgiveness for letting this happen.

Instead, I grabbed the first aid kit from the side table and settled beside her. The room was quiet, save for her shallow breaths and the crackle of the fireplace. I tore open a packet of gauze and pressed it gently against the wound, ignoring her wince.

"It's deep," I said, more to myself than to her. "You'll need stitches."

Her voice was small when she finally spoke. "He followed me."

I nodded. "From Dublin."

She swallowed, her hands twisting in her lap. "I didn't know. I didn't mean to—" Guilt hovered in her eyes, and I wanted to rage and roar at it being there. That this dumbfuck thought he could make her feel bad about the joy she took in her exploration of her art.

"You don't have to explain," I said firmly, turning her chin so she saw my intent clearly. "This isn't your fault. It's *mine*. I should have protected you better."

She blinked, startled by the admission, and I looked away, focusing on cleaning the wound. When the knock came at the door, Lev let the doctor in.

"He could have hurt one of you. I never thought that something like that would ever happen." Her voice was soft as she watched me carefully.

I didn't give two shits about someone coming for me, but coming for her was bullshit. There was a code that should have been followed anyway. The O'Gara's broke that. We never touched women and children.

O'Flannery was a wiry man with quick hands and a sharp tongue, but his demeanor softened as he examined Cora. "You're a lucky young lady. Another inch and that knife could've done real damage."

She nodded mutely.

He doused the wound with numbing spray, then moved quickly and efficiently as he sewed even tiny stitches. As O'Flannery worked, stitching the gash below her collarbone, I stayed close, watching every wince and flinch. When he finished, he glanced at me. I didn't need the reminder that she was lucky. That fucker could have chosen to cut her deeper or sliced her throat, and I couldn't have done anything.

"The other cuts and scrapes don't need stitches but should be cleaned," he said. "She needs rest. Keep an eye on her for signs of infection. If there's anything else, call me."

I nodded, and he packed his bag, pausing to give me a nod. "Take care of her, Mr. Volkov. She's tougher than she looks, but she's not invincible."

Once he was gone, I turned back to her. She looked exhausted, her face pale against the dark fabric of the couch.

"Cora," I said softly.

She opened her eyes, the vulnerability in them cutting deeper than I expected. "You're angry," she said.

"Yes."

"At me?"

I shook my head, brushing my knuckles against her cheek. "At myself. But not you."

She searched my face as if looking for something, then relaxed slightly. "Thank you," she whispered. "For saving me."

For a moment, I just looked at her, the fire-light casting flickering shadows across her face. "You don't need to thank me," I said quietly. "You're mine to protect."

She frowned, but before she could argue, I stood. I needed to plan. Joe O'Gara had made this personal, and the O'Gara family would pay in blood for what they'd done. I'd wipe them all from the earth.

But first, I needed to make sure Cora was safe. I would die before I let anyone else touch her.

A scratching at my trouser leg drew my attention, breaking through the storm of rage that churned in my chest. Frowning, I looked down, half-expecting to see nothing. Instead, that small, bedraggled kitten—a grey mix with matted fur and wide, imploring eyes—stared up at me. Its tiny claws clung to my pant leg like it had decided I was its last hope.

I stiffened. Of all the creatures in the world, cats were the ones I liked least. Their unpredictable movements and the way they seemed to see through people unnerved me in ways I hated to admit, and now, one was trying to climb me like a tree.

Cora's soft giggle made me glance up. She watched Clyde, her lips parting in a mixture of surprise and something that looked suspiciously like delight. "Max," she breathed, her voice tinged with wonder. "He likes you."

I looked back at the kitten, gently dislodging it with my foot. It refused to let go, meowing pathetically as its claws stuck to my pant leg.

"It's just a cat," I muttered, stepping back.

"It's not just a cat," Cora said, her tone firm despite her weariness. "Look at it—he was abandoned. Left alone by his family. We have to be his family now."

I tried not to look too closely, but I couldn't ignore the thinness of its frame or the small cut along one ear. Its meow was barely more than a squeak, and even my unease couldn't smother the faint pang of pity it stirred.

"I'll call Lev," I said, already reaching for my phone. "He can take it somewhere—"

"No!" Cora's protest was so sharp it startled me. She struggled to sit up, wincing as she moved too quickly. "Don't send him away. Please."

I hesitated, torn between wanting to argue and the soft plea in her voice. Her fingers trembled as she reached toward the kitten, her movements slow and careful. "Come here, sweetheart," she murmured.

"Stop moving," I ordered. "I'll give it to you." The reluctance wasn't faked as I reached for the kitten. "Why doesn't it have bones?" It felt like it had no skeleton inside. "Am I going to squish it? How do you hold these things?

My hands weren't made to hold delicate things. Clyde made soft little huffing noises, looking completely unconcerned as I heaved it off the ground.

"They have bones. You can feel the tiny ribs."

I was appalled and dropped it on her without preamble. I didn't want to feel its ribs or any part of it. The kitten felt too fragile in my hands.

"There," she whispered, stroking its fur with gentle fingers. "You're safe now."

The words hit me harder than I expected, echoing the ones I'd said to her not long ago. I watched her cradling it, her eyes soft despite the pain she was in.

"You can't keep it," I said gruffly, though the fight was already leaving me.

Cora looked up at me, her expression so unguarded it made my chest ache. "Why not?"

"It's a cat," I said, as though that explained everything.

"I'm keeping it," she countered, her voice gaining strength.

I opened my mouth to argue but closed it again when the kitten released a contented purr, nestling closer to her. My dislike of cats warred with the realization that I'd lost this battle the moment it had appeared.

"Fine," I said finally, pinching the bridge of my nose. "But it stays in the kitchen, and Lev feeds it."

Cora's smile was small but victorious.

I growled, turning away to hide the way her gratitude affected me. I'd let her have this small victory.

The kitten kept its eyes on me, its unblinking stare making my skin crawl. It was as though it knew I was afraid and liked it.

Perfect. Now I had two lives to protect: my wife and her damn cat.

cora

THE SMELL of warm pizza drifted through the air, the tangy scent of olives and spiced sausage making my mouth water. I hadn't realized how hungry I was until Maxim set the box down in front of me, its grease-stained surface a familiar comfort.

"Donna's?" I asked, my voice still rough from earlier.

He nodded, his expression unreadable. "Lev picked it up."

"Thank you," I murmured, tearing off a slice. It was still too hot, the cheese stretching in long strings, but I didn't care. I needed the normalcy, the small joy of eating my favorite food.

Maxim sat beside me on the couch, closer than usual. Clyde perched on the armrest, its tiny body leaning toward him as if it knew he didn't want it there.

"Eat your food," he grumbled when he caught me watching him.

I hid a smile behind my slice, taking another bite. He'd been hovering all day, fussing in ways I hadn't expected. When I'd tried to get up earlier, insisting I didn't need to be coddled, he'd silenced me with a look so stern it had rooted me to the spot.

Now, he glanced at Clyde and frowned. Its unrelenting gaze seemed to wear him down, and with a deep sigh, he reached out a hand.

"Be nice," I teased, unable to resist.

His fingers awkwardly brushed Clyde's head like he was touching something alien. Clyde responded with a soft purr, leaning into his touch.

"This thing is going to get spoiled," he muttered, pulling his hand back as if burned.

"Maybe," I smirked, leaning back against the cushions. "But he's cute, isn't he?"

He didn't answer, but his silence was answer enough.

Later, we ended up sprawled on the couch together, *Warm Bodies* streaming on the TV. It was one I loved—corny and over-the-top—and Maxim complained the entire time.

"This is ridiculous," he said as a horde of zombies stumbled after the heroes.

"It's supposed to be," I replied, stifling a laugh.

He grumbled something in Russian under his breath but didn't move. His arm was around my shoulders, his warmth chasing away the last of the chill from earlier. At some point, I fell asleep, my head resting against his chest, lulled by the steady rhythm of his breathing.

When I woke, it was to the sound of Lev muttering angrily near the door. Maxim was slipping on his coat, his expression grim.

"You don't need me here for this," Lev said, folding his arms.

"Yes, I do." Maxim's tone was final.

Lev cursed in Russian, his voice rising. "You're being an idiot. This is not how we handle—"

"Enough." Maxim's sharp command cut him off. "This is where I want you. Your most important duty."

Lev nodded soberly. "Yes, pakhan."

I sat up, wincing as the movement pulled at my stitches. "Are you leaving?" I asked, my voice soft but steady.

Maxim turned to me, his expression softening just slightly. "I need to speak with Conall. Lev will stay with you."

Lev groaned audibly, throwing his hands in the air. "Babysitting duty."

"You'll survive," Maxim said dryly before stepping closer to me. He crouched, his dark eyes locking with mine. "Rest, Cora. I won't be gone long."

I nodded, unease coiling in my stomach. "Be careful."

His lips quirked in a faint smile, and for a moment, I thought he might kiss me. But he only brushed his fingers against my cheek before straightening and walking out the door.

Lev cursed again as it closed behind him. "Your husband is leaving me out of the fun stuff."

"Sounds like you'll get to be a couch potato with me and Clyde," I murmured, leaning back against the cushions.

I must have fallen asleep again because the next thing I knew, the faint sound of running water pulled me from sleep. Groggy, I pushed myself up and wandered toward the mudroom, drawn by the low hum of activity.

The sight that greeted me stopped me in my tracks. Maxim stood in the dim light, stripped down to his boxer briefs. His clothes —a dark shirt and jeans—were stuffed into what looked like a small incinerator built into the wall.

The flames flared briefly, then died down as the lid closed with a soft hiss.

"What…?" I began, but my voice trailed off as he turned, his gaze meeting mine.

His expression was unreadable, his face shadowed with exhaustion. "Go back to bed, Cora."

I didn't move, my eyes flicking to the blood smeared faintly across his hands, his arms. My stomach twisted, but I forced myself to speak. "Are you okay?"

His shoulders sagged slightly, and for a moment, he looked so tired it made my chest ache. "Yes."

Without another word, he stepped into the adjoining bathroom, the sound of the shower turning on soon after.

I stood there for a long moment, my heart pounding as I stared at the closed door. Whatever had happened tonight, it was bad.

* * *

I HAD DONE as Max asked. I returned to the master bedroom and slid into the king-sized bed with Clyde, but I stayed turned on my side, watching the hallway, waiting and hoping he'd come to bed.

The sheets smelled like him, a mix of cedar

and something faintly spicy, and it was a small comfort as I lay there, the kitten curled up against the headboard. Clyde's tiny purring was steady, a metronome against the storm of thoughts swirling in my head.

I kept my eyes on the hallway, listening for any sign of Maxim coming upstairs. The house was too quiet, the kind of stillness that amplified every creak and whisper of the wind outside. The events of the day replayed in my mind like a broken record: the knife, the blood, the fear in my chest as I realized how close I'd come to losing everything.

And yet, through it all, Maxim had been there. Unyielding. Steady.

When I finally heard the soft tread of his footsteps, my breath caught. I didn't move, didn't call out, just stayed still, watching the doorway like it held the answers to the questions I was too afraid to ask.

The door opened slowly, the light from the hallway spilling in to cast his silhouette in sharp relief. He paused when he saw me awake, his dark eyes meeting mine.

"You're supposed to be sleeping," he said softly, his voice rough with exhaustion.

"I couldn't," I admitted.

He stepped inside, closing the door behind him. The room was dark except for the faint glow of the moon through the curtains, and I could see the tension in his frame as he crossed the room.

Maxim sat on the edge of the bed, his movements slow and deliberate. I reached out, my hand brushing his arm. "Are you okay?"

For a moment, he didn't answer, his gaze fixed on some distant point. Then he turned to me, his expression softer than I expected. "I'm fine."

It was a lie. I could see it in the way his shoulders were too stiff, the way his hands flexed as if they still itched for violence.

"Max…" I hesitated, unsure how to ask what I wanted to know. "What happened tonight?"

His jaw tightened, and for a moment, I thought he might brush me off. Instead, he reached for my hand, threading his fingers through mine.

"Nothing you need to worry about," he said quietly.

"That's not an answer."

He sighed, the sound heavy with things left unsaid. "Cora," he began, his thumb brushing over the back of my hand. "I'll tell you what you need to know when the time is right. But tonight, all that matters is that you're safe."

I wanted to argue, to push for more, but the

turmoil in his eyes stopped me. Whatever he'd done, whatever weight he was carrying, it was for me. For us.

So, instead, I nodded, shifting closer to him. "Come to bed."

He hesitated, but when I tugged gently on his arm, he relented, lying down beside me.

"I'm not sure it's a good idea to come to bed."

I curled into him, my head resting against his chest. His heartbeat was steady beneath my ear, a rhythm that slowly eased the tightness in my chest.

"Why?"

"Because all I want is to touch you."

"I want you to," I whispered, unsure if he could hear me.

His arm tightened around me, his lips brushing the top of my head. "You're playing with fire, zayka."

CHAPTER TWENTY-EIGHT

maxim

SHE RUBBED UP AGAINST ME, deliberately taunting me. My cock had already been hard when I'd come home and seen her in the mud room. Torture and death wound me up. There was an energy to it that put me on edge. Before Cora, I'd have a whore over or two if the mood was right.

"I was waiting up for you, Max," she said.

My hand drifted to her hip. Did she mean she was up like a little cat in heat? Wanting me? I let my fingers curl beneath her panties. She was soaking — the silk fabric drenched.

"God. You're weeping for me," I moaned. "Get that pussy up here and those fucking panties off. I want you on my face right now."

Her face wrinkled in confusion for a minute,

and her eyes sparked with excitement. "Up there?"

"Be a good girl. Face the headboard. Hurry up. I don't want to wait."

She scrambled to obey, even though I could see she was shy as her slit approached my face. Growling even as she let out an adorable squeak, I grabbed her ass cheeks and yanked her firmly down against my face, fastening her to me.

Fuck.

I wanted to die like this.

Smothered.

Her hands gripped the iron rail, her nails curling around it, pumping it as if in time to her hips as she rocked — locked in her pleasure.

I was coming to know Cora. When she fucked, she did it without holding back.

I loved that.

She moaned long and low as she came, my fingers clutching her ass cheeks, spreading them as I sucked every drop from her.

"Oh God. Max."

Her movements stopped, and she tried to move from me, but I held her to me as I continued my ministrations until I'd gotten every drop of goodness before I let her move away.

"Now on your knees, zayka. I've got plans for that pussy."

I wanted to imbed myself in her. Impale her. Fuck her forever. She angled her ass up towards me with a smirk, her dripping slit swollen from my mouth. I couldn't help but run my fingers through it before I lined up and notched my cock there. Sliding forward, I drove home, letting my balls slap hard, the wet sound echoing in the room. Each glide was so good that I wanted it to last.

"I wish you could see this view, baby. My cock going into your hole is so pretty." She gushed in response, pushing against me. The thought turned her on.

Glide.

Stroke.

My balls tightened, and that tingle started at the small of my back, warning me that I was about to come.

"Touch your clit," I demanded. "Give me another. Put your ass up. Head down so I can fuck you harder. I'm going to blow my load in a minute, paint that pussy of yours. Would you like that?"

"Yes." She put her head down and ass up, her hand working between her legs furiously as I slammed into her.

"That's it, baby. Tweak that clit so I can fill you up," I growled.

She screamed as she came, almost losing the rhythm as she spasmed, but I was so far gone that I held tight to her as I did as I promised — filled her to the brim — coming in ropes into her channel.

Hot.

Warm.

Heaven.

Worth dying for.

* * *

CORA LAY BESIDE ME AFTERWARD, and I flinched at the sight of the stitches. They still made me furious. She traced lazy patterns over my tattoos with her fingertips.

"Will you tell me about the scars on your back? How you got them?"

Her hair had fallen over her face, her dark lashes feathering around those jewel-colored eyes as they gleamed at me. I'd been wondering if she'd ask. It wasn't a time of my life that I was proud of or liked to speak of, but she had every right to know about it.

"My father believed in very little in life. The bratva, money, power. He didn't respect family, women, or children. Those things meant little to him unless they could be a source of income, provide for his bratva, or increase his power." She edged closer so her nipples touched my chest, and those silken strands fell over me, and she could continue her path over my scars. "From the time when we were very young, my mother had allowed my father free rein over the two of us. She'd given birth, and that was all she'd been able to do. He beat her, raped her, and starved her when she tried to intervene. She died when I was nine." Cora's fingers brushed my cheekbones. She didn't speak, and I was grateful she didn't interrupt with empty words.

"After her death, my father didn't have a leash anymore — not that my mother had been much of a deterrent, it had been something."

It had meant something to me as a boy that she had tried. It had killed me that he had beaten her. I knew what happened in that room. Night after night, I had been angry with her when she defied him, knowing what it cost. I had wished that she would stop. Then, he had silenced her for good. He finally went too far and killed her. For many years, I had carried a childhood guilt that my wish had made something terrible come true.

"Dimitri was only three when she died, but I was old enough to join my father in his work, so

I was taken along. Dimitri was left with the maids until I could return home to take care of him. If I didn't obey, I was whipped or beaten by my father or his vors."

"You killed him?" she finally asked. There was no condemnation in her gaze, no judgment.

"Not until I was nineteen. It took me a long time to gain enough men to my side to plan a takeover of the bratva. I would never have been able to leave without killing him. He would have hunted my brother and me down unless I had been able to, and even that wouldn't have been enough. You must have the men on your side in a power struggle in a bratva, or the new pakhan will take out the remaining heirs." Her eyes widened.

"You have a very expressive face, zayka. Did you know that?" I nudged some hair behind her ears for a better view and pulled one of her legs over my hip.

"Do I?" She kissed me softly. "So, then, were you and Dimitri safe?"

"Well, then Dimitri decided he'd rather take off. He didn't want to be part of the bratva anymore." I frowned, remembering that moment.

"Wasn't he just …" I could see her doing the mental math. "Fifteen?"

"Maybe in years, but we were much older.

He deserved to choose his own way if he wanted." I didn't begrudge him his choice, but it had stung.

"You were lonely without him." She leaned forward again for a kiss.

"Yes, but I'm not lonely anymore. How are your stitches?"

"They're fine."

She rubbed against me greedily. This was what love felt like, I thought, just before I slid into her.

CHAPTER TWENTY-NINE

maxim

THE SMELL of Joe O'Gara's blood still clung to me, even after scrubbing it off in the shower before coming to meet the others. A man didn't just wash away the kind of night I'd had. Dumping his body at the doorstep of his crew leader's mansion had been deliberate—loud, messy, and unsubtle—a message written in crimson, bone, and sinew.

The air in the dimly lit room was thick with smoke and tension. Conall leaned back in his chair, his face as unreadable as ever, his fingers drumming against the table in an uneven rhythm. Angelo sat across from him, his sharp suit impeccable despite the early hour, frowning at Conall as if they still had some hold over beef that hadn't been solved. Ilias, as usual, looked like he'd rather be anywhere else, his disdain for meetings barely masked beneath his cool demeanor.

"Joe's body sent a strong message," Conall said, breaking the silence. His Irish lilt carried a sharp edge, his green eyes flicking to me. "Though I imagine the O'Gara crew won't take it lightly."

"That was the point," I said flatly, leaning back in my chair. "Joe broke the code. Women and children are off-limits, but he went after Cora. He knew what he was doing, and he paid the price. It was bullshit to come to the States for those fucking pictures."

It still pissed me off. The whole fucking thing.

What an idiot Joe was. Claimed that Conall had sent a spy. Seriously whacked. The guy had been stubborn right up until I did what I'd promised.

He'd died screaming. Skinned that fucker. Eli would have loved it.

Angelo nodded, his fingers toying with the cigar in his hand. "His crew won't have much they can do about it." He chuckled darkly. "The O'Gara's power is thin at best. They'll be scrambling to stay afloat. Still, we'll need to keep an eye on them."

"I feel good about my plan to kill them all for thinking about touching my wife. I'm okay with carrying that out." It wasn't a lie. I'd thought about it last night as Cora lay beside me, sleeping.

Conall's jaw tightened, but he didn't argue. Instead, he turned to Ilias. "Maybe let's put a pin in killing *all* of them for now. What's the word on who burned down *Fortune*?"

Ilias shrugged, his gaze sharp despite his casual posture. "No proof yet, but there's plenty of speculation. Rumor has it that Dante Caruso is behind it. Angelo seems to agree."

Angelo's lips curved into a humorless smile. "It's got Caruso's fingerprints all over it. The timing, the method—it's his style. He's been itching for an excuse to poke the bear, and *Fortune* gave him one. Well, and Dante has a bone to pick with Maxim there."

"*Fortune* wasn't just a club," I said, my voice hard. "It was a hub for our operations, a symbol of our presence in this city. Burning it down wasn't just a move against us but a declaration of war. If Caruso was behind it, then the Olivetos have a problem."

Conall nodded, his face grim. "That's why I called for this meeting. If Caruso is making a play, we need to decide how we're responding —and fast. If he's being a dick, then we still need to answer, but we should let the Olivetos know that we are taking him out."

Conall wasn't wrong. I hadn't taken Caruso off the board from the beginning because of that reason. The Five Families were their own animal in the boroughs. Our crews and our united front made us strong, but against all of the families? Well, that'd be stupid. Taking out a made man like Dante Caruso wasn't smart if it pulled down some of the other mob families on our heads.

Angelo exhaled a long stream of smoke, his expression dark. "I've already arranged a sit-down with the Olivetos. They'll want to keep their hands clean, but they know as well as we do that Dante's ambition isn't good for business. If we can pressure them to rein him in, we might avoid an all-out war," he paused. "If it's Dante."

"'Might' isn't good enough," I said, my tone sharp. "Cora's safety is non-negotiable. If Dante so much as breathes in her direction, I'll gut him myself. I don't care if he's a made man or works with the Olivetos."

The room went silent, my words hanging heavy in the air. They all looked at me like they'd never seen me before. I paced and narrowed my eyes at each of them in turn. Were they going to back me or not? I was pretty sure they would.

Conall leaned forward, his expression unreadable. "I understand, Maxim. She's my fucking sister, you know. Asswipe. Just remember that burning down *Fortune* had nothing to do with Cora, to our knowledge."

Ilias frowned at Conall's words. "We're with you. This is an attack, and we'll figure it out. The fucking O'Gara deserved what he got." Ilias spit on the ground. "I don't care that you skinned the fucker, and we can't let the attack on the *Fortune* go unanswered."

"But?" Angelo stubbed out the cigarette he had been smoking half-heartedly. Pinning Ilias with an annoyed look. "Spit it out, *fratello*. You have something on your chest. We," he motioned to all of us. "Want to hear it."

"Fine," Ilias blew out a long breath, and I knew already he was going to piss me off. "This marriage bullshit was supposed to be in name only. Now we're dropping bodies?"

I met his gaze, unflinching. "I'm not talking about emotions, Ilias. I'm talking about principles. If we don't make it clear that coming for us means death, we'll lose more than just *Fortune*. That fucker deserved what he got."

Angelo nodded, his eyes glinting with approval. "He's right. A show of strength now will save us trouble later. The O'Garas will see that we aren't to be fucked with. If Caruso was behind the *Fortune* — well, the Olivetos might not like it, but they'll respect our intent. And if they don't…" He shrugged, his smile cold. "Well, accidents happen."

Ilias sighed, running a hand through his dark hair. "We're walking a tightrope here. Push too hard, and we risk a full-blown war. Play it too soft, and we look weak. Either way, the fallout's going to be messy."

"It always is," I said. I had more experience than most at the metaphorical table when going to the mat with other organizations. If some of these people wanted war — I'd give them war.

The meeting continued, each of us laying out plans and contingencies, but my mind drifted back to Cora. To the way she'd looked at me earlier, her eyes filled with questions she was too afraid to ask.

"I'll set a meeting with the Olivetos," Angelo finally said. "It'll be a neutral location, and we'll go from there. In the meantime, let's send out feelers about other players."

It was well into the afternoon by the time we adjourned, and I'd been itching to get home. I walked out of the building with Conall at my side, his expression unusually solemn.

"Maxim," he said quietly, stopping me before I could get to my car.

I turned to him, raising an eyebrow. "What?"

"Be careful," he said. "There might be blow-back from the O'Gara's."

I nodded, but I didn't answer. I didn't need him to tell me that could be true, but no pissant O'Gara was going to take me out. They'd die trying.

cora

THE TOWNHOUSE WAS QUIET, except for Clyde's occasional meow as he batted at a crumpled piece of paper near the coffee table. The little kitten was relentless, pouncing and rolling with the intensity of a lion on the savanna. I watched him from the couch, my laptop propped open but forgotten as I nibbled on the edge of my thumb.

"Clyde's clearly the apex predator of this household," I said aloud, glancing at Lev, who stood near the door with his arms crossed.

Lev grunted in response, his eyes scanning the room like there was a threat lurking in every shadow.

"Relax, Lev. The only thing attacking us today is Clyde." I smiled, pointing at the kitten as he launched himself at the paper ball again.

Lev didn't look convinced. "I'm here to protect you, not to be entertained by a cat."

"Oh, come on," I teased. "What if we watched something? You can't just stand there all day, looking like a statue. Have you ever seen *The Walking Dead*? It's a classic."

Lev's brow furrowed. "Zombies?"

"Zombies," I confirmed, grinning. "It's got action, drama, survival—it's basically a training video for any apocalypse scenario. You'd love it. And … if there's a plague, you might have to protect me from zombies. It's important for you to know how to kill them. It's a survival skill."

He coughed to cover up a laugh. "I doubt zombies are ever going to happen."

"You never know," I said, laughing. "Fine. Be a grump. But if Clyde and I get bitten by zombies while you're brooding over there, it's on you. You'll have to explain to Max why I'm one of the undead."

He rolled his eyes but said nothing, which I took as a victory.

* * *

AROUND LUNCHTIME, I wandered into the kitchen, Clyde trailing behind me like a tiny shadow. I pulled ingredients from the fridge— romaine, cherry tomatoes, cucumbers, and some leftover grilled chicken. It wasn't much, but it would do. The supplies in Maxim's kitchen were lacking, and we needed to do a serious grocery run. The first thing I needed was Lucky Charms. I almost died this morning without my fix.

Clyde darted around my feet as I chopped the veggies, his wide eyes watching every movement with fascination.

"Sorry, buddy," I said, tossing a tiny cube of cucumber his way. He sniffed it, then batted it around the floor with disdain. "I know. Not as exciting as the kitten food Kolya got you."

The thought of Maxim made my stomach twist. He'd been gone all day, and I hadn't heard a word from him since the morning. My mind wandered to the meeting he'd mentioned—something with Conall and the others. I didn't ask for details, but the tension in his jaw before he left said enough.

"You're worrying again," I muttered to myself, dumping the salad into a bowl.

* * *

Natasha: U ok? Heard Max's club burnt down.

Me: Yeah. Some trouble with some guy I took a picture of in Dublin. He chased me here, I guess. Grabbed me.

GROUP: **Ronnie, Hollis & Natasha**

Ronnie: wtf happened? Natty says you were attacked?

Hollis: are u ok?

Me: I'm ok. Max rescued me. I needed some stitches.

Natasha: The same guy burn down the club?

Me: I don't think so. The guy who grabbed me was from Dublin. Joe O'Gara. I took a picture of him in an alley that he didn't like. I didn't tell anyone, though. I was afraid.

I bit my lip, my fingers hovering.

Hollis: Hey. That's not your responsibility what this Joe guy did. You weren't doing anything with that picture you took. Fuck that guy.

Ronnie: u alright?

Me: Yeah. I'm good. I've got
Clyde and Max.

Natasha: Speaking of Max ...
how'd he take it?

Ronnie: Well, looking at the
body on the sidewalk of Declan
O'Gara's home, I'd say that he
was upset.

Me: Let me see.

Natasha: Absolutely not.

Ronnie: Let's just say that it
was a clear message.

I googled 'bodies left on sidewalks' in NYC, but nothing came up, and decided that it was probably best that I didn't see it anyway. Not to mention, it didn't bother me that O'Gara was dead. He had plans to hurt me — now he couldn't.

* * *

THE KNOCK on the door startled both me and Clyde, who darted under the table like the coward he was. Lev was at the door in seconds, his hand on his sidearm, speaking into his walkie-talkie like he was on the set of some spy film.

"It's fine," I said, peeking around the corner as Lev opened the door to reveal Paddy and Brody.

"Hello, little sis," Paddy said, grinning as he stepped inside. His wild auburn hair was as untamed as ever, and his freckled face was split with a mischievous smile. Brody followed, quieter but no less imposing.

"Hi," I said, setting the salad bowl on the counter. "What are you two doing here?"

"Checking on you," Brody said, his sharp eyes scanning the room in a way that reminded me of Maxim. "And bringing you this." He held up a box.

"Is that…" I peeked inside and grinned. "Pizza?"

Paddy smirked. "I heard you liked the sausage and olive. Figured you'd appreciate it more than whatever rabbit food you're making."

"It was a salad," I said, feigning offense, but I'd never say no to pizza. I could eat pizza every day of the year and never get tired of it. I had been eating an awfully large amount of it lately, but I'd never complain.

"Rabbit food," Paddy repeated, stealing a cherry tomato from the counter.

Lev muttered something in Russian, and Paddy turned to him with a raised eyebrow. "What's that, big guy?"

"Don't worry about it," I said, smiling sweetly. "He's always grumpy."

* * *

THE AFTERNOON DRAGGED ON,

and the townhouse felt smaller with every passing hour. Even with my brothers here, my mind was elsewhere, the weight of Maxim's absence pressing down on me.

It was close to five when the front door opened. Clyde bolted from his perch on the couch, skidding across the hardwood to greet Maxim like an overeager dog.

"About time," Paddy said, leaning against the kitchen counter. "Your girl's been worrying herself sick over you."

Maxim stepped inside, his expression unreadable, though his eyes softened when they landed on me. "I see you've made yourself at home," he said dryly, nodding at Paddy and Brody.

"Someone had to keep her company," Brody said.

"And feed her," Paddy added, gesturing to the pizza box.

Maxim smirked. "Good. Saves me the trouble."

He crossed the room, his hand brushing against my waist as he passed, a subtle but reassuring gesture. "Lev, thanks for staying with her."

Lev muttered something under his breath, and Maxim raised an eyebrow. "What was that?"

"Nothing," Lev said, though the corner of his mouth twitched.

"Uh-huh," Maxim said, unimpressed.

"Alright, we're off," Paddy announced, grabbing his jacket. "You two lovebirds enjoy your night. Try not to keep him up too late, sis. He's got a business to run."

"Go away, Paddy," I said, rolling my eyes as he and Brody headed for the door.

Once they were gone, Maxim turned to me, his hand finding the small of my back. "You okay?"

"Now I am," I said softly, leaning into him.

Clyde meowed from the floor, demanding attention. Maxim sighed, scooping the kitten up with a resigned look. "Your guard cat needs work," he said, his voice laced with humor.

I laughed, the sound breaking through the lingering tension. For now, Maxim was home, and that was all that mattered.

・ ・ ・

I LEANED back against the plush sofa in Maxim's townhouse, the hum of the city muted by the thick glass of the windows. The faint scent of sandalwood and spice filled the air, unmistakably Maxim's, grounding me in the moment. Maxim loosened his tie and removed his jacket. His dark hair was slightly disheveled —a rare sight for the typically composed pakhan.

"So, you're back," I said, sitting up. I pushed my hair behind my ear and pulled my legs up into a crisscross. "Let me guess. Another day of plotting and posturing?"

Maxim smirked, his sharp features softening as he approached. "Something like that. I'll tell you all about it, but first, I'm starving. What are we eating?"

I grabbed the takeout menu I had been eyeing. "I was thinking Thai. Something spicy to match your charming personality."

"Clever." His grin widened. "Order whatever you want. I'll take my usual."

"Let me guess, you're a green curry kind of guy?" I teased, already dialing the restaurant.

"Pad Thai, actually," he replied, settling into the armchair opposite me. He leaned back, stretching out as if he finally allowed himself to relax. "It's reliable."

"Boring," I quipped, my tone light. I placed the order and set my phone down. "So, tell me. What happened today? You've got that look— like you just got away with something."

Maxim's eyes gleamed, the faintest trace of amusement flickering behind them. "The Commission meeting went as expected. Ilias still thinks he's the smartest one in the room, Angelo tried to play peacemaker, and your brother…" He paused, his gaze sharpening. "Conall's being clever, but he's hiding something."

I frowned. "What do you mean?"

"He's got something going on." Maxim's voice was calm, but the edge of calculation was impossible to miss.

"Sounds exhausting," I said, leaning my chin on my palm. "Why do you even deal with them? I'd just fake my death and move to Bali."

Maxim chuckled, a deep, warm sound that seemed almost out of place coming from him. "Tempting, but I'm not quite ready to abandon my empire for a beachside bungalow."

"You're missing out," I said. "Imagine it: no meetings, no power struggles, just endless cock-tails and sunsets."

He leaned forward, resting his elbows on his

knees. "And what would you do in Bali, zayka?"

"Photograph every inch of it," I replied without hesitation. "Then sell the prints and make a fortune."

Maxim shook his head, his smile softening. "Always a dreamer."

Before I could retort, the doorbell rang. I stood to get the food, but Maxim waved me off. "Sit. Kolya will bring it."

A few moments later, he returned with bags of steaming takeout. We laid the containers out on the coffee table, the aroma filling the room.

As we ate, I pressed him for more details about the meeting. Maxim indulged me, recounting snippets of the conversation with each leader and the subtle power plays at work. I could see the faintest flicker of tension in his expression as he spoke about Conall.

"You don't think he'll double-cross you or anything?" I asked.

It never would have occurred to me that my brother would be untrustworthy, but it made sense that they were all purveyors of secrets.

"No. I don't. We have been friends for more than twenty years. I was twelve when I met him. We were barely boys when we first sat down together in that club." Maxim's gaze met mine, steady and unyielding.

We fell into a comfortable silence, the clink of chopsticks against containers the only sound. When we finished, Maxim leaned back, his gaze lingering on me.

"They made you sign?"

"Yes. Angelo fought like a wildcat, but the rest of us were beaten down, and we all had things to lose." He folded his hands together. "My father knew my weak point."

"Your brother."

"There was no reason to deny him something like a marriage in the future. I was twelve. A wife? It was so abstract to me at the time. I was busy trying to survive a horror show."

I reached over to place my hand on his. "I'm always here if you want to talk."

"I appreciate that, zayka." He considered me for a moment, refilling his glass. "We all have our dark moments, don't we?"

"That's true," I admitted. I had been chewing on my thumbnail and tried to consciously stop, sticking my hand under my thigh. He had shared so much of his childhood I could give him a little of mine. Right? "I was just a little girl when my father died. I don't remember very much. Conall was just a teenager himself — seventeen, but he came and woke me up and wrapped me in my blankets." The memory of it hits me, the smell of blood, the carnage. "Conall had told me to close my eyes, but I peeked."

"You should have kept them closed."

I'm surprised to find Maxim sitting beside me, tucking me close, stroking my hair.

"I wasn't very good at obeying, even then," I gave him a sleepy smile and leaned over for a kiss.

CHAPTER THIRTY-ONE

maxim

I LOVED HAVING her in my bed.

Pineapples.

She tasted of pineapples.

Licking her slit, I felt her explode. Her walls fluttered as she came.

Her breasts heaved as she clutched the sheets, calling my name out to the ceiling.

Fuck I was a lucky bastard.

She whimpered and groaned — wiggled against my cock as I slammed into her gripping her thighs in an iron grip that I knew might leave marks, but I couldn't help myself.

"I can't —" The words were lost as I came in a rush. I'd never had it happen so fast. I was almost embarrassed as the orgasm went on and on as I emptied into her. I flushed. "Give me a minute, zayka. I'll be right as rain in a minute."

Rolling us so she was on top so I could admire her, she smiled at me. "I love that I drive you as wild as you drive me, Max. That's how it's supposed to be."

"You're so sexy. Do you know that?"

She was an image that was burned into my mind—her curves. The softer ones intrigued me the most: the slopes of her belly, the way her nipples puckered, and how her breasts filled my hands. I loved her softness against my calluses and scars.

Running my palms up to her tits, I weighed them in my hands, pinching her nipples, rolling them, and tweaking them while I watched her face. Her dark hair fell in waves around her shoulders, the strands framing her heart-shaped face. Pleasure made her cheeks pinken and flushed as she watched me with those green eyes, her hands planted on my chest.

This was what love felt like. It was a lightning bolt.

My cock stiffened inside her as she groaned against me, rocking. I could feel cum sliding between us, and all I wanted to do was to fill her again.

"Zayka," I moaned, rotating my hips and grinding up into her. "Ride me the way you like. Let me watch you get your pleasure."

"Hmm, I like that idea," she hummed.

Balancing her hands on my chest, she rode and ground—humped my cock while she leaned over me, kissing me like we were on the precipice of something. A fine sheen of sweat coated her body. Watching her was like a window into her soul. I wanted the pleasure to go on forever.

She bit into my shoulder hard enough to draw blood as she came, but the pain was sharp enough for me to grab both of her ass cheeks and thrust into her as I finished.

"I love you, Max."

"I love you back, baby. I love you back," I swore.

* * *

THE MIDDAY SUN filtered through the high windows of the old conference room, casting sharp streaks of light onto the polished mahogany table. This was neutral ground—a private estate in the Hudson Valley, far from our strongholds. The Olivetos had chosen the location, a calculated move to show they were just as wary of us as we were of them. I couldn't fault them for that; trust was a rare commodity.

Too bad for them. We'd come prepared anyway. If they thought we hadn't, they were stupid.

I arrived early, taking in the room's layout and ensuring my men had secured the perimeter. It was standard procedure. I'd learned the hard way never to underestimate a seemingly cordial meeting. Angelo, Conall, and Ilias arrived shortly after me, each bringing their distinct energy. Ever the diplomat, Angelo nodded in greeting while Conall's gaze swept the room with casual scrutiny. Ilias strode in last, his predatory confidence unmistakable.

"Neutral ground," Ilias said with a smirk as he sank into his chair. "How quaint."

"It's practical," Angelo countered, his tone light but firm. "And considering the stakes, practical is what we need."

Conall leaned back, his expression unreadable. "Let's just hope the Olivetos see it the same way."

When the Olivetos finally arrived, they were led by Cosimo Oliveto himself. I'd never met him, but he looked decent enough. I'd suspect he was in his thirties, his dark hair styled back and tailored suit doing little to soften the sharpness of his features. Behind him, his men fanned out, their postures tense. As Cosimo entered, his eyes flicked toward me, assessing, measuring. I stood, extending a hand.

"Cosimo," I greeted, keeping my tone neutral. "A pleasure."

"Maxim," he replied, his handshake firm but brief. "Gentlemen, shall we get to it?"

The room settled as we all took our seats. Conall leaned back in his chair again, his expression carefully neutral. Angelo clasped his hands in front of him, the picture of calm. Ilias watched Cosimo with a faint, amused smile as if the whole situation was a game he was already winning.

"We're here to address two issues," I began, my tone clipped. "The first: the fire at *Fortune*."

Cosimo's brow furrowed slightly, but his composure didn't falter. "A tragedy," he said. "But surely you don't believe the Oliveto family had anything to do with that."

"Tragedy, yes," I said, my voice cold. "Coincidence, no. *Fortune* was a known location of ours. It's hard to believe anyone else would benefit from its destruction."

"I'll admit," Angelo interjected smoothly, "the timing was… unfortunate, but let's not jump to conclusions."

Cosimo's fingers tapped lightly against the table. "We've heard similar accusations before, but I assure you, Maxim, my family had no hand in it. Fires… happen."

"Fires don't happen without a spark," I countered. "And this spark has your name written all over it. I'm in no mood for games."

"Well, that was evident with the state of O'Gara's body," he mumbled.

I didn't bother responding to him. O'Gara got everything he deserved. I narrowed my eyes at Oliveto and his underboss.

Ilias chuckled softly, leaning forward. "It's interesting, isn't it? The Olivetos always seem to be near the fire but never get burned."

Cosimo's eyes narrowed. "Careful, Ilias. Baseless accusations can ignite fires of their own. I came in good faith."

"And what of Caruso?" I asked, steering the conversation. "His name keeps coming up in my inquiries. Erratic behavior. Moves that don't make sense. Perhaps you can shed some light on that?"

Cosimo's reaction was instant and telling. His jaw tightened, and his carefully maintained mask slipped for a fraction of a second. "Caruso's been... difficult," he admitted reluctantly. "But he's not acting on our behalf. If he's caused you trouble, I assure you, it's not at my family's direction."

"Difficult?" I repeated, my tone heavy with skepticism. "Difficult doesn't explain the trail of chaos he's left behind. Or his proximity to my interests."

"He's gone rogue," Cosimo said, a hint of frustration seeping into his voice. "We've been dealing with him internally, but he's… unpredictable." He paused for a moment and put both elbows on the table, leaning forward and clasping his hands. "I'll be honest. It's one of the reasons that I agreed to this meeting."

"Unpredictable is a liability," I said sharply. "One we won't tolerate anywhere near our operations."

"We have been patient, Don Oliveto," Ilias added. "Caruso has always held a particular disdain for all of us." I guffawed. That was putting it lightly. "He has something against Maxim in particular because of his father, but that isn't our responsibility, as I'm sure you sympathize."

Interesting.

I wasn't aware of the Oliveto family background or how Cosimo became head of his family, but now I was curious. Ilias knew something that was evident by the way he was needling him and the way Cosimo was reacting.

"He's still family," Cosimo said tightly. "We've been reluctant to cut him completely loose. But …"

"Family or not," Conall cut in, his voice low and even, "he's jeopardizing more than just your interests. If this continues, we all pay the price."

Angelo nodded, his diplomatic tone returning. "Perhaps it's time we consider... neutralizing the issue."

Cosimo's lips pressed into a thin line. "He's still family," he repeated, but his conviction wavered.

"Family," I said, leaning forward, "isn't an excuse for recklessness."

The room fell into silence again, the weight of my words settling over everyone. Cosimo's unease was palpable, but he gave a curt nod, his expression unreadable.

"I don't disagree," he said finally. "It is past time for this to be put to rest. I'll handle this matter in the next twenty-four hours. You have my word."

"Of course, with the understanding that you'll be asking about the arson and if he was involved." Angelo gave a lazy shrug. "Maybe we're off base."

I didn't like it, but the others weren't wrong that business was better if we weren't losing resources to fighting an unnecessary war. If Cosimo Oliveto wanted to be an ally, then fuck it ... we'd be allies.

"Very well."

I leaned back, satisfied for the moment. "Good. Then we have an understanding."

"I've been watching the progress you've been making." He made careful eye contact with each of us. "*All of you.* With your businesses. Loyalty is a trait I admire."

"Obviously, we agree," Conall said pointedly. "Our friendship has served us well over the years."

"You know. I'd turn an eye toward Vallone if you thought someone wanted to cause you problems."

"Vallone," Angelo fairly spat out. "He is a piece of work." Angelo shot a glance in our direction. "Vallone still dabbles."

We knew what that meant—the flesh trade. We had done our best to close out all our contracts and cut ties, but it was amazing how insidious it was. Certain organizations seemed to breed and grow, which seemed to continue no matter how much you stamped them out. It turned my stomach. My brother's wife, Hollis, had been a victim of the flesh trade. I'd be damned if I let it happen in this city.

"You think he might have an eye toward our business?"

Cosimo shrugged, but it was practiced. "I'm just pointing out that Vallone doesn't care for any of you and doesn't admire the bond that you share. Some might be intimidated by the fact that you work together the way you do. Your fathers had quite the idea that they cemented with that blood oath."

We all went still. We hadn't heard that anyone knew about the oath.

"How did you hear about that?"

"My father. He was ranting and raving about it at dinner one night. Your fathers bragged about it to the other dons. Their scheme made them rich. My father was incensed. He had been counting on securing his contracts with Stefano Santelli."

Cosimo paused, his eyes glinting with barely concealed animosity. "You see, my father never let go of the insult. Losing that business—those contracts—it broke him. He blamed your fathers for it until his dying day, and he wasn't alone. Vallone was there, watching it all unfold, watching my father descend into fury and obsession. It was a shared grievance."

Angelo's brow furrowed as he exchanged a glance with Ilias. "Vallone was never one to let go of a grudge," Angelo said slowly. "But the idea that he'd still be nursing wounds from something that happened decades ago?"

"Don't underestimate him," Cosimo said. "He might be older now, but he's more dangerous than ever. He has no love for your families—or this alliance you've built."

I narrowed my eyes, leaning forward. "You're telling me Vallone is behind Caruso's chaos? Or are you suggesting something bigger?"

Cosimo exhaled, his fingers drumming lightly on the table. "I don't have definitive proof, but I'd bet my life Vallone's been pulling strings. Caruso is erratic, yes, but not without purpose. And Vallone—he's always preferred to operate from the shadows, letting others take the heat. I've been curious about Caruso's motivations. We've been looking for a mole in our organization. Caruso has always felt he was owed, but he has always been an underperformer, if I'm honest."

Ilias let out a low chuckle, though his smile was humorless. "If this is true, Vallone's overplayed his hand. If he wants to provoke a response, he's about to get one."

"Easy," Angelo said, his calm voice cutting through the tension. "If Vallone has been biding his time all these years, it's because he's patient. He wants us to act rashly. We need to figure out his endgame first."

"And where do you stand in all this, Cosimo?" Conall asked, his sharp gaze boring into the Oliveto heir. "You've just admitted your father held a vendetta against us. That doesn't inspire much trust."

Cosimo's jaw tightened. "My father's grudges were his own. I'm not here to settle old scores. My interests lie in ensuring the stability of my family's future. A war with the four of you? That's not a future I want."

"You could've fooled me," I said dryly, my tone laced with suspicion. "If Vallone's been conspiring with your family, then this peace you're offering might just be a Trojan horse."

"I came here at your request and to warn you," Cosimo shot back, his voice rising. "If you don't want to listen, that's your choice. But make no mistake—Vallone isn't content to sit on the sidelines anymore. He sees your alliance as a threat, and he's moving to dismantle it. I'm not the enemy here."

The room fell into a weighted silence, his words settling over us. Vallone hadn't been on our radar. That was a mistake.

"We need to watch his movements," I said finally, breaking the silence. "Every deal, every contact—no stone unturned. If Vallone thinks he can manipulate us into self-destruction, he'll regret it."

Angelo nodded. "I'll have my people start digging. He won't stay in the shadows long if Vallone's involved."

"Cosimo," Conall said, his voice low but firm, "if you're playing both sides, we'll know. And there won't be any neutral ground to hide behind."

Cosimo didn't flinch under Conall's glare. "I've told you where I stand. Believe me or don't—it doesn't change the fact that Vallone's your real threat."

"Then you won't mind proving it. That you're interested in peace with us," I said coldly. "Start with Caruso."

Cosimo gave a sharp nod, though the tension in his posture betrayed his unease. "As agreed. I'll be in touch."

As the Oliveto men left, the four of us lingered, the atmosphere charged with unspoken resolve.

"Vallone," Ilias muttered, his voice dripping with disdain. "I should've known he'd be a problem. The old bastard never knew when to quit."

"This isn't just about the past," Angelo said thoughtfully. "If Vallone's causing problems now, it's because he sees an opportunity. We need to figure out what he's really after."

"We will," I said, my voice steely. "And when we do, he'll wish he'd stayed buried in history."

* * *

Me: I want full family backgrounds on all family members for those connected to mob families in NYC

Ronnie: like?

Me: Everyone

Ronnie: 😐

Ronnie: I'll start with the main families and go from there.

Me: Dig hard. Look first at the Vallone family and the Olivetos.

Ronnie: 🫡

CHAPTER THIRTY-TWO

cora

THE SOFT HUM of the computer was the only sound in the room as I sat at my desk, my fingers brushing over the keyboard. My new office space was pristine, every detail meticulously arranged—a quiet testament to Maxim's peculiar way of showing care. A sleek monitor dominated the desk, with my damaged camera set to the side. Though the camera's body was a lost cause from the attack, the SD card had survived. It now sat safely in a card reader, revealing the gritty, raw photos I had captured at the scene of the *Fortune* fire.

I had other photos that I needed to edit, but I wanted to revisit the scene — so to speak. Taking a deep breath, I steadied myself.

I was safe. I knew that O'Gara was dead thanks to Ronnie's comment in our text chat yesterday. I'd kept myself from asking Maxim about it since I already knew the outcome. What would I say anyway? It wasn't as if I disagreed that he'd killed him.

I leaned closer to the screen, adjusting the exposure on a striking shot. The image showed flames licking at the edges of the building, their light contrasting sharply with the shadows of the onlookers. My breath caught as I zoomed in on the faces of the workers on the fringes of the parking lot. Fear and curiosity painted their expressions. A strange pang of guilt twisted in my chest as I edited—like I was intruding on something —but this was why I loved photography, this opportunity to catch a glimpse behind the veil.

Clyde leaped onto the desk, batting at the corner of the monitor with his tiny paw. I smiled and scratched behind his ears. "You're not helping, Clyde." The kitten mewed in protest, flopping onto the keyboard.

"If you delete this photo, we're going to have a serious problem," I warned playfully, lifting him into my lap. He purred contentedly as I continued my work, one hand occasionally straying to pet his soft fur.

I lost myself in the editing rhythm: adjusting contrasts, sharpening details, and cropping distractions. Each photo pulled me deeper into the memory of the fire—the heat, the chaos, and the moment I realized the danger I had been in. My hand hovered over a photo of a charred sign, its letters barely legible: *Fortune.*

There was no sign of O'Gara anywhere in the shots. I wasn't sure what I thought I'd find or why my brain had been so insistent that I do these pictures first.

I began to understand that our lives were messy and entangled—his world of power and shadows collided with my quieter one, and somehow, I didn't mind.

Pausing on a photo, I focused on the man standing in the shadows watching Maxim and Conall. My finger hovered for a minute, and after a quick edit, I sent it to Maxim's email. I wouldn't repeat the mistake of not sharing a photo that tugged at my gut. Maybe it was nothing, or maybe it was important.

A knock at the doorframe startled me. I turned to see Kolya, my apparent guard at the townhouse that day. His large frame nearly filled the doorway, and his expression was as impassive as ever. He was wincing today and walking gingerly. I suspected he might have gotten a couple of gut punches from my husband for letting me wander off. My insides squirmed with guilt. It wasn't Kolya's fault that

I'd been taking pictures and moved away from the group.

"Everything all right, Mrs. Volkova?" he asked, his deep voice carrying a hint of concern.

"Yes, Kolya," I said, stretching. "Just editing. It's… consuming work. Please use my first name." I rolled my eyes at him. "It's Cora."

His gaze shifted to the damaged camera on my desk. "I can't do that. The pakhan is already not happy with me. A shame about your camera."

"I am sorry you got in trouble," I offered.

He stiffened. "It is my job to watch you. I failed both you and the Volkov Bratva when you were attacked. I was distracted. You don't apologize to me. I apologize to you. I am sorry that you were injured." He looked pained while he spoke, but I knew he was sincere.

I wanted to argue, but I also understood that this was a time I needed to understand what our roles were. He was doing his job, and I needed to let him.

"Thank you for coming for me, Kolya. I knew you and Maxim would," I said instead of what my heart wanted to say — *I'm sorry*.

"We will always come for you. You are our queen." He cleared his throat and looked away, gesturing to the wall where Maxim had some camera equipment. "Will one of these work for

337

you as a replacement?" Kolya plucked Clyde off the floor, handling him so gently that I wanted to reach for a camera.

"Yeah, I think one of those will work. They're beautiful and a little fancier than I'm used to." I took a glance at the wall of equipment. It was like a camera shop with five different complete bodies, lenses to match, flashes, lighting equipment, tripods, and other things I wasn't sure I'd ever touch ... but I was excited about those cameras.

Kolya gave a slight nod of understanding, his stern features softening slightly. "Is there anything you need?"

"Actually, yes. I want to go to the grocery store. I need Lucky Charms, and I'm craving .. Something."

Kolya raised an eyebrow. "Something?"

"Something specific. I'll know it when I see it," I said with a grin. "And I need fresh air. I've been cooped up all day."

He hesitated, clearly weighing the risks, but eventually nodded. "Very well, but we'll take precautions."

"Of course," I said breezily, grabbing my coat. "Let me get my bag."

Kolya's watchful eyes scanned the street as we walked to the car. He moved with practiced ease, his hand always near his concealed weapon. Despite his intimidating presence, I found his vigilance oddly comforting. Maxim chose well.

"You don't talk much, do you?" I teased as we settled into the car.

"Not much to say," he replied, his tone even.

"I'll take that as a challenge," I said with a smirk.

To my surprise, his lips twitched, almost forming a smile. "Good luck, Mrs. Volkova."

The grocery store was a welcome change of pace. I wandered the aisles, tossing items into the cart while Kolya followed a step behind. I laughed at the absurdity of having a bodyguard in the produce section. Still, Kolya remained unfazed, even as I jokingly held up a head of lettuce like a trophy.

When we returned home, the sun was dipping low, casting warm hues over the townhouse. I unpacked the groceries while Clyde darted between my feet, chasing imaginary prey. I couldn't help but laugh, scooping him up for a quick cuddle before setting him down again.

As I cooked dinner, my thoughts drifted to Maxim. I'd caught glimpses of the man behind the pakhan—the man who painstakingly set up my office space, told me he loved me, and exacted vengeance on my behalf.

My feelings for him were still new, still

surprising, but they were real. As Clyde meowed at my feet, demanding attention, I smiled, feeling a quiet contentment I hadn't expected to find in this life.

"Maybe it's not so bad being Mrs. Volkova," I murmured, scratching Clyde behind the ears. "Maybe it's exactly who I was always meant to be."

THE TOWNHOUSE FELT different in the evenings—quieter, yet alive with possibilities. After dinner, I decided I needed to escape the confines of the house. Maxim was still traveling back from his meeting with the Olivetos, and while Kolya was stationed as my shadow, I wanted to breathe the night air and test out one of the new cameras Maxim had bought for me. They were fancier than I had ever had, and I had no idea how they'd function compared to my trusty old camera.

"I'm stepping out for a bit," I announced, poking my head into the living room where Kolya sat, ever watchful. Clyde had claimed the couch, sprawled out on a blanket like he owned the place. Maxim would have a baby cow if he saw him on the couch.

Kolya's sharp eyes met mine. "Where to?"

"Just outside. I want to test a new camera," I said, holding up the sleek device. It still felt foreign in my hands, the buttons not yet familiar. "I won't go far."

He stood without hesitation. "Okay. Let's go. I'm coming with you."

"You don't need to hover," I teased, slipping on a light jacket. "I'm just going to the courtyard," I said, knowing he'd insist. I savored my alone time when I took my photos, but I supposed I'd have to get used to it. There was no way I'd be able not to have protection. It wouldn't be allowed, and there were too many risks.

Kolya didn't reply, but his presence was answer enough. I gave a resigned shrug and opened the door, letting the frigid evening air wash over me. The city sounds hummed in the distance, but here, in this quiet little pocket Maxim called home, it felt worlds away.

I found a spot near the wrought-iron fence where the streetlights cast a golden glow. The camera's lens captured how the light filtered through the trees, the shadows stretching long and elegant against the pavement. I adjusted the settings, experimenting with shutter speeds and apertures. Each click of the shutter felt like a small triumph as I began to get a feel for the new equipment.

Clyde had followed us to the door, his tiny face pressed against the glass. I smiled, waving at him between shots. "He's mad he can't come," I said to Kolya, who stood a few feet away, his gaze scanning the perimeter.

"He'll survive," Kolya replied dryly.

I laughed softly. "You Russians are not cat people, are you?"

"I prefer animals that earn their keep," he said, a faint smirk betraying his otherwise stoic demeanor.

"Clyde earns his keep," I countered. "Emotional support is a full-time job."

Kolya's lips twitched, the barest hint of a smile. "If you say so."

"I do say so," I insisted. "And I think you secretly like him. Don't think I haven't noticed you sneaking him pets."

Kolya didn't reply, but his lack of denial was answer enough. I grinned, feeling victorious.

I turned my attention back to the camera, capturing the details of the townhouse—the intricate balcony ironwork and the frost creeping up the brick facade. Each image felt like a puzzle piece, tiny glimpses into this strange, beautiful life I'd stumbled into.

"How long do you think Maxim will be?" I asked, lowering the camera to glance at Kolya.

He checked his watch. "Late. Meetings like this aren't quick, and this was complicated."

I nodded, feeling a pang of something I couldn't quite name. It wasn't loneliness, exactly. It was more like... anticipation. Maxim and I were still figuring each other out, and every absence felt like an opportunity missed.

"He'll be back soon enough," Kolya said as if sensing my thoughts.

"I know," I said softly, adjusting the camera strap on my shoulder. "I just... I don't know. It's hard to explain."

Kolya didn't press me for details, and I appreciated that. Instead, he gave me space to lose myself in my photography again. The night deepened around us, the air crisp and cool. For the first time in days, I felt a sense of calm. The camera's viewfinder framed the world in a way that made it feel manageable, even beautiful.

Clyde eventually gave up his vigil at the door and disappeared into the house. When Kolya and I finally stepped back inside, the warmth of the townhouse was a welcome contrast to the night air. Clyde reappeared instantly, weaving between my legs as if to scold me for leaving.

I scooped him up, pressing a kiss to his soft fur. "You're so needy," I said with a laugh.

Kolya shook his head, a rare smile ghosting across his face. "He's your cat, all right."

Later, with Clyde settled on my lap, I curled up on the couch and turned on an episode of *The Walking Dead*. The show was just the distraction I needed, though Clyde didn't seem impressed. He swiped lazily at a passing zombie on the screen, his tiny paw batting at the movement.

"Relax, Clyde," I said, scratching behind his ears. "You'd never survive the apocalypse. Too soft."

Kolya's voice came from the doorway. "You wouldn't last long either, Mrs. Volkova."

I turned, mock-offended. "Excuse me? I'd be the ultimate survivor. Charming the enemy, sneaking supplies, and probably running a black-market trade in cat food."

Kolya's brows lifted in faint amusement. "I'd give you a week."

"A week?" I threw a pillow at him, laughing. "You're underestimating me, Kolya. I'd be unstoppable."

Clyde leapt off my lap to chase the pillow as it landed, biting at the corner with ferocious determination. I pointed at him triumphantly. "See? I'd have Clyde as my secret weapon."

Kolya shook his head, his rare smile making

another appearance. "Both of you would be doomed."

"Rude," I muttered, turning back to the screen, but I couldn't help smiling. As strange as my life had become, moments like this—playful, unexpected, and oddly normal—were what made it feel like home.

* * *

HOURS LATER, I was still curled up on the couch, though the episode had long since ended. Clyde had claimed the blanket as his throne, and I was absentmindedly scrolling through photos on my phone when I heard the sound of the front door opening. My heart jumped, and I sat up straighter, my pulse quickening.

Maxim was home.

He stepped inside, his presence immediately filling the space. He looked tired but composed, his sharp features shadowed by the dim light. His gaze swept over the room and landed on me.

"You're still awake," he said, his voice low and slightly surprised.

I smiled softly. "I wanted to wait up for you. How was your trip?"

He hesitated, his expression unreadable. "Long."

"Come sit," I said, patting the spot beside

me on the couch. "You look exhausted. Did you eat? I can make you a sandwich, and there are leftovers."

Maxim gave a small nod and crossed the room, his movements deliberate. He sat down, and the couch dipped slightly under his weight. Clyde lifted his head briefly before deciding Maxim's arrival wasn't worth leaving his blanket for.

"Yes, I ate zayka." He leaned in for a kiss. "Did you miss me?"

I inhaled that scent of his, lifting my hands to his cheeks. "Yes."

"Clyde and I missed you too. It was a long day." I indicated the tiny fur ball, who hadn't noticed Maxim was gone at all.

"Did the little monster miss me," he sounded skeptical. "I doubt it."

"How did the meeting go?" I asked, my voice gentle. "It must have been important to travel all that way."

Maxim sighed, leaning back against the couch. For a moment, he looked as though he might brush off the question, but then he spoke. "It was productive, but... tense. There are several Italian families in New York that are mafia. We'd had some suspicion that one of them could have been involved in the fire at the club, but it seems we were wrong." He chewed his lip a little.

"Who are the families?" I asked instead. "If I'm going to be in this life, I'd like to know who the players are. Even if it is just to follow the conversation when you talk to me."

He examined me closely for a moment and nodded. "The Italian families are old," he smiled. "Even more old-fashioned than the bratva. The Olivetos, the Vallones, the Scarpatos, the Santellis, and the Cardonis."

I nodded, trying to commit the names to memory, reciting them over in my head. "The Santellis is Angelo, right?"

"Yes. The Vallones and the Cardonis are still run by dons that go back a generation," he hedged.

"Those dons worked with your father? With my father?" I clarified.

Maxim got to his feet, paced a little, and poured himself a whiskey. "We learned today from Cosimo Oliveto that the blood oath agreement wasn't a secret." He turned to face me, and I could see that this had upset him.

"It was supposed to be?"

"We had thought it was just between the four of them. We hadn't thought it was common knowledge. Now that we know that others know about it, it is even more important that the others hold up their end of the bargain," he paused. "But some weren't happy about the original agreement."

"Because they didn't get included or what?" I wrinkled my nose in disgust. "Conall said the whole thing was about trafficking. That's what the gross assholes were into, right?"

I picked up Clyde, who grumbled as I pushed him up against my chin, taking comfort from his limp body. One of the things that I loved about cats was how they let themselves hang like little dishrags when they trusted you.

"They were all involved in it. They wanted to make sure they got the best deal and that their business with each other thrived. With the agreement, nobody could back out. Not only were they trafficking other people's children, but they sold their own with that blood oath," he said with disgust. "Now Oliveto tells us that it was known and that some people have a grudge about how it shook out." Worry lines creased his eyes.

"A grudge? Because?" I was confused. "I know that Conall had something to do with my father's death…" I trailed off. I knew that Maxim killed his, but I wasn't sure it was common knowledge among the other mob families. I didn't care that he had killed his father. Sounds like he was a scumbag.

"We all didn't exactly have the best upbringing. I've told you that mine was hard, zayka. My father was a cruel man. Bratvas are run with blood and cruelty as a rule in the old country. He viewed Dimitri and me as property to be trained. It took me a long time to gain enough power to extricate us. Too long, but I was able to bring enough soldiers to my side and take over eventually."

"All four of us had vowed to stop the lines of flesh peddling that had happened under our fathers, but it seems like there is some resentment that we didn't anticipate."

"You met with Oliveto. He's not the one upset?" I asked, petting Clyde and eyeing my husband.

"The Olivetos are cautious. Cosimo mentioned that Vallone has been resentful this whole time about the deal that was made. That he could be a viable threat. Maybe behind the arson and your hit, or it could have been Oliveto's man Caruso." Maxim's jaw tightened.

I frowned, tilting my head thoughtfully. "Does Oliveto agree with you about Caruso?"

"Caruso is a made man. Do you know what that means?"

"Not really," I admitted. "What does it mean?"

"Once you've paid your dues and you've

pledged to your don or your pakhan, then you are 'made,'" he held up quotes.

"Meaning they're untouchable?" I ventured, watching his expression for confirmation.

"In theory," Maxim replied, his voice cold. "A made man is supposed to be under the protection of their family, a symbol of loyalty and obedience. Dante Caruso has been giving me quite a bit of trouble lately, but I've been reluctant to take him off the board since he is part of the Olivetos. Cosimo has agreed to take him out, but he wants to do it." He watched me carefully with his toffee-colored eyes. "Cosimo believes he might be playing two sides. If he is, his status doesn't protect him. Betrayal erases all oaths."

I nodded slowly, processing this. "So, if Caruso is involved in any of this—be it the arson or this supposed grudge—he could be eliminated without retaliation from his family?"

Maxim sipped his whiskey, his gaze narrowing. "Yes. Cosimo won't have any worries about taking him out. He's promised us information about what Caruso has been up to."

"And Vallone?" I asked. "If he's the one holding a grudge, what does he gain from picking a fight with all of you?"

Maxim hesitated, swirling the amber liquid in his glass. "Angelo claims that Vallone has always been power-hungry. Maybe he sees an opportunity. It could be that his resentment over the original agreement isn't just about what he didn't get—it's about what he sees as having been taken."

I let out a slow breath, the weight of his words settling over me. "So, this isn't just about the past. It's about what Vallone wants now. He was part of trafficking then," I guessed. "Or still part of it."

Maxim nodded. "Exactly, and that makes him dangerous. Cosimo may be cautious, but Vallone is bold, reckless even. If he sees an opening, he'll take it."

Maxim moved back over to the couch and sat down next to me. "We believe he wants to expand his paltry schemes again, and our current operations are impeding him. Oliveto doesn't hold with trafficking, either."

I shifted, the cat squirming in my arms as he hopped back onto the couch. "So, what's your next move? I'm sure you've got one."

A faint smirk tugged at his lips, but his eyes remained serious. "I need to shore up our alliances. Make sure Oliveto stays on our side and keep a close watch on Vallone's movements. Conall will also need to get a move on with his marriage deal with Angelo's side of the family — Francesca. If Vallone thinks there's a crack in our foundation, he'll exploit it."

I nodded, my heart twisting at the thought of what was at stake. "And what about you? You've been handling so much. Are you—are we okay?"

His gaze softened as he set his glass down and leaned forward, taking my hands in his. "Zayka, *we* are solid. You are my home. Everything else is noise. I handle it because I must, but never doubt where my heart lies."

I smiled faintly, the tension in my chest easing as his words sank in. "Good. Because I'll be right here, doing what I can to help."

He raised an eyebrow, a flicker of amusement breaking through the weight of his worry. "And what do you think you can do to help?"

I grinned, leaning closer. "I've got Clyde, and I've got questions. Maybe I'll interrogate them both until they crack."

He chuckled, his deep laugh rumbling through the room. "The Italians don't stand a chance." He quirked an eyebrow at me. "Maybe there's something else you can do to help."

"Hmm, what's that, Mr. Volkov?"

CHAPTER THIRTY-THREE

maxim

I LOWERED myself to my knees and moved her robe out of the way, watching her as I caressed the soft skin of the bones of her kneecaps. Her breath hitched, her pulse fluttering in her throat as her eyes dilated.

"Mrs. Volkova," I breathed. "You're like an angel." My fingers made small circles on her skin. I wanted to savor the moment. Every moan, every heady sigh that she made.

"Max," she breathed.

Brushing the fabric off her thighs, I let it fall on either side, exposing each long limb and her panties beneath. Rubbing my knuckles over the apex of her thighs and the wetness there, I watched as she threw her head back against the couch, her hips lifting infinitesimally.

"I can't wait to taste you. You're going to come for me."

Leaning forward, I nuzzled her slit through the silk, breathing in her scent. I bit her clit lightly as she gasped and arched into my face.

"That's it, zayka. That's it."

I leaned on my haunches and pulled out my knife, watching Cora steadily as I cut off her panties. She was glistening, dripping, her pussy swollen and pink. Rubbing my thumb over her, I watched as goosebumps scattered across her skin.

"Please, Max," she moaned. "Please."

Licking her slit, I let out a sigh of pleasure, that pineapple taste that was uniquely hers spreading over my tongue. God, I'd never get enough of her. Setting myself to the task, I took my time, eating her pussy like it was my life's work, using my thumb to circle her clit steadily until she pushed into my face and gripped my hair.

"I'm so close. Don't stop."

I wouldn't stop for anything. She cried out, her body bowing in its pleasure, her hips stuttering, and her pussy clenching, and then gushing into my mouth as I drank her down.

Easing away, I rubbed her lazily. "Bend over the couch for me, baby."

My cock was fairly pulsing in my pants, and

I was sure that I had a wet spot on my trousers. I couldn't wait to bury myself in her. Her eyes lit up as she moved into position, holding onto the back of the couch.

"Push that ass out for me, bend further forward, and hold on tight."

"Hurry," she urged.

I laughed. My wife was perfect for me — so needy and eager. Gripping my cock, I squeezed it hard, trying to remind it who was boss. Notching it to her, I eased into her sheath, each movement an exquisite torture as she stretched to accommodate me. She was still dripping wet. I could feel the wetness between us, and there was nothing more intoxicating than the realization that I turned her on.

"Baby, you're so wet. You're taking my cock so well."

"It feels so good, Max."

I rammed into her, fucking her hard as I angled her hips so I could drive deeper, sliding my hands up her hips, kneading both cheeks, my hands digging into the flesh and her crack. Reaching forward, I pinched her clit, letting my fingers run over her flesh as I drove us both until I felt her flutter around me as she came.

I came in spurts before collapsing over her back for a moment, laying kisses on her spine. I'd never thought to find her.

* * *

I SAT at the head of the oak table, a steaming mug of coffee cradled between my hands, the smell wafting into my nostrils. Coffee was one of my rituals — I suppose that wasn't unusual. It was the smell more than the taste. Something about it reminded me of my mother in better times. She always had a cup of coffee by the windows, looking towards the gardens. It was one of the few things that had brought a smile to her face, even in bleak times.

Morning sunlight filtered through the curtains, casting long shadows across the room, but I was already focused on the day ahead. Lev stood across from me, his posture rigid as he flipped through a leather-bound notebook filled with figures, names, and the day's priorities.

"Collections are running behind in Brooklyn," Lev began, his voice steady. "One of the crews reported resistance from the local distributors. They're claiming pressure from an independent group moving in from Jersey."

I sipped my coffee, letting the bitterness settle on my tongue as I considered the implications. "Jersey? We've got no gaps there. If someone's pressing up against our territory, they're testing us."

Lev nodded, his dark eyes narrowing.

"Exactly. I've already sent a team to handle it. They'll make an example of whoever's stepping out of line."

"Make sure it's thorough," I said. "If they're bold enough to test us, we send a message they won't forget. Anything else?"

"Supply chain issues from the docks. One of our contacts has been dragging his feet on deliveries," Lev continued. "I'll visit him personally if it continues."

"See to it," I replied. "We can't afford delays. Not with everything in motion."

Lev made a note in his book before flipping to another page. "Then there's the Oliveto situation. Cosimo has a few more hours to deliver Caruso's body. If he doesn't, we're looking at a serious breach."

I placed the mug on the table with deliberate care, the slight clink echoing in the quiet room. "Cosimo knows the stakes. Caruso's a liability, and we clarified that he's responsible for closing it. If he fails, the consequences fall squarely on his shoulders."

Lev's lips tightened into a grim line. "And the information Caruso was supposed to bring? Without it, we're going to be blind."

Lev hadn't been pleased that we'd let Oliveto have the concessions that we had, but there hadn't been much of a choice.

"We're not blind," I said, my tone sharpening. "We know who we're dealing with. If Cosimo delivers, we gain leverage. If he doesn't, he's out of play. Either way, the Olivetos don't get a second chance to prove their loyalty."

Lev leaned forward, lowering his voice. "Do you think Cosimo has it under control? Or do we need to start preparing for a cleanup operation?"

I leaned back in my chair, considering the question. Cosimo was seasoned but not infallible, and the situation with Caruso reeked of instability. "Prepare the cleanup. If Cosimo fails, we'll move decisively. Caruso is a dead man one way or another."

Lev gave a single, firm nod before closing his notebook. "Understood, pakhan. I'll set everything in motion."

The conversation paused, and the room briefly filled with the soft hum of the refrigerator. I picked up my coffee again, taking a slower sip as my mind churned through the web of alliances and betrayals that defined our world. Time was always against us, and hesitation cost lives if you weren't careful.

The footsteps on the stairs drew my attention, and I turned my head toward the doorway. Cora appeared, her hair slightly tousled, her expression soft but curious. She paused at the threshold, her gaze flicking between Lev and me.

"Good morning," she said, her voice light yet carrying the subtle undertone of someone assessing the room's mood.

"Morning," I replied, a hint of warmth creeping into my tone. "You're up early."

"Couldn't sleep," she admitted, stepping fully into the room. "What's going on?"

Lev's gaze shifted to me, waiting for direction. I gave him a slight nod, and he quietly gathered his things before heading toward the door. "I'll report in later," he said, his voice low as he exited, leaving me alone with Cora.

She moved toward the counter, fixing herself a cup of tea before taking the seat Lev had vacated. Her presence brought an odd sense of calm, a reminder of why the chaos and violence were worth enduring.

"Anything I should know about?" she asked, her tone casual but her eyes sharp.

I let out a faint chuckle. "Plenty, but nothing that can't wait."

Her lips quirked into a small smile, and the weight of the morning's discussions faded into the background for a moment.

She wrapped her hands around the mug and

studied me for a long beat. "You look tired, Max. We should take a vacation."

I exhaled softly, leaning back in my chair. "I didn't sleep much either. Too much on my mind. A vacation sounds nice."

Her brows furrowed, a flicker of concern in her gaze. "Is it about last night? Or something else?"

"Both," I admitted. There was no point in pretending otherwise—Cora was sharp and knew enough to see through deflection. "The Oliveto situation is a mess; we can't afford mistakes. I'm a little stressed, baby," I admitted.

"Cosimo?" she guessed, tilting her head slightly.

I nodded. "He's running out of time. If he doesn't deliver, it's his head. Ronnie sent me some of the backgrounds on the other families. The Vallones are in deep with a lot of nasty stuff."

The Vallones were their own quagmire of shit that I was going to have to bring to the boys to help sort through. I should have dug into the families before arriving in New York to be more prepared. Now, I was kicking myself for having to play catch up.

Cora took a sip of her coffee, her expression thoughtful. "Do you trust Cosimo to come through?"

"No. Trust is a dangerous luxury." I studied her across the table, curious at the direction of her thoughts. "Why do you ask?"

She shrugged one shoulder, though her gaze remained steady. "Because if you don't trust him, you're already preparing for him to fail."

I smiled faintly, impressed as always by her perception. "I am."

"Then what happens next?"

"Today, we go to Conall's and see if Cosimo fails." I raised a brow. "If he does … well, that's a clusterfuck."

Cora didn't look away, her expression holding mine. There was no fear there—only understanding and something else I couldn't quite name. Finally, she spoke, her voice quiet but resolute.

"I want to come."

I looked at her for a long moment. The kitchen was silent except for the faint ticking of the clock on the wall.

"Are you sure," I said finally, though the words felt heavier than they should. Things should be stable. That was the thought, anyway. "It should be safe, but there aren't any guarantees in this line of work. It could be dangerous — and messy."

"I know, but I don't want to be someone who sits at home all the time waiting for the other shoe to drop." She bit her lip. "I'd like to go with you when I can. I'm willing to learn to shoot and stuff." She shifted on her feet.

There was a part of me that hated the idea and the other part that loved the idea. The meeting was going to be at Conall's anyway. His building was virtually impregnable, the paranoid motherfucker.

"Okay, zayka, we can take it slow. Today you can come. We can see how you do." Her face lit up like a beacon, and my cock tightened. Too bad we didn't have time for a quickie.

* * *

A-HOLE *Chat*

> Ilias: T minus 15 to find out what Cosimo found out. 5k that he delivers

> Angelo: 10k he says he found out nothing

> Me: 100k that cut off Dante's hands

> Conall: wtf dude

> Angelo: you're whacked, Maxim

Ilias: just out of curiosity …
nevermind — I'll raise that 500k
that he cut off the hands

Conall: fine, 500k he didn't

Me: See you soon.

cora

I ZIPPED up my puffer coat as I followed Maxim through the fortified entrance of Conall's building in Vinegar Hill, Brooklyn. The industrial-modern space was a testament to my brother's meticulous nature: wood floors polished to a gleam, glass walls reflecting warm, muted lighting, and the faint hum of a security system embedded in every inch of the structure. Armored guards flanked the hallways, their eyes sharp as they acknowledged Maxim with slight nods.

Nerves had skittered across my skin during the drive with the thought of what was supposed to happen at this meeting, but I wasn't going to change my mind. If my husband was going to be some kind of bratva pakhan-thing, I would make sure I would be a match for him. Not one iota of my being ever wanted to be the kind of wife waiting at home making meatloaf, and I never wanted to be the one waiting to find out if my husband was dead.

I knew Maxim had a terrifying profession or calling—whatever he wanted to call it. Maybe if I were with him during some of his days, I wouldn't have be so worried.

Finn was waiting as we entered the building, frowning at Maxim as if he'd personally insulted him.

"Hi, Finn." I made sure to inject the right amount of cheer into my voice. "How've you been?" Even though I'd only known him briefly, I had still come to like him.

"Cora. Good to see you. How's Clyde?" he asked.

"Growing and becoming more of a handful by the day. Still super cute."

Maxim stalked next to me, a force, as much an immovable object as an unstoppable one. Today, bringing me into the heart of business felt like a test I had demanded to take. We headed to the fourth floor, where the offices and conference rooms were.

The room buzzed with low conversation until we strode in. Conversations halted. Conall, Angelo, and Ilias turned their heads, each man radiating their unique authority. The surprise on their faces was unmistakable when they saw me beside Maxim.

"Cora?" Conall's voice was a mix of warmth and irritation. He crossed the room in a few strides, pulling me into a brief, firm hug. "You didn't mention you'd be coming."

"I asked to come," I replied evenly, meeting his gaze with a determined tilt of my chin. "This involves our family. I have a right to be here."

Maxim's lips twitched in what might have been amusement. "Cora is here because she insisted," he said simply, his voice leaving no room for argument. "And because she's my wife, she can go where she wants. If she wants to be part of the business — she can."

Angelo raised an eyebrow. "Family, maybe. But this isn't exactly a family dinner, Maxim. This is business."

"I don't give a fuck," Maxim answered. "She'll go where I go if I say so." Maxim looked like he could care less, but I knew he did. He squeezed my hand as if to say it was all right, which I appreciated — just like I appreciated him sticking up for me.

Ilias, with his usual Greek charm, chuckled. "We're not questioning her presence, merely your unorthodox methods. It's good to see you, Cora."

"It's good to see you too," I replied, my voice steady despite the tension in the room.

Conall gestured for me to sit beside him on one of the leather sofas. I obliged, though I could feel the weight of everyone's eyes on me. Maxim remained standing, a looming figure of authority as he addressed the room.

"Cosimo will arrive shortly," Maxim began. "When he does, we'll have answers about Caruso."

Conall's jaw tightened. "If Caruso was working against us, we need to know who else was involved."

Conall looked at his phone for a minute. "He's here. Down in the back bay."

"I think you should stay here with Finn while I verify the body." Max leaned close to me, ensuring his words were for my ears only. "I'm not sure Caruso's body will be a pretty sight."

My belly tightened and pitched. Was this really what I wanted to see? Some gangster with bodies that they were trading around like Pokémon cards? Still, what came out of my mouth was, "I'm going." Maxim's expression didn't change, but his jaw clenched. I was going to guess that he hadn't expected me to insist.

"Alright," he said with resignation.

We trooped toward the elevator bank, with

the others giving glances that ranged from hostile to disapproving. Finally, Conall leaned over and said, "I don't think you should be involved. I specifically didn't want you to be." He was grinding his teeth so hard I could practically hear the enamel being worn down.

"Well, maybe you should have thought about that before you married me off." I winked at him. "Too late now. You have no say."

He glared, but there wasn't any rebuke he could offer since he was the one who set the wheels in motion for the whole arranged marriage situation. I glared back at him for good measure. The poor girl who ended up with my grumpy brother would need all the help she could get to deal with him.

We rode down together in the elevator, and additional security filed in behind us. Maxim spoke in Russian to Lev and Kolya, who tightened up beside me, and I made a mental note to download a language app to start learning. If I was going to be married to a Russian and be around men who spoke a foreign language, then it was going to be something I would need to learn.

The back bay led to the alleyway behind the building, so it was obvious why they'd asked Oliveto to meet them at this specific spot. It was essentially a concrete box with a few drains that you could drive several vehicles into. I was in no doubt that some unsavory things happened here.

One of the men by the doors spoke into his walkie-talkie and looked to my brother for his approval. At his nod, they opened the double steel doors to admit an SUV that rolled forward into the space.

"Stay close to me, zayka."

The room fell into a tense silence until the SUV doors opened, and men exited. I picked out Oliveto immediately. He was about Maxim's age, handsome with a Mediterranean look, his hair swept back from his face. Three other men accompanied him, who, between them, unloaded a large, bloodied tarp from the back of the SUV. The metallic tang of blood filled the air as they set it down with a heavy thud.

Oliveto's sharp eyes scanned the room, pausing for a minute on me with speculation as I hovered between Kolya and Lev before settling on Maxim at my side.

"Caruso didn't go quietly," he said, "Shall we?"

"By all means." Maxim made a lazy motion as if this was an everyday occurrence.

Watching them as Oliveto pulled back the tarp to reveal the battered body made me believe that I wasn't wrong. This was normal for them

— looking at dead bodies. Not a single one of them flinched — as opposed to me. My belly twisted, and my gorge rose.

I inhaled sharply, almost turning my face away, but Lev touched the back of my arm, gripping it hard enough to ground me. I straightened my shoulders. The reality of our world was brutal, and I had asked to be here. This was what I wanted—to be part of the 'business.'

"What did you get out of him?" Maxim asked, his tone devoid of emotion.

Cosimo's gaze flicked to the corpse, then back to Maxim. "Caruso was working for Vallone. He's been feeding them information about our operations for months. The leak is bigger than we thought," he admitted. "He was also the one to put the hit on your wife."

Maxim clenched his fist, and tendons stood out in his neck. His fury was unmistakable, but I breathed a sigh of relief.

Angelo cursed under his breath. "Vallone has been a constant issue for years, but this?" He gestured to the body. "Planting a mole in your organization this high up? Putting a hit on Cora?"

Ilias's expression darkened. "We're all vulnerable."

I wasn't sure why that would be, but I kept quiet and kept my eyes off the corpse on the tarp. He was hardly recognizable as a man anymore, and Maxim had been right — he was missing his hands. How had he known?

"Vallone was responsible for burning down *Fortune*. Dante had some sort of very specific vendetta against you, Volkov. He had some kind of relative who was caught up in your father's organization years ago. He blamed you."

Maxim's jaw tightened. "We're going to need to come up with a plan to eliminate the threat. No half-measures."

"And how do you propose we do that?" Conall asked, his tone wary.

"We take out Vallone and anyone loyal to him," Maxim said. His gaze swept over the room, landing on me for a moment longer than necessary. "No one betrays the Commission and lives to tell the tale. We can probably get a few of the other families to side with us."

Oliveto nodded. "I figured you'd all feel that way. I'll work with you on this if you're interested. If you're not, then I'll still be going down the list on Vallone's network because they came after me. Caruso's confession gave us enough to pinpoint key players in Vallone's network."

"Might as well work together," Angelo shrugged. "Boys?"

"I agree," Ilias said, sounding bored. "Conall? Maxim?"

"The men exchanged glances, unspoken agreements passing between them. Finally, Conall nodded. "Fine."

"I agree. No reason not to work together," Maxim stuck his hand out to Oliveto. "Let's go to war."

CHAPTER THIRTY-FIVE

maxim

THE CITY STREETS buzzed with their usual chaos as we exited Conall's building, stepping into the biting cold of a New York evening. My mind was a whirlwind of thoughts—Cosimo's revelations about Caruso being a mole within the Oliveto organization for Vallone had rocked the foundation of my plans. Caruso's betrayal explained much, but it also complicated everything.

I wouldn't miss the fucker. He'd been a pain in our ass for a long time, always making comments even when we were just teenagers. The mention of a relative yesterday had me wondering what that was about—some victim of my father's trafficking ring. I wondered if I could get some kind of information about that. I wished I had a little more to go on, but the man was dead now, so that was … well, a dead end.

The bratva was much like the mafia. All organized crime families were balanced on a knife's edge. We operated on fear, yes, but also respect and loyalty. If those currencies were violated, you had trouble in the ranks.

Cora walked a step ahead of me, her coat pulled tight around her, her gaze sweeping the street with an intensity I hadn't seen in her before. Lev and Kolya flanked her, their hands resting under their coats where their weapons lay concealed. The atmosphere felt… charged. I didn't like the feel of it.

In Russian, I ordered Lev and Kolya to tighten up and hurry. The sooner they had Cora to safety, the better. I swiveled my head, watching the streets.

We had barely made it halfway to the car when chaos erupted. The first shot came from a black SUV parked across the street, the sharp crack of gunfire slicing through the din of the evening. The bullet missed me by inches, embedding itself in the brick wall behind us.

"Down," Kolya barked, shoving Cora toward the cover of a parked car. I dropped instinctively, drawing my pistol as Lev pulled me behind a metal trash bin. More shots followed, this time from a second vehicle further down the street. A Vallone hit squad — motherfuckers.

The cacophony of gunfire drowned out Cora's shouts back to me, but I could see Kolya curved around her, shielding her as best he could with his body as he fired off a volley of shots at the attackers. It looked like she was furiously texting something. Lev was already returning fire, his movements precise and calculated, the picture of professional lethality.

"They're flanking from the right!" Lev shouted, his voice cutting through the chaos. I shifted my position, firing at the two men attempting to approach us from the sidewalk. One went down with a gurgling cry; the other ducked behind a mailbox.

Conall's men emerged from the building, guns blazing. I saw Conall himself, his face a mask of grim determination as he joined the fray. He moved with the ease of someone accustomed to violence, taking down two attackers with clean, efficient shots. But there were a lot of them, and they were better equipped than we were. This was planned.

A bullet grazed my shoulder, the searing pain momentarily distracting me. I clenched my teeth, forcing myself to stay focused. Lev noticed, his eyes narrowing as he fired to cover me, his teeth bared with a ferocity that bordered on recklessness.

"Kolya, status on Cora?" I barked in Russian, my voice sharp despite the chaos.

"She's safe, boss. For now." Kolya's tone was strained but resolute. He was taking fire from two directions, his cover rapidly deteriorating.

The hit squad began advancing, their superior numbers fading but forcing us into tighter positions. Conall's men held their ground, their return fire keeping the attackers from overwhelming us completely. Then I saw Conall stagger, a bullet catching him in the abdomen. He fell to one knee, his hand pressed against the wound as blood seeped through his fingers.

"Conall!" I shouted, breaking cover to reach him. Lev swore under his breath, moving to provide cover fire as I sprinted across the street. Another bullet grazed my thigh, the pain barely registering as adrenaline surged through me. I reached Conall, dragging him behind a car.

"Stay down," I ordered, my voice harsh. Conall's face was pale, but his eyes burned with fury.

"Like hell, I will," he growled, raising his gun to fire at an advancing attacker. The movement cost him; he grimaced, fresh blood pouring from his wound.

Ilias, Angelo, and their men were sprinting from the building, eyes wide with confusion and rage as they took in the scene on the street and the scent of gunpowder.

The tide began to turn as Kolya and Lev coordinated with Conall's men, methodically picking off the hit squad. The attackers, realizing they were outmatched, started to retreat, leaving their dead where they lay. Lev took down two more as they scrambled into their vehicles, tires screeching as they sped off down the street.

It fell eerily silent, the air thick with the acrid smell of gunpowder and blood. I leaned against the car, my shoulder and thigh throbbing in time with my heartbeat. Conall was slumped beside me, his breathing shallow but steady. Kolya and Lev approached, their expressions grim but victorious.

"They'll regroup," Kolya said, his tone devoid of optimism. "We'll need to call in more men, be more careful from now on. We can't be taken off guard like this again."

"Let them come," I replied, my voice cold. "Next time, we'll be ready. We were sloppy today. Careless. It won't happen again."

Cora appeared then, her face pale but resolute. She knelt beside Conall, pressing her hands against his wound to stem the bleeding.

"We need to get him inside," she said, her voice shaking but determined.

Lev nodded, already moving to help lift Conall as Angelo and Ilias came forward to help. I straightened, ignoring the pain that lanced through me. This wasn't over. Not by a long shot.

"Jesus, old man, you got fucked up," Angelo teased.

"Fuck off," Conall answered, but his voice was thready.

"Whatever. You need more practice at ducking," Ilias continued cheerily as if his friend wasn't bleeding out, but he was trying to keep him talking and awake.

As we made our way back toward the building, the sound of distant sirens began to rise above the silence. Kolya and Lev stayed vigilant, their weapons drawn, scanning the surrounding streets for any signs of lingering threats. Cora walked beside Conall. Her hand was still pressed firmly against his wound to slow the bleeding.

Conall's men moved quickly inside the lobby, clearing a path and barking orders to secure the area. The room was a flurry of motion, but my focus remained on Conall. His breathing had grown more labored, and his skin was ghostly pale. I knew I was dripping on the flooring, but I was pretty sure they were through-and-throughs even though Cora cast me worried looks.

"Get a doctor," I ordered, my tone leaving no room for argument. "That O'Flannery guy." Lev nodded and disappeared into the crowd, his phone already to his ear.

Cora glanced up at me, her expression a mix of worry and determination. "He's losing a lot of blood."

I crouched beside her, ignoring the sharp protest from my injured leg. "Stay with him. He's strong, and we'll get him through this."

Conall's eyes fluttered open, and he fixed me with a weak glare. "You're... not rid of me yet," he muttered, his voice barely audible.

I couldn't help but smirk despite the gravity of the situation. "Good. I'd hate to lose the only Irishman stubborn enough to keep up with me."

Dr. O'Flannery arrived moments later, rushing in with a harried look and swinging his case in one hand onto the table where we'd set Conall in the conference room. He wasted no time assessing Conall's condition. As he worked, I felt Cora's hand brush against mine. I glanced at her, and for a brief moment, her resolve faltered, her eyes glistening with unshed tears.

"He should be in a hospital," Dr. O'Flannery muttered. "I'm going to need things."

Ilias crossed his arms and scowled. "Give me a list. I'll have everything in less than half an hour. Whatever you need."

"And you. You're bleeding." O'Flannery pointed at me.

"Conall first. These can wait."

"Fine. I need a nurse, too." O'Flannery snapped as he turned his attention back to Conall before rattling off a list to Ilias. "And a nurse!" he said again.

"I can get a nurse," Angelo said quietly.

Levering myself into a chair, I tugged Cora beside me. "We'll make it through this," I said, more for her sake than anyone else's.

She nodded, her grip tightening. The chaos outside might have subsided, but the war was far from over. Tonight's ambush was just the beginning, and I'd be damned if I let the Vallones think they could win. We'd regroup, strike back harder, and remind them exactly who they were dealing with.

CHAPTER THIRTY-SIX

cora

CONALL'S CONFERENCE room smelled faintly of whiskey and cigar smoke, the scents mingling with the sharp tang of antiseptic. Dr. O'Flannery worked quietly, tending to the stomach wound on Conall, his steady hands belying his gruff demeanor. On the opposite end of the room, Maxim reclined on the leather couch, pale but defiant as Angelo's sister Francesca, currently in her clinical rotation at a trauma hospital, cleaned the wounds on his shoulder and thigh.

I'd not met her before, but she was not what I expected. She'd arrived in a huff and given Angelo a look that told him he was in big trouble later, but she was efficient and professional.

"You two look like you've been through a

blender," Paddy quipped, leaning against the doorframe. Brody stood beside him, his arms crossed and a smirk plastered across his face. "But hey, at least your faces are still pretty. Maxim might lose his leg, though. That's a shame. You're less intimidating without both feet on the ground."

Maxim gave Paddy a withering look, though it lacked its usual intensity. "Don't you have a pub to be annoying in? Or a rainbow to find?"

Brody barked a laugh. "Not until we're sure you're not dying, big guy. Gotta make sure our investment in this alliance isn't a bust. Maybe we'll take our sister back while you're laid up."

I rolled my eyes, though the tension in the room eased just a little. Leave it to my brothers to make a medical emergency feel like a pub crawl. "Can we save the banter until after the stitches are in place? Or better yet, keep it outside?"

Brody's gaze met mine, and for a moment, the usual bravado in his eyes softened. "You okay, Cora?"

"I'm fine," I said quickly, though the truth was harder to swallow. The ambush had rattled me more than I wanted to admit. Watching Conall and Maxim bleed, seeing Lev and Kolya's grim faces as they secured the perimeter, had left a cold knot in my chest that refused to loosen. Kolya had wrapped himself so tightly over me that I knew I wasn't in any danger, but the sight of bullets hitting people I loved wasn't going to leave me anytime soon.

The first item on my list was to learn how to contribute. I was not going to be the only person who couldn't shoot. All I had been able to do was text my brother for help.

"Sure?" Brody pressed, his teasing tone gone.

"Positive," I said firmly, though my voice wavered just enough to betray me. Maxim's jaw tightened, but he didn't push further. Thank God.

After what felt like an eternity, Francesca finished with Maxim's wounds and stepped back, wiping her hands on a towel. "He'll live," she said, her tone light but professional. "But you're not moving that shoulder much, and you're certainly not walking on that leg for at least a week."

Maxim swung his legs over the side of the couch, but when he tried to stand, he winced and leaned heavily on Kolya.

"You're not walking on that," I said, stepping forward.

He arched a brow at me. "It's not up for discussion."

"Neither is you falling on your face," I shot back.

Lev, ever the diplomat, moved between us. "Let's get him to the car before he decides to prove his point."

"We've got the car in the bay where it's protected. That's standard protocol from now on," Paddy said.

"Smart. Cora, say goodbye to your brother. We'll leave together," Kolya ordered, and I went to give my brother a kiss.

He was sleeping heavily, his face screwed up in pain, but I hoped that I could come and check on him tomorrow. Dr. O'Flannery was sitting in a chair next to his bed.

"He'll be fine. He's strong. I just gave him something to rest, lass," he said kindly.

The ride back to the townhouse was quiet, except for Kolya's occasional humor attempts and Lev's exasperated groans. "You're both useless," Maxim muttered when Kolya started humming an off-key version of an old ballad.

Once home, Lev and Kolya helped Maxim to the couch, where he collapsed with a heavy sigh. I disappeared into the kitchen, returning with a glass of water and a couple of Ibuprofen.

"Take these," I said, holding them out.

He took the pills without protest, which only made me more worried. Maxim never admitted to pain, let alone took anything for it. As he settled back, I moved Clyde from his usual spot on the couch. The kitten's soulful eyes followed me before he jumped into my lap as soon as I sat down.

"Hi, monster," I muttered, scratching behind his ears. Clyde wiggled against me, oblivious to the chaos of the day.

"He has good taste," Maxim said, his voice low. He reached over, his fingers brushing against mine. The contact shivered down my spine, though I tried to play it cool. "Come here."

I hesitated for a moment before sliding over, careful not to jostle his injured leg or shoulder. He lifted his arm, allowing me to tuck against his side.

"You need rest," I said softly, leaning into him. The warmth of his body chased away some of the lingering chill.

"So do you," he murmured, his lips brushing the top of my head. "I'm sorry, zayka. I'm sure that was scary. You did well."

Clyde settled on my chest as Maxim grabbed the remote, flipping through channels until he landed on a movie.

"A romantic comedy?" I teased, glancing up at him.

"Only you would think that," he replied, a

faint smirk tugging at his lips as *Warm Bodies* started to play.

For the first time that day, I let myself relax, the steady rise and fall of Maxim's chest grounding me. Whatever chaos awaited tomorrow, tonight we had this—a quiet moment in the eye of the storm.

maxim

CORA HAD INSISTED that I couldn't navigate the stairs on my crutches, so she'd set us up in the guest room. I wouldn't admit that she was probably right. My leg hurt like an absolute bitch, throbbing and pulsing like it had a heartbeat of its own despite the two tumblers of whiskey I'd downed and two ibuprofen.

Somehow, the beast was snuggled up on my chest, and despite everything, the little maniac was kind of comforting. The furball was purring like he was twice the size of one of those Abominable Snowmen on crack and kneading his little claws into my chest, but I couldn't find it in me to mind.

"Here's a glass of water and an extra couple of Ibuprofen for later tonight." Cora set them on my nightstand, squinting at the sight of the kitten. "Made friends?" she snorted.

"I didn't put him there. He just climbed up," I defended myself.

"You're warm. He knows a good thing when he sees it."

"That's right. Maybe you should climb on," I suggested, hopefully.

She laughed. "Not a chance, big guy. You're injured. You get kitten therapy. That's it. Maybe tomorrow. Let's see how you're doing and if you can rest."

"You'll sleep with me, though, right?" Her gaze softened, and she brushed her hair back.

"Yes, Max. I'm sleeping here." She slipped up onto the bed with me. "I wouldn't be anywhere else."

Music to my ears. I clasped her hand, and I let myself drift off, holding Clyde with the other.

THE TENSION in the room was palpable as I watched Conall ease himself into the leather armchair at the head of the table. I wasn't sure it was so advisable for him to be out of bed, but he'd insisted, and he was nothing but a stubborn son-of-a-bitch.

His face was pale but resolute, and the strain of the gunshot wound to his abdomen was evident in every movement. The lines of pain etched across his features reminded me of the toll this war was already taking. I followed him into the room, my crutches clicking softly against the marble floor as I moved to a seat beside Cora. She stayed close to her brother, her expression calm but watchful.

Angelo and Ilias were already seated, their presence commanding despite the casual elegance of their attire. Oliveto, an unexpected addition to the meeting, leaned against the back of his chair, his sharp eyes scanning the room as if sizing up the players on a chessboard.

I shifted uncomfortably, the weight of the discussion ahead pressing heavily on me. Gripping my crutches, I spoke, keeping my voice steady. "Let's get to it. Vallone has made his move. He's gone beyond posturing. An attack on us here … right on O'Kelly turf is a declaration of war. The other families won't have anything to complain about when we hit back."

Conall's jaw tightened, and he nodded. "He should have made sure to kill us the first time around."

Angelo's smooth voice cut in, laced with menace. "Vallone's ambition has always been his weakness. He's overextended himself, and now we have an opportunity to strike. We need precision. Anything less will cost us more than we gain."

"Agreed," Ilias added, his tone measured. "But we also need to consider the collateral. Vallone isn't just playing for power; he's playing for chaos. He wants to draw us into a war we can't control."

That made a lot of sense.

Cosimo leaned forward, his voice cutting through the discussion with authority. "Chaos is exactly what we can't afford. The question is, what's our leverage? What do we have that he doesn't?"

I glanced at Cora, feeling the weight of everyone's gaze. For a moment, the room seemed to hold its breath. "We have information," I said, quieting my voice but no less firm. "Vallone thinks he's untouchable, but he's made mistakes. We have some of his accounts, but we need to get them all. We need to catalog all of his movements and… other vulnerabilities. I've asked a hacker friend to help me, but we need to set up some of our resources to do our own spying. Vallone is dedicating resources to this — we need to do the same." I was gratified to see nods around the table.

Cora's brow furrowed slightly, but she didn't interrupt. She had seen the files I had gone over with Ronnie, and we had pored over the details late into the night. It was damning, but it also meant we were playing a high-stakes game.

"We need to hit him where it hurts," Conall said, his voice like steel. "Trafficking, for one, but we do it on our terms. No more reacting. We plan, we coordinate, and we finish this."

"And we do it quickly," I added. "Vallone isn't going to sit back and wait for us to retaliate. He'll be moving already."

"What about his alliances?" Angelo asked, glancing at Ilias. "Do we know who's backing him?"

"Some," I admitted. "The Albanians are one of his major alliances, but there are more. That's another piece we need before we strike. Any cracks in his foundation need to be exploited."

The room fell silent for a moment, the weight of the decision settling over us. Cora glanced at Conall, her voice soft but firm. "Whatever we do, we need to be certain. Vallone won't just retaliate; he'll escalate. Innocent people could get caught in the crossfire."

"We'll keep it clean," Conall assured her. "But we can't let him walk away from this. Not after what he's done."

"He's made his decision. He's not walking away," I pointed out.

Cosimo stood, his movements deliberate.

"Then let's start—no more hypotheticals. We draw up the plan, assign the players, and make the move."

"It's going to be a process we can't rush," I warned.

As the men leaned forward, the conversation turning to logistics and strategy, I caught Cora's gaze lingering on her brother. She could see the fire in his eyes, the determination to protect what was his. And as much as I knew she hated the violence, she also knew there was no turning back.

This was war, and we would all see it through.

CHAPTER THIRTY-EIGHT

cora

THE SUN DIPPED low on the horizon, setting the sky colored with hues of orange and pink, the colors reflecting off the crystal-clear waters of Bali's shoreline. I sat on a lounge chair, my bare feet digging into the soft, warm sand as gentle waves reached my ears. The world there felt distant from the chaos we had left behind in New York. It was a sanctuary—a rare, precious moment of peace.

It had been a wonderful few days that we'd spent here. Maxim had let me spend as much time as I wanted with my camera, following me everywhere with tiny, tempting touches. He'd corner me and take me against the nearest available surface every few hours. It was paradise.

I glanced over my shoulder at Maxim, who stood near the villa's infinity pool, a drink in his hand, his sharp features softened by the warm light of the setting sun. Even on vacation, he exuded an aura of control and authority. But there was a different side to him, away from the weight of the bratva and the pressures of our world. He wore a loose linen shirt, the top buttons were undone, and the faintest hint of a smile pulled at his lips as he watched me.

"You're quiet," he said, his deep voice cutting through the air as he approached me. "What's on your mind, Cora?"

I tilted my head, a smile playing on my lips. "Just thinking how unreal this feels. Like we've stepped into another life." Maxim placed his glass on the side table and lowered himself onto the lounge chair beside me. "It's not another life. It's our life. This—" he gestured at the serene beach, the soft waves, the golden glow of the sunset, "—is what we're fighting for. To carve out moments like this, away from everything. Conall, Angelo, and Ilias have things under control while we are gone this week. Lev will help — he's bringing in more men while we get ready for the next stage of our fight against Vallone."

I turned to face him fully, the sincerity in his words striking a chord deep within me. "Do you think it'll last? Moments like this?"

Maxim's smile faded slightly, but his eyes

never left mine. "It will last because I'll make it last. For you. For us."

I reached out, my fingers lightly brushing his. "I don't want to lose this, Maxim. Or you."

He took my hand in his, his grip firm but comforting. "You won't. I promised you, Cora. I don't break my promises."

I leaned into him, my head resting on his shoulder, as we watched the sun slip beneath the horizon. The world seemed to hold its breath, and the transition between day and night was a perfect metaphor for our lives. We had come from darkness, clawing our way into the light, and now, together, we stood on the edge of something brighter.

"You know," I said, my voice teasing, "you're almost convincing as a romantic."

Maxim's laugh was low and rich, vibrating through his chest. "Don't let it fool you. I'm still the same man. When we return to New York in a few days, there will be just as much blood and chaos." He gave me a stern glower. "And you're going to learn to shoot."

I pulled back, studying his face. "I'm not fooled."

Maxim's expression softened, and for a moment, the formidable pakhan was replaced by a man who loved me fiercely, without hesitation or regret. "You make me want to be more."

We stayed like that for a long while, the world around us fading into the background. When the stars began to sprinkle the sky, Maxim stood and offered me his hand.

"Come," he said. "There's a promise I made you."

I let him pull me to my feet, the warmth of his hand in mine grounding me. As we walked back to our villa, the lights from the pool casting a soft glow around us,

"What promise is that?" I said coyly as we reached the bedroom, looking at him from my lashes and reaching from my bikini strings.

"Don't untie those yet, zayka," he warned with a growl.

"Don't untie them?" I teased. "Or … what will happen?" I pulled the string slowly.

"You're going to get punished." His jaw clenched.

I let the bikini fall to the floor as it unraveled and scooted back to the bed, watching while Maxim picked the bikini up and pulled the string out of the top and the bottoms. Wetness pooled between my thighs, and I thought about finding relief myself. I slipped my hands over my breasts, tweaking my nipples. The sensation sparked as I pulled and twisted each nub.

"I'm so close, Max."

"No, my bad little girl." He tsk'ed. "Get on

your knees. Hands on the headboard. I don't want you coming until I say."

Eagerly, I did as he asked as he prowled forward. He rubbed a palm over one of my flanks, caressing them, pinching gently until his blunt fingers edged toward my slit as he positioned himself behind me. I groaned with need, dropping my head to the pillows. I was aching to be filled.

"I've promised you a spanking for a while now, haven't I?" Maxim crooned, returning his palms to rubbing my ass.

"Yes," I managed. He had promised, and the thought was tantalizing, but I was having second thoughts now. My hips swiveled as his fingers dipped and whirled in the wetness that had gathered.

"We need to cure you of that wandering, zayka. Make you obedient." His cock dipped into me, and I groaned. The sensation was electric as he pumped the tip inside. It wasn't nearly enough. "Maybe this will be your fate every time. I'll fuck you into submission."

"More Max. More. Please," I begged, trying to thrust back against his cock and the feelings that were expanding inside me.

"Bad girl," he chastened, but I could feel how he was restraining himself – how he pulsed inside me.

The spank surprised me. It was hard enough to sting and startle me, but his palm soothed the sting immediately after, stimulating the skin underneath in a new way that made my senses fire on all cylinders.

"You like that, don't you?" Maxim kept up his steady, teasing pace.

"Noooo," I whined. "Let me come, please." I was going to explode.

"Don't lie, zayka. That's bad."

Smack. His palm hit the same spot, and pain sparked, but the hit seemed to go straight to my clit, and I almost came right then. Maxim started to slide into me lazily as I squirmed.

"Don't come," he warned, but I was already gone like a shooting star, the lights blazing behind my eyes as the orgasm hit me.

"We'll have to start again, baby," he said with a sigh pulling his cock from me.

Turning me over, he tweaked my nipples, laving them with his tongue and kneading them while he spread my legs and speared my center with his fingers. Just when I was about to come, he withdrew and flipped me back over, making me nearly cry.

"Should I punish you for coming before I told you?" he asked me as he positioned me how he wanted.

I was quivering with need by now and

wasn't sure how I felt about this new round of sexual frustration. Did I like it?

"No?" It came out in a whine.

Smack.

He soothed the sting as he pumped into me. "Don't you dare come."

His thumbs dug into sore spots on my ass and thighs as he thrust harder and harder just as he reached forward to my clit, pinching it hard.

"Now, zayka," he groaned.

The explosion went on forever, the pleasure bursting forth as he bent over me, pressing and kissing against my skin and rolling me to the sheets. I closed my eyes and let my head fall against my husband.

"Are you going to be good now?" he whispered.

"Never," I whispered back.

conall's reign

Tropes: Revenge, Billionaire, Irish Mob,
Arranged Marriage, Plot & Spice, Jealous Hero,
OCD (MMC), He Helps Her Heal,
Nurse (FMC)
*This book is not recommended for sensitive
readers.*

Conall's Reign
Estimated Release: Spring of 2025

FRANCESCA

I'm on a new path in my life.

I've been moving away from my persona as a mafia principessa.

My brother thinks I don't know about my father's stupid blood oath that he signed, but I know all about it. The oath that promises me to one of the men of the Commission. I'm not sure which one I'll have to marry, but I'll worry about that later.

For now, I'll go to nursing school like I always wanted and live a real life away from the mafia.

Help people instead of hurting them.

Too bad it's never about what I want.

Old oaths and promises are about to come due.

CONALL

We are in a war that might be impossible to win.

It won't stop me from taking the wife I've dreamed of for years.

Francesca Santelli has been my obsession for longer than she knows.

I've been patient, giving her time for a life, but I'm done waiting.

I also might have rigged things so she could be mine, but I'll never tell.

NO CHEATING. *HEAs. All books are part of the interconnected worlds that Haven creates. Expect to see all characters more than once. While these can be read as standalone novels, they are best read sequentially.*

THIS IS *the second book in the Commission Mafia series. Each book features a different couple and can be read independently, but I recommend the following reading order.*

MAXIM'S PROMISE
   Conall's Reign
   Angelo's Vengeance
   Belonging to Ilias

please consider ...

If you liked this book, please consider leaving a review. Every star and every comment counts for authors like me who are out here on our own. We appreciate it so much. Reviews don't have to be long, either. Throw us a like. 🩶

want more?

Sign up for monthly news, opportunities to ARC read, and more.